PEG AND ROSE SOLVE A MURDER

Center Point
Large Print

Also by Laurien Berenson and available from
Center Point Large Print:

Murder at the Puppy Fest
Ruff Justice
Wagging Through the Snow
Bite Club
Here Comes Santa Paws
Pup Fiction
Game of Dog Bones
Show Me the Bunny
Howloween Murder

PEG AND ROSE SOLVE A MURDER

A Senior Sleuths Mystery

Laurien Berenson

CENTER POINT LARGE PRINT
THORNDIKE, MAINE

This Center Point Large Print edition
is published in the year 2022 by arrangement with
Kensington Publishing Corp.

The text of this Large Print edition is unabridged.
In other aspects, this book may vary
from the original edition.
Printed in the United States of America
on permanent paper sourced using
environmentally responsible foresting methods.
Set in 16-point Times New Roman type.

ISBN: 978-1-63808-490-7

The Library of Congress has cataloged this record
under Library of Congress Control Number: 2022940830

PEG AND ROSE
SOLVE A
MURDER

"Poodles are Labs with a college education. My Poodle will do anything your Labrador will do. After a day of retrieving in the field, your Lab wants to curl up and snore in front of the fire. My Poodle wants to be a fourth at bridge and tell naughty stories."

—Anne Rogers Clark

Chapter 1

Peg Turnbull was standing in the hot sun on a plot of hard-packed grass, staring at a row of Standard Poodles that was lined up along one side of her show ring. She'd been hired to judge a dozen breeds at the Rowayton Kennel Club Dog Show, and she couldn't imagine a better way to spend a clear summer day. Judging dogs involved three of her favorite things: telling people what to do; airing her own opinions; and of course, interacting with the dogs themselves.

A tall woman in her early seventies, Peg had a discerning eye and a wicked sense of humor. In this job she needed both. Aware that she'd be on her feet for most of the day, she had dressed that morning with comfort in mind. A cotton shirtwaist dress swirled around her legs. A broad brimmed straw hat shaded her face and neck. Her feet wore rubber-soled sneakers, size ten.

Though her career as a dog show judge had taken her around the world, today's show was local to her home in Greenwich, Connecticut. Peg had arrived at the showground early. She'd begun her assignment at nine o'clock with a selection of breeds from the Toy Group. Now, two and a half hours later, she finally found herself facing her beloved Standard Poodles.

As she gazed at the beautifully coiffed entrants in front of her, Peg knew exactly what she was looking for—a sound, elegant, typey dog displaying the exuberant Poodle temperament. Having devoted her life to the betterment of the Poodle breed, and spent the previous decade judging numerous dog shows, Peg was well aware there were days when those coveted canine attributes could be in short supply. Thankfully, this first glimpse of her Open Dog class had already indicated that this wasn't going to be one of them.

Peg flexed her fingers happily. She couldn't wait to get her hands on the Poodles. She was eager to delve through their copious, hair-sprayed coats to assess the muscle and structure that lay beneath. It was time to get to work.

A throat cleared behind her. "Peg?"

Marnie Clark was Peg's ring steward for the day. While Peg evaluated her entries and picked the winners and losers, it was Marnie's job to keep things running smoothly. That was no small feat. To the uninitiated, the arrangement of classes, record keeping, and points awarded could appear to rival a Rubik's Cube in complexity.

Marnie was an officer of the show-sponsoring kennel club. She was bright, vivacious, and two decades younger than Peg. Peg's Poodles and Marnie's Tibetan Terriers were both Non-Sporting Group breeds. The two women had known and competed against each other for years.

Reluctantly, Peg turned away from the four appealing Open dogs to see what Marnie wanted. The woman was holding up an unclaimed armband. The fifth Standard Poodle entered in the class had yet to arrive.

Absent? Peg wondered. *Or merely late?*

Each exhibitor was responsible for being at the ring on schedule. However, busy professional handlers with numerous breeds to show could sometimes find their presence required in more than one ring at the same time. In those cases, it was up to the judge to decide whether or not a concession would be made.

Peg glanced at the armband and lifted a brow.

Marnie wasn't supposed to tell her the missing exhibitor's name—a nod to impartiality that didn't fool anyone. The dog show world wasn't large. As soon as the handler arrived, Peg would recognize him or her, just as she knew the other exhibitors currently in her ring. As long as a judge remembered to evaluate the dogs on their merits and not their connections, that didn't have to be a problem.

Marnie obviously agreed. "It's Harvey," she said under her breath.

The steward nodded toward a big, black Poodle waiting just outside the gate with the handler's harried-looking assistant. Peg hadn't seen the young man before. He must be new. He was casting frantic glances toward the Lhasa Apso ring farther down the row of enclosures.

Peg took a quick look herself. Yes, indeed, there was Harvey—standing in the middle of a class of Lhasas that he very clearly wasn't winning. The handler was glaring at the indecisive judge as if he wanted to throttle her.

Peg felt much the same way. In her opinion, anyone who didn't want to have to make tough choices shouldn't apply for a judging license. Peg presided over her ring with the deft precision of a general inspecting troops. People might not agree with every decision she made, but they all respected her ability to get the job done.

Peg turned back to Marnie. "Give the young man the armband. Tell him to bring the dog in the ring and take him to the end of the line. You can switch Harvey in when he gets here."

"I already tried that," Marnie told her with a sidelong smirk. "The poor guy looked like he might faint. I wouldn't be surprised if this was his first dog show."

"And possibly his last." Peg felt an unwanted twinge of sympathy. It was no wonder that Harvey's assistants always looked stressed. The handler had entirely too many clients to do each one justice.

On the other hand, she was well aware that Harvey's Open dog was a handsome Standard

Poodle who compared favorably with the others now in the ring. Unless she was mistaken, the dog only needed to win today's major to finish his championship. Harvey would be devastated if he missed this chance.

Peg sighed. Time was a valuable commodity for a dog show judge. And now hers was passing. She was done dithering.

"I'll start the class but take things slow," she said to Marnie. "Harvey has my permission to enter the ring when he gets here. But for pity's sake, do try to hurry him along."

Ten minutes later, Harvey made it to the ring in time, but only just. Peg leveled a beady-eyed glare in the handler's direction as he took possession of the big Poodle at the end of the line. Her meaning was clear to everyone in the vicinity. She'd granted Harvey leniency this time, but he shouldn't make a habit of needing it.

After weighing the merits and flaws of her male Standard Poodle entry, Peg was further annoyed when her earlier speculation proved to be true. She ended up awarding Harvey's dog the title of Winners Dog and the coveted three point major that went with it. With an outcome like that, Harvey would never learn better manners. But darn it, the dog had deserved the win. So what else was she supposed to do?

Peg hated it when her principles found themselves at odds with each other.

It didn't help that Marnie was laughing behind her hand as she called the Standard Puppy Bitch class into the ring.

"Wait until you get approved to judge," Peg said as they crossed paths at the judge's table. "Then I'll come and make fun of you."

"As if you'd stoop to stewarding," Marnie sniffed. Then winked. Stewarding was a difficult and often thankless job and they both knew it.

The Standard Poodle bitch classes passed without incident. Peg took the time to reassure a nervous novice handler whose lively puppy couldn't keep all four feet on the ground. The woman left the ring delighted with her red second-place ribbon in a class of just two.

In the Open class, Peg purposely paid scant attention to a local handler who'd brought her a black Standard bitch that wasn't at all her type. The man had shown under Peg on many previous occasions. He would have known that she preferred a more refined Poodle, not to mention one with a correct bite. He would also have been aware, however, that Peg and the Poodle's owner were friends.

No doubt he was hoping to capitalize on that relationship.

The implication made Peg steam. If the handler had the nerve to think that would sway her decision, he deserved the rebuke she was about to deliver. With a dismissive flick of her hand,

Peg sent the pair to cool their heels at the back of the line. Then she awarded the class, and subsequently the purple Winners Bitch ribbon, to a charming apricot bitch she hadn't previously had the pleasure of judging.

After that, Best of Variety was an easy decision. It went to a gorgeous Standard who was currently the top winning Poodle on the East Coast. The apricot bitch was Best of Winners, which meant she shared the three-point major from the dog classes. Her elated owner-handler pumped Peg's hand energetically when she handed him his ribbon.

"You certainly made someone happy," Marnie commented as she turned the pages of her catalog to the next breed on the schedule.

"Yes, and my fingers may never recover." Peg smiled. "He was so excited by the win, I was afraid for a moment that he might burst into tears. Were we ever that young and enthusiastic?"

"Of course we were. It's just that it was so long ago, we're too old to remember what it was like."

Peg turned away and surveyed her table. If Marnie was old, what did that make her? Perhaps it was better not to think about that.

She grabbed a sip of water from her bottle, then flipped her judge's book to a new page. Miniature Poodles were up next, and they'd drawn a big entry. Dogs and handlers were already beginning to gather outside the ring.

More fun coming right up.

"I wonder what that lady's story is," Marnie said. "Even in beautiful weather like this, dog shows hardly ever draw spectators anymore."

Not like in the good old days, Peg thought. She was arranging her ribbons and had yet to look up. "What lady?"

"Over there." Marnie gestured discreetly. "She's sat through four different breeds. There's a catalog in her lap but she looks like she hasn't the slightest idea how to read it."

"Maybe she just loves dogs," Peg said happily. *Welcome to the club.* She straightened to have a look, then abruptly went still. "Oh dear."

Marnie was heading to the in-gate. It was time to start handing out numbered armbands. She glanced back at Peg over her shoulder. "What?"

"That's my sister-in-law, Rose."

"Okay. Then that makes sense."

"Not to me," Peg muttered.

Marnie returned to her side. "She's really a relative of yours?"

Peg nodded.

"And you hadn't noticed she's been sitting there for an hour?"

"Apparently not." Why would she waste time perusing the ringside when she had all those lovely dogs in her ring?

"Right." Marnie didn't sound convinced.

Now that Marnie and Peg were both looking in her direction, Rose lifted a slender hand in a tentative wave. Her pleasant features were framed by a firm jaw and a cap of short gray hair was brushed back off her forehead. She was perched on the seat of a folding chair with her head up and her back straight. Rose had always had excellent posture.

Marnie smiled and waved back. Peg remained still.

Marnie gave Peg a little push. "Go say hello to her."

"I think not."

"Don't be silly. You have plenty of time."

Peg drew herself up to her full height. Even in sneakers, she neared six feet. "Not now. I have Minis to judge—"

"You're running early. I won't call the puppy dogs into the ring for at least two minutes."

"Rose can wait. I have a lunch break after Minis. She and I will talk then. Or maybe we won't." Peg pulled her gaze away. "Her choice."

"I see." Marnie bit her lip. It suddenly sounded as though this had ceased to be any of her business. "Then let me just finish handing out these armbands and we can get started."

Peg refused to let herself be distracted by her sister-in-law's presence as the first class of Miniature Poodle dogs filed into the ring. She had a job to do. Numerous exhibitors had honored her with an entry, and each of them deserved her complete attention.

Still, it was hard not to sneak a peek in Rose's direction every so often. What on earth was she doing here? As far as Peg knew, Rose didn't like dogs. Nor did she like Peg.

That feeling was mutual.

Animosity had sizzled between the two women since Peg became engaged to her beloved, and now dearly departed husband, Max, more than four decades earlier. In all the intervening years, neither Rose nor Peg had managed to put the things that were said during that rocky time entirely behind them. Max was Rose's older brother—and a man for whom Peg would have done anything. Yet even he had never succeeded in forging a friendship between the two most important women in his life.

Peg plucked a stunning white youngster from the Puppy class and awarded him the points over the older dogs. She suspected once she'd seen the rest of her Mini entry, he would win Best of Variety too. That would be a bold move on her part. People would take notice. There was bound to be talk.

As she waited for the first bitches to enter the ring, Peg allowed herself a small smile of satisfaction. The white puppy was a star in the making. He would finish his championship handily, and she would be known as the judge who'd discovered him.

Buoyed by the prospect of that success, she

allowed her gaze to flicker briefly in Rose's direction. It aggravated Peg that she felt compelled to gauge her sister-in-law's reaction. It aggravated her even more than to see that there was none.

Rose had set aside her catalog. Now her hands were folded demurely in her lap. Her expression was bland, her features arranged in a mask of resigned complacency that Peg knew infuriatingly well.

Of course Rose hadn't noticed anything unusual. She probably couldn't tell the difference between a Miniature Poodle and a hamster.

That brought Peg back to her earlier thought.

It was never good news when Rose appeared. Peg wondered what the woman wanted now.

Chapter 2

Peg finished her Mini Poodle judging by making the handsome white puppy her Best of Variety winner. Since she put the dog up over two finished champions, her selection caused some minor grumbling among the other exhibitors. Not that anyone would dare say anything to her face, of course.

"Don't worry," Marnie told her. The show photographer had been called to the ring so they could take pictures of the morning's winners before the lunch break. They were waiting for the man to appear. "I've got your back."

"Thank you," Peg replied. "I wasn't worried, however. Should I be?"

"You didn't hear what Dan Fogel said as he left the ring."

Fogel was a busy and successful professional handler with a very high opinion of himself and his dogs. He clearly hadn't been pleased when Peg moved the white puppy up from the middle of the line and placed it in front of his specials dog.

"And I don't want to either," Peg said firmly. "Considering all the breeds he handles, Dan shows under me frequently. If a momentary lapse in judgment caused him to say something

21

unfortunate, I'm better off not knowing about it. I'd hate for it to taint my opinion of him in the future."

"Your loss. He used some rather colorful language." Marnie grinned. "For what it's worth, I'd have done the same thing you did. There wasn't a better moving dog in the variety ring than that puppy."

Once the photographer arrived, a dozen pictures were taken in quick succession. Everybody knew the drill. Pose the dog, hold up the ribbon, smile, flash! Done, and on to the next.

"Lunchtime," Marnie said happily when they were finished. "I can't wait to get off my feet for a few minutes."

"You go ahead." Peg glanced toward the side of the ring. "I'll catch up."

Apparently the extra time Peg had spent taking photographs had been the last straw for Rose. Now she was squirming in her seat. Peg didn't blame her. Those folding chairs weren't meant for long-term use.

"Sounds good." Marnie followed the direction of Peg's gaze. "I'll save you a place."

The two women exited the show ring together. Marnie headed toward the hospitality tent. Peg went the other way, striding around the low, slatted barrier that formed the sides of the enclosure. She stopped in front of Rose, who looked up and smiled.

"Good morning, Peg."

"Afternoon, now," Peg replied smartly. There was another chair nearby. She dragged it over and sat down. "Imagine my surprise to find you sitting outside my ring. What are you doing here?"

"I was curious. I came to see what you do for a living."

Peg wasn't buying that for a moment. But she was willing to play along. "And?"

"It's rather boring, isn't it?"

"Not to me." Peg's smile had a wolflike quality, more a matter of bared teeth than shared humor.

"Perhaps not. I'm sure you know more about these things than I do."

Having been immersed in the sport of purebred dogs for the majority of her adult life, Peg knew more about *these things* than ninety-nine percent of the world's population. She might have been tempted to point that out except it sounded as though Rose was trying to be agreeable. And that immediately made Peg suspicious.

"If you found the judging boring, why did you stay?" she asked pleasantly.

Rose shifted sideways in her seat. Now she and Peg were face-to-face.

"I think it's time you and I got to know each other better."

Peg's mouth opened. Then closed. She could have sworn she already knew more about Rose than any sane person would ever want to know.

"Why would we want to do that?"

"Because despite our differences, we're family."

Family. Huh. As if that was a good excuse.

Peg's eyes narrowed. "What are you up to?"

"What do you mean?" Rose's reply was all innocence.

Abruptly, Peg was reminded that her sister-in-law had found a vocation early in life. She'd entered the convent straight out of high school and spent most of the intervening years as Sister Anne Marie of the Order of Divine Mercy. Rose had perfected that serenely guileless look during her time in the convent. She still used it to great effect on occasion.

Peg wasn't fooled. Having been called both a heathen and a sinner by Rose in the past, she disdainfully thought of the expression as Rose's *nun face.*

"As entertaining as it is to spar with you," she said, "I'm sure you can see that I'm quite busy today. If you have something to say to me, please do so. If not, it's time for my lunch."

The other woman sighed heavily. That was Peg's cue to stand up. Somewhere on the showgrounds there was a rubbery prewrapped sandwich calling her name. And a trip to the porta-potty wouldn't go amiss either.

"Wait," Rose said. "Give me a minute."

"I've already given you three."

"Sit back down. Please?"

It was the novelty of hearing the word *please* that did it. Peg thought that might be the first time she'd ever heard Rose voice such an appeal. She swished the skirt of her shirtwaist dress to one side and sat.

"Go on," she said.

"I want to join a bridge club. And I want you to join with me as my partner."

"You're joking."

"No." Rose frowned. "Why would I joke about something like that?"

"Because it's funny?"

It was funny, wasn't it? Any moment now, the two of them would dissolve into laughter. Not that they'd ever done so before. Belatedly it occurred to Peg that it didn't appear to be happening this time either.

Instead, Rose was simply sitting there, staring at her. Her calm manner was almost unnerving.

"A bridge club," Peg repeated. Apparently it wasn't a joke. "I would think you'd be too busy for a frivolous pastime like that."

"Of course I'm busy. But I can't spend all my time doing good works." Rose managed to deliver that statement with a straight face. "Besides, bridge isn't a frivolous game. You should know that. You used to play."

Yes, she had. But how did Rose know that?

"You mentioned it once." Rose answered the unspoken question. "You were talking about living in a dorm when you were in college. You said every night after dinner, you and your friends would go down to the living room for demitasse and bridge."

Peg was slightly stunned. "That was fifty years ago."

"Even so. You talked about it."

Peg shook her head. She barely remembered playing bridge, much less having a conversation about it later. And with Rose of all people. How had that come about? She had no idea.

"I never went to college," Rose said in a small voice.

"No. You left home to become a nun instead."

"I had a vocation."

Even Peg wasn't mean enough to point out that Rose's vocation had apparently vanished like a puff of smoke when—after more than three decades in the convent—she had met a priest and fallen in love. Peter and Rose had recently celebrated their tenth wedding anniversary, however. So there was that.

"I realize now that there are many things I missed out on in my youth," Rose said.

"That was your choice," Peg pointed out.

"I didn't know that then. I was young enough and naive enough to think that God had made the choice for me. Now that I'm older, I realize that there are many paths to eternal salvation."

"And one of them includes playing bridge?"

Peg regretted the words as soon as they'd left her mouth. In all the years she and Rose had known each other, they'd never had a conversation quite like this. All at once, Peg didn't want to be the one responsible for shutting it down. "I'm sorry. That was uncalled for."

"No, I get it. You're skeptical. I probably deserve that."

"Yes, you do."

"That goes both ways."

Peg snorted. "Don't tell me you're waiting for an apology."

"Of course not." A small smile played around the corners of Rose's mouth. "I know better than that. But I didn't come here today to fight with you."

After a pause, Peg shrugged. "It wasn't on my calendar either."

The two women shared a look of mild accord. It wasn't quite rapprochement, but perhaps a small step in that direction.

"I gather you're missing lunch on my account," Rose said. "I passed a food concession on my way in. Maybe I could buy you a salad?"

Peg nearly laughed. "Thank you, but no. Obviously you've never had dog show food."

"That bad?"

"Probably even worse than you're imagining."

"All right, then." Rose reached down into a canvas tote beside her chair and pulled out a shiny red orb. "Apple?"

Peg accepted the piece of fruit. She studied the apple from all angles, then took her first bite. "Maybe you should tell me something about your bridge club. I haven't played the game in years. I may not be up to their standards." She cocked a brow in Rose's direction. "Or yours."

"You don't have to worry about that. My friend, Carrie, belongs to the group. From what she's told me, the members enjoy getting together to play bridge, but they aren't seriously dedicated to the game. They don't play duplicate or anything like that. Just plain old rubber bridge, and it's mostly for fun and socializing."

"What about Peter?" Peg asked. "I would think you'd want to play with him."

"His game is chess, not bridge," Rose told her. "Besides, just because he and I are married doesn't mean we have to do everything together."

Peg helped herself to another bite of the apple and stared off into the distance. She and Max had done everything together. Their relationship had been one of moving in tandem toward shared goals and accomplishments. They'd created a family of renowned Standard Poodles, while building a life that suited each of them perfectly. Max had been the other half of Peg's whole. Even a decade after his death, she still felt incomplete without him. Peg would have given anything to have those days to live over again.

"Plus, I like to win," Rose was saying. "So I'd prefer to have a partner who's competitive. Someone cutthroat like you."

Peg blinked, yanking her thoughts back to the present. "Cutthroat?"

"You know what I mean. You make Genghis Khan look like a sissy."

Peg suspected she was meant to be offended. In truth, she didn't mind the comparison. Strength was a virtue in her eyes. Speaking of which, Rose wasn't giving in and going away like she usually did whenever the two of them crossed paths. Maybe she possessed more backbone than Peg knew about.

"Apparently you're not as mild-mannered as you'd like people to believe," she said.

"Then perhaps we'd make a good team."

"We'd probably end up fighting with one another."

Rose shrugged. "We fight now, so what's the difference? Who knows? Maybe after all these years, we could become friends."

Peg nearly choked on her last bite of the apple. "I highly doubt that."

"Now you sound like a quitter."

"I do *not*."

"A coward, then?"

"I see what you're doing," Peg said mildly. "You think if you back me into a corner, I will give you what you want."

"Not at all," Rose replied. "It seems to me this should be something we both want."

"How do you figure that?"

"Neither of us is getting any younger."

"So?"

"At our ages, life is all about personal connections. It's inevitable that we'll start losing people from our lives. Doesn't that make it even more important to appreciate the friends and family we have with us?"

Family. This was the second time Rose had referenced that relationship. As if things were really that simple. Unfortunately, where the Turnbull family was concerned, complications had always been a way of life.

Peg's heart squeezed painfully in her chest. Rose did have a point about losing loved ones, however. Peg hadn't needed to reach the age of seventy-two before realizing that.

Still, she hated having to admit that Rose might be right about something. So instead she said, "I'll think about your offer and get back to you."

"Don't wait too long." Rose picked up her tote and stood. "This isn't an open-ended invitation. If you dawdle, I might find someone better."

Someone better. Peg blew out a breath. *Right.* Like that was going to happen.

Chapter 3

It was almost four o'clock by the time Peg finished her last breed, awarded her last ribbon, and signed and turned in her judge's book. By that time, the group judging was already in progress. Peg paused at ringside to take a look at the Terrier Group. As the dogs gaited around the ring, her gaze immediately went to an impressive Kerry Blue. He would be her pick.

Usually after she'd finished judging, Peg remained at the show until the very end of competition. That was the time to chat with friends, compare notes on the day's entries, and debate which dog deserved to win the ultimate prize of Best in Show. Spending an entire day putting her hands on one gorgeous purebred dog after another was a privilege Peg didn't take for granted. Instead of being tired, normally she would have been exhilarated.

Today was different, however. Having completed her assignment, Peg felt moody and unsettled. Rather than summoning up the enthusiasm to stay and socialize, she was ready to go home.

Peg could guess what was responsible for her unaccustomed malaise. The visit from Rose had disrupted her routine and distracted her from doing her job. It was yet another thing for which her sister-in-law could be blamed.

Before today, it had been at least four months since the two women had spoken to each other. Their previous conversation had taken place shortly after Peter and Rose arrived back in Connecticut after a two year missionary trip to Central America. As far as Peg was concerned, one chat with Rose every two years was just about the right interval.

From the moment they'd first met, the two women had disliked each other. Peg wasn't sure she could ever imagine that changing. After all this time, she wasn't even sure she wanted their relationship to change. Despite the fact that on this occasion, Rose had seemed to be in a particularly conciliatory mood.

Bridge, indeed.

Rose and Peter had opened a women's shelter in downtown Stamford early in the year. By all accounts, the Gallagher House was a much-needed addition to the city's social service options. Surely running that philanthropic establishment was enough to keep Rose busy.

And if not, why did that have to be Peg's problem?

The drive home took less twenty minutes, much of it on shaded country roads that were lined with low stone walls almost as old as the trees around them. Peg lived on five acres of land in back country Greenwich, the area north of the Merritt Parkway. Her home was a remodeled farmhouse that dated from early in the previous century. Originally it had served as the core of a working farm. She and Max had purchased the sprawling property shortly after they were married. That was before the rich and famous had discovered Greenwich's many charms, elevating both the town's profile and its real estate prices.

In the decades that Peg had lived in her cozy home, the properties that surrounded hers had sold and resold numerous times. Now her formerly rustic lane boasted a hedge fund manager, a dotcom millionaire, and a top tennis player from the Czech Republic among its notable residents. Fortunately, her neighbors were as intent on preserving their privacy as Peg was, and they all got along splendidly.

Having purchased enough land on which to house a whole collection of Standard Poodles, Peg and Max had initially moved into their first home with just one: a beguiling, black puppy whom Max presented to Peg as a wedding present. Peg had cradled the wriggling ball of fluff in her arms, and immediately fallen in love. Over the following years, that puppy's descendants had grown into a first-class family of dogs, known throughout the Poodle world for their beauty, health, and superb temperaments.

Back then, Peg and Max had exhibited their dogs weekly at venues up and down the East Coast. As many as a dozen Standard Poodles shared their home and the kennel building out back. All their Poodles were finished champions. Some were group and Best in Show winners.

Busy and successful, Peg hadn't bothered looking toward the future. She and Max already had everything they needed or wanted. They were so in love and so in sync, it somehow felt as though the lovely life they shared would be able to cocoon them from having to face the harsher realities of life.

Until everything changed at once. Max's fatal heart attack and the subsequent theft of their top winning Poodle had quickly taught Peg that nothing, not even dreams, lasted forever. When she was younger, she'd believed in fairy tales. But that kind of cheery optimism was well behind her now.

Peg turned in her driveway and coasted toward the house. Set on a small rise, the clapboard-sided structure had been built for comfort and practicality rather than to impress. Large windows let in plenty of light. The peaked roofline added space and promoted air flow. A front porch helped to shade the home's interior. The house was stained a weathered shade of gray that blended harmoniously with its surroundings. Old and unapologetic about its age, the home projected a sturdy sense of constancy that Peg had always found comforting.

As her minivan neared the garage, three black Standard Poodle heads popped up in the front windows. Peg's face immediately creased in a smile. The sight of her canine welcoming committee never failed to lift her spirits.

Hope was the grand dame of the house. Eleven years old, the bitch was still spritely despite her age. Peg and Hope had been companions and confidantes for so long that a subliminal thread of understanding seemed to connect their thoughts. Peg knew that Hope would have been waiting near the front door for the first sound of her return.

Beside her was Coral, a lovely younger bitch who'd been handled to her championship by Peg's fifteen-year-old nephew, Davey. The third face staring through the window belonged to Peg's ten-month-old puppy, Joker. The youngest and only male Poodle, he was bouncing up and down on his hind legs in excitement.

Peg hopped out of the minivan, ran up the front steps, and threw open the front door. "Thank goodness I'm home!" she cried, laughing as she voiced the sentiment she knew her dogs were thinking.

Peg stooped down and opened her arms wide to absorb the effusive greeting. The Poodle pack didn't disappoint. Immediately she was swarmed by three warm, wiggling bodies. Each dog vied to be first in line to receive her attention. Together, the three big Poodles nearly bowled her over.

"I know," she crooned happily. "I missed you too."

Hope whined softly and pressed her nose into the hollow beneath Peg's shoulder. Coral's long pink tongue licked her chin. Joker, who'd been pushed to the rear of the group by his elders, began to bounce again.

"I know what that means," Peg said. "Everyone needs to go outside, right?"

There was a sudden scrambling of feet as the Poodles spun around and raced toward the rear of the house. Peg closed the front door and followed. On the way in, she'd stopped to get her mail from the box at the end of the driveway. Passing through the kitchen to open the back door, Peg tossed the small stack of envelopes on the butcher block table in the middle of the room.

Behind the house was a fully fenced acre field. Peg barely had the door open before the three black Poodles went flying past her out into the yard. As soon as the necessities had been taken care of, Joker grabbed up a thick length of knotted rope and whipped it up into the air, trying to entice Coral and Hope into a game of tug-of-war.

Peg was instantly on alert. When she wasn't

busy judging, she'd started taking the puppy to his first dog shows. Joker's show coat was long and still growing. It would need to be cosseted until he was finished in the ring.

"No hair pulling, you three!" she called out across the yard.

Hope sent her a baleful look. *She knew that.* Coral did, too, for that matter. Both former show dogs, the two bitches had been indoctrinated since birth about the care and handling of a Poodle show coat.

Peg harrumphed under her breath. A gentle reminder never hurt.

Leaving the back door open, she picked up the water bowl on the floor, rinsed it out, and refilled it. Then she set the kettle on the stove to make herself a cup of tea. After a glance outside confirmed that all was still good, Peg picked up the mail and thumbed through it.

The first two envelopes weren't interesting. Both held bills. Beneath them, however, was a postcard from her niece, Melanie. It had been sent from Nashville, Tennessee, and there was a picture of the Grand Ole Opry on the front.

With school out for the summer, Melanie and her husband, Sam, had rented an RV and taken their two boys, Davey and Kevin, on a month-long driving tour around the country. The family had been away for a week so far. Peg was an independent woman. She was strong, self-sufficient, and accustomed to filling her days with activities. So it was surprising how much she missed all of them.

She flipped the postcard over to read the message.

The boys are having a great time cruising the open road. Graceland coming up next. It turns out Kevin does a great Elvis impersonation. Who knew? Hope all is well with you!

Peg frowned as she tossed the postcard back on the table. Of course all was well. Why wouldn't it be? She'd just spent a lovely day judging dogs and now she was home with three delightful Poodles for company. What could be better than that?

Peg gazed around her quiet kitchen. Perhaps having someone to talk to besides a Poodle. Not that they weren't wonderful conversationalists, but still. She was loathe to admit it, but even with three big dogs crowding around her legs, the house had still felt empty when she arrived home. *Lonely*. Like something was missing.

She thought back to what Rose had said earlier. Even without trying, her sister-in-law had managed to disrupt her life once again. Peg had talked to Rose. And Rose had made her think of

Max. No wonder she was feeling out of sorts.

The kettle whistled, interrupting Peg's reflections. She checked on the Poodles once more, then poured the steaming water over the tea bag she'd placed in a ceramic mug. The postcard on the tabletop caught her eye again.

After Max's death, Peg and Melanie had become great friends. One could even call them partners in crime. Except that in their case, they'd been solving crimes rather than committing them. Peg relished unraveling puzzles, and her collaborations with Melanie had proven to be surprisingly enjoyable.

She swallowed a sip of her tea and sighed. If she was being entirely honest, it wasn't just the conversation with Rose that had been a problem. With Melanie and her family out of town for a whole month, her life seemed flatter somehow. And maybe just the tiniest bit . . . boring.

That wouldn't do at all.

Clearly Peg needed to shake things up. That thought brought her straight back to Rose with her ridiculous suggestion. Which maybe wasn't entirely ridiculous after all.

A bridge club would broaden Peg's circle of friends. And bridge was a thinking person's game. That was another plus in its favor. But good gracious, it had been decades since she'd played. Did she even remember how?

Perhaps she could find a good refresher course

online. It wouldn't hurt to sharpen up the old skills again.

Peg put down her mug and took out her phone. "So," she said when Rose picked up, "just how cutthroat do you need me to be?"

Chapter 4

Rose disconnected the call and stared at her phone with a bemused expression on her face.

"That was Peg, wasn't it?" On the other side of the living room, her husband, Peter, was sitting in an overstuffed armchair. A pair of tortoiseshell glasses was perched on the bridge of his nose and he was holding a book open in his lap.

An affable man in his late sixties, Peter had devoted his life to helping others, first within the priesthood, and then later as a lay counselor. He had comfortable features, a soothing manner, and the enviable ability to put others around him at ease. Having come through a recent health scare, he was slowly working his way back to full-time activity.

"It was," Rose confirmed.

"Bad news?"

"Not exactly."

"Good news?"

Rose smiled. "Honestly, I'm not sure."

Peter set his book aside. It looked as though this conversation could take a while. "What did Peg say?"

"That she'd be willing to attend a bridge club meeting with me and give it a provisional try."

"That's what you wanted, right?"

"I guess so." Rose shrugged her slender shoulders. She had on a neon pink polo shirt, paired with knee-length madras shorts. After so many years of wearing the same dark habit every day, she reveled in the ability to dress in bright colors. "Minus the provisional part. Maybe."

Peter rose and walked over to where his wife was standing beside an open window. She was still holding her phone. He took the device from her hand and placed it on a nearby table.

Early in the year, he and Rose had returned from Honduras to found a women's shelter in Stamford. Initially, they'd resided in the cramped, dark apartment in the basement of the building. By May their finances had stabilized, however, and they'd been able to move into a small ranch house in Springdale, just a few miles away.

The view from their windows wasn't much— there were neighboring houses close to them on either side. But now that Rose could see out again, there were times when she was content to simply gaze up at the open sky. Until talking to Peg brought her back down to earth and made her serenity vanish.

"Maybe?" Peter lifted a brow. "This morning you seemed to think that was a good idea. Have you changed your mind?"

"No, but . . ." Rose turned around to face him. "Why does that woman always have to make everything so difficult?"

"As far as I've been able to tell, it's Peg's nature to avoid doing things the easy way."

Peter expected Rose to laugh, or at least smile in acknowledgment. She did neither.

"Why didn't you remind me of that this morning when I got the harebrained idea to track her down at a dog show and ask her to be my bridge partner?" she grumbled.

"Because after all these years, it seems to me that it's time for you and Peg to finally heal the rift between you. And because I was proud of you for being the one to take the first step."

Rose sighed. "Darn it. I was trying to stay mad and now you've gone and ruined it."

"Good. That was my intent." Peter led her to the sofa where they sat down together. "Perhaps this introductory outing to the bridge club should be approached as a provisional arrangement on both sides."

"You mean, if I take the time to get to know Peg better, I might like her even less than I do now?"

"I don't know. Is that possible?" Peter was gratified by the fact that this time Rose did smile.

"Peg and I are both grown women," she said. "Adults in every sense of the word except when it comes to our relationship. Why is it so hard for us to move past something that happened more than forty years ago?"

"Because up until now, neither of you has really tried, have you?" Peter pointed out. "Sometimes there's comfort in maintaining the status quo. Remaking your connection with Peg will involve throwing out old prejudices and preconceived notions. Change, even when it's welcome, can be a complicated process."

"Dealing with Peg is a complicated process too," Rose retorted.

"And yet you asked her to partner with you in joining a bridge club."

"I must have been out of my mind."

"I sincerely doubt that." Peter waited a minute, then said, "You've never entirely explained what it was that started the problems between the two of you."

"Peg married my older brother Max," Rose replied. "After that, everything went straight downhill."

" 'Everything' encompasses quite a lot." Peter reached over and took one of her hands in his. "Perhaps we should try to narrow it down. Were you in the convent at the time?"

Rose nodded.

"And you became acquainted with Peg because she was engaged to marry Max?"

"Yes. She and Max visited the convent and we met briefly. By then, Peg's engagement to Max was already a fait accompli."

"Interesting," Peter mused. "Had you expected to have input as to whom your brother chose to marry?"

"No, of course not." Rose shot her husband an annoyed look. "But I didn't expect him to choose a woman with low morals, an absurdly high opinion of herself, and a temper that could blister paint."

Peter bit back a smile and squeezed his wife's fingers, perhaps a bit harder than necessary. "Rose, you know I love you dearly, but you're sounding rather judgmental."

"Looking back now, I suppose that's how I acted when Peg and I first met," she admitted. "My only excuse is that I was young, and very naive. I was barely eighteen when I entered the convent. I knew almost nothing about the ways of the real world."

Peter nodded and waited for her to continue.

"I idolized Max. Michael was our older brother, but when we were children, he always seemed to be somewhere else, doing something more important than spending time with us. Max was the one who listened to me, played games with me, and walked me to school. I thought he could do no wrong."

"It sounds as though the two of you shared a wonderful bond. And that maybe you were a bit jealous when Peg came along and intruded upon your relationship?"

"It wasn't that," Rose said.

"Are you sure? It seems to me that a supportive sister would have welcomed the woman your brother wanted to marry with open arms."

"Peg was pregnant at the time."

"I see." Peter took a moment to digest that. "I'm tempted to say, 'It happens, even in the best of families,' but under the circumstances, I suppose that would sound dismissive."

"I was outraged," Rose told him. "I'd spent my childhood in Catholic school. When I met Peg, I'd just taken my vows after two years as a novice. At that point in my life, I was as indoctrinated in the teachings of the Church as anyone could possibly be. All I knew was that Peg had been guilty of living in sin. In my eyes, that meant she wasn't good enough for Max."

Peter cleared his throat softly. "Now that you've had plenty of time to think about your initial reaction, I hope you've realized that for Peg to have found herself in that condition, your brother Max must have been living in sin too?"

"Of course," Rose snapped. Then her voice softened. "There are any number of life lessons that are clearer to me now than they were when I was twenty. I'm not proud of the way I behaved. Looking back now, it makes me shudder to even think about it."

"Perhaps you should admit that to Peg."

"I tried." Rose's chin lifted. "Several times. Peg's a tough woman. She didn't want to listen."

"Peg's not the only tough woman in your family," Peter said. "Maybe you should try again."

"It feels like it's too late now."

"Trust me," he said. "It's never too late."

Rose remained silent. She moved over so she could rest her head on Peter's shoulder.

"I never had a chance to meet Max," he mused. "I seem to recall he died shortly before I left the priesthood."

"Yes, that's right. It's a shame you never got to know him. You and Max have a lot in common. I'm sure you would have liked him."

"I don't recall ever meeting Peg and Max's child either."

There was a long pause before Rose replied. "There was no child. Peg lost the baby. It would have been a little girl. I'm not sure what went wrong, but after that Peg wasn't able to have any more children."

"How tragic," Peter murmured.

"Yes, it was tragic. Obviously I know that now. But at the time, I was filled with the hubris of my calling, and I'm afraid I behaved like a fool. I told Peg that the loss she'd suffered was God's punishment for the immoral way she'd conducted herself."

"Oh dear."

Rose felt Peter stiffen. She lifted her head and looked at him across the small distance between them. "Now you know the most unforgiveable thing I've ever done. It's something I'll regret for the rest of my life. Please tell me you don't despise me for the way I behaved."

"I could never do that," he replied. "You are the dearest woman in the world to me. Never doubt that for a single moment."

"Peg hates me," Rose said in a small voice.

"I doubt that. *Hate* is a strong word. And even the harshest emotions have a way of mellowing with time. You and Peg are talking to each other now. That's a good sign. It could be that you'll find out the two of you make a good team when you join the bridge club together."

Rose frowned. "Or maybe she'll bid me up to slam then lay down a hand with three points, just so she can have the pleasure of watching me go down in flames."

"I'd like to see that," Peter said with a laugh. "If I were her, I might be tempted."

"So you think maybe she deserves a little payback?"

"Not exactly. What I'm saying is that rather than the two of you sniping at each other all the time, maybe you and Peg should try letting go of the past and give each other a little leeway for once. Life is hard. Stuff happens. Deal with it and move on."

Now Rose was the one who was laughing. "You were in school for years. You have advanced degrees in both counseling and social work. And that's the best you can come up with? 'Deal with it and move on'?"

"Damn straight," Peter replied. "You'd be

surprised how many contentious situations could be neutralized if only people would listen to that advice."

"All right," said Rose. "Then I'm in. Let's hope that Peg agrees."

Chapter 5

"This is the place?" Peg asked dubiously.

She and Rose were standing outside the community center in Old Greenwich, preparing to enter. The building was one story tall and constructed of brick. A row of windows brightened an otherwise plain facade. Peg thought the place resembled the elementary school where she'd learned to read and write. There was even a playground and a soccer field off to one side.

Two days had passed since Peg agreed to become Rose's bridge partner. She'd had plenty of time to change her mind since then. It hadn't happened though. Mostly because Peg had tried to think about the upcoming commitment as little as possible.

So now, for better or worse, here she was.

"Of course it's the place," Rose said briskly, striding toward the door. "What did you expect?"

When she'd been told that the bridge club met on Tuesday afternoons at a community center, Peg had pictured someplace, well, homier. All her memories of playing bridge harked back to a much earlier time. She and her friends had sat cross-legged on the floor of their dorm's living room, playing cards in front of a large, cozy fireplace.

51

Clearly this was going to be a very different experience.

Not that Old Greenwich didn't have plenty of small town appeal. Peg had always thought of the charming coastal community as "her" Greenwich's little sister. The community center wasn't located in the village, however. Instead it was north of those delightful shops, nearer to the Post Road than Long Island Sound. Perhaps that accounted for its functional appearance.

"Well, you know," Peg said, still looking around as she followed along behind, "you did say Old Greenwich."

"This is Old Greenwich." Rose sounded exasperated. She was holding the door open for Peg. "Come *on*. Especially our first time, we don't want to be late."

"Late," Peg huffed. She was never late. That was a point of pride.

By her watch, they were fifteen minutes early. She barely had time to take more than a quick glance around the center's reception area, however. Rose was already hurrying down a side hallway, her heels clicking a brisk tattoo on the linoleum floor.

"This way," she said.

Peg's gaze slid over the walls as they passed by. They were lined with team pictures, colorful banners, and posters announcing upcoming activities. "How do you know where you're going?"

"Carrie Maynard, my friend who's in the club, told me that they meet in the Elk Room," Rose tossed back over her shoulder. "I looked up a map of the building online."

Elk Room? Peg could hardly imagine a building less qualified to advertise itself as a habitat for wildlife of any kind.

All at once she was tired of being rushed along. Peg stopped walking. "You know, you're not at Divine Mercy anymore."

Rose's steps slowed, then stopped altogether. She turned around. "What does that mean?"

"Mother Superior isn't watching you now. You're not setting an example for impressionable young children. There's no need to go racing along as if it's a sin to waste even a single moment of time."

"That's not what I'm doing."

Peg lifted an eloquent brow.

Rose's eyes narrowed. "And you're not at a dog show. Which means you have better things to do than stand in one place while everyone twirls a circle around you, hoping you'll decide that their dog is the fluffiest one."

"That is not what I do."

"No? That's what it looked like to me."

"That's because you have an uneducated eye," Peg snapped.

"Right." Rose shook her head. "You're never going to let me forget that I didn't attend college, are you?"

"Don't be ridiculous. College has nothing to do with judging dogs."

"I'm glad to hear you admit that, at least."

"At least?" Peg frowned. "What are you complaining about now?"

"Asks the woman who can never, ever, admit when she's wrong."

"That's because it happens so seldom, it hardly seems worth the bother."

Rose blew out an annoyed breath. "And to think, I'd almost convinced myself that I owed you an apology."

Peg stared at her sister-in-law incredulously. She heard the words, but they took a moment to sink in. Then it felt as though she should say *something*. But for once in her life she had no idea what that should be.

An apology? *From Rose?* Peg didn't know such a thing was even possible.

Then the front door to the community center opened behind her and the moment was lost. Four people entered the building at once. Two men and two women were chatting and laughing together like old friends. The couples started down the hallway toward them.

Peg turned back to Rose, but she was too late. In the few seconds she'd delayed before answering, her sister-in-law had already moved on. Rose's fingers clutched the curved metal handle of a nearby door. She yanked it open.

"I'll see you inside," Rose said.

Peg had no idea what had just happened. Nevertheless, she was pretty sure it was at least partly her fault. Why did Rose always have to be so prickly about the things she'd missed during those years she'd spent in the convent? If she'd only stop reacting every time the subject came up, Peg would lose the urge to keep goading her about it.

Besides, it wasn't as though Peg had never changed her mind about a decision—though none of her misjudgments had been of such life-altering magnitude. Luckily, Rose had never been around to witness any of Peg's missteps.

The group of four had almost reached her. Peg strode over to the door, drew it open, and went inside. The room was medium in size—a meeting room rather than an auditorium—and brightly lit. Industrial carpeting covered the floor. The space was air-conditioned to a temperature just slightly south of arctic. Peg was happy she'd thought to bring a cotton sweater with her.

Four card tables with chairs were set up in the center of the room. They were placed far enough apart to discourage kibitzing, but near enough that the players could converse from table to table if they needed to. Set out on each tabletop were just two decks of cards, a scorepad, and a pencil.

Old school, Peg thought happily. At least that part looked familiar. There weren't any fancy bidding boxes or card holders, just the basic equipment needed to play and score the games. Somehow it made the whole endeavor seem less intimidating.

Rose was standing beside a refreshment table toward the back of the room. She was holding a cup of coffee in her hand and talking to a plump, older woman whose blond bouffant hairdo had last been fashionable in the 1960s.

Carrie Maynard, Peg assumed. She made her way across the floor to join them.

"There you are," Rose said, as if she hadn't just abandoned Peg in the hallway outside. "I'd like you to meet my friend Carrie."

The two women shook hands. Peg was careful not to squeeze too hard. Carrie's fingers were adorned with an assortment of rings whose stones were large enough to inflict pain. Several matched the heavy turquoise pendant that hung from a chain around her neck.

"Welcome to our little club," Carrie said. "It's a pleasure to meet you. I'm the informal director of the group, mostly because I'm the one who originally came up with the idea and found us a place to meet. That all happened years ago, of course. But nobody else has volunteered to step up and take charge in the meantime, so it still all falls to me."

"I'm sure you do a wonderful job," Peg said.

"Thank you, I try." Carrie looked pleased by the compliment. "When the Harrelsons moved away last month, I was afraid it might take some time to replace them. And having only seven pairs for bridge means one couple would have to sit out. So it was a lucky thing that I happened to be talking to Rose, and she offered to find a partner and come join us. She told me you've played bridge for years."

"Not exactly," Peg replied. "What Rose meant was that I used to play bridge years ago. I'm afraid I might be a little rusty."

"Don't worry about that," said Carrie. "I'm sure we'll have you up to speed in no time. Most of us have been playing together forever, and we're all here to have a good time. Everyone will understand if it takes you a few games to find your footing."

"Thank you," Peg said. "I appreciate that."

"Of course your partner may not be as patient with you as we are." Carrie winked at Rose, and the two of them laughed together.

Peg wasn't amused. In almost any situation, she was accustomed to being the competent one. Now she hated feeling that her skills might not be up to scratch.

Not only that, but she and Rose had never partnered one another before. They'd spoken earlier to compare notes on their preferred strategies for bidding and play. Even so, there was bound to be a learning process as they figured out each other's idiosyncrasies.

Rose didn't seem to be too concerned about any of that, however. Peg had decided that meant she shouldn't worry either. If the worst that could happen was that she embarrassed herself in front of a group of people whom she'd never met before and might never have to see again, well, it wouldn't be the first time.

While Carrie and Rose continued their conversation, Peg checked out the refreshment table. Coffee and bottled water were the only drinks available. There wasn't a single tea bag in sight. She picked up a napkin and helped herself to a cheese mini-Danish. Carrie left to talk to someone else, so Peg turned back to face the room with Rose.

Another pair, two men this time, came through the doorway. Both were nearing Peg's age. One man was tall and scrawny looking. The second, shorter man had a paunch that strained against the buttons of his patterned shirt. Both men were wearing ball caps on their heads.

By now, most of the other bridge players had arrived. People were helping themselves to refreshments and conversing in small groups.

Looking around at the assembled company, Peg realized there was a reason why the members of this club played bridge the same way that she'd originally learned the game. There wasn't a single person in the room under the age of sixty.

"You might have warned me," she said mildly.

Rose glanced her way. "About what?"

"This looks like an old folks' club."

"Why would I have warned you about that? I hate to break it you, Peg, but you and I are old folks. We fit right in."

Carrie stepped to the middle of the room and clapped her hands several times. The buzz of conversation died away. Heads turned in her direction.

"Everyone, I'd like you to meet our new players, Rose Donovan and her partner, Peg Turnbull. Both of them are avid bridge players, and I know they can't wait to jump right in."

Peg and Rose shared a startled look, but Carrie didn't seem to notice. She was still talking. "Let's make them feel welcome by going around the room and introducing ourselves. And please take a moment to tell Rose and Peg a little bit about yourselves."

"I'll start." One of the men who'd entered the room behind Peg took a step forward. He was trim and handsome, and he sported a golfer's tan. "I'm John Severson, and this is my wife, Violet." He indicated the smiling woman standing beside him. She was wearing a flower-sprigged sundress and had a cardigan sweater draped around her shoulders. "We're from Greenwich, and we've been part of this group for more years than we'd like to count," John finished with a laugh.

Florence and Franny Grover were two sisters from south Stamford. The two women not only resembled each other, they were also wearing matching outfits. Their silver hair was styled in the same short pixie cut. When they spoke, they even sounded alike.

Good Lord, thought Peg. That was what too much togetherness could do to sisters. She glanced over at Rose. It was a good thing the two of them had never been in danger of that happening.

Stanley Peters went next. "You can call me Stan," he said. He was the tall, skinny man Peg had seen earlier. "I enjoy all sorts of card games, and now that I'm retired I have more time to devote to them. I can't say bridge is at the top of my list, but it's close enough."

Stan smiled broadly, like that was a joke. Peg wondered what other kinds of card games he enjoyed. Maybe poker or blackjack?

"This is my good buddy, Mick Doran," Stan continued, gesturing to the stocky man next to him. "He's probably forgotten more about bidding conventions than I'll ever bother to learn." Mick lifted a hand in greeting.

After that, Sue Richey introduced herself and her fiancé, Bennett Jones. There was a sizable age gap between them, with Bennett being the younger partner. The couple looked good together, however, standing closer to each other than was strictly necessary, and listening to each other's words when they spoke.

Sue gazed up at Bennett the same way that Peg had once looked at Max. The realization brought a lump to Peg's throat. She hoped that couple was as happy as she and Max had been.

"Standing next to Bennett is my partner, Lacey Duvall," Carrie announced, pulling Peg's attention back to the matter at hand. Lacey had bright blue eyes and long gray hair was gathered on top of her head in a bun. She favored Peg and Rose with a tight smile and a nod.

"Lacey and I met in college," Carrie said. "And believe it or not, after all these years we're still friends."

"Stan, Reg, and I have known each other since high school, and I guess we still tolerate each other well enough." Jerry Watkins was a portly man with a gruff voice. After sharing that tidbit, he declared himself too uninteresting to be worth talking about and nudged his "better half" forward. "This is my wife, Mae. She's shy."

Mae shook her head. "Oh, Jerry, don't be ridiculous. You'll give the new ladies the wrong idea." Even wearing tall wedge sandals, Mae barely came up to her husband's shoulder. She giggled as she turned to Peg and Rose. "He's only saying that to make fun of me. Jerry thinks I talk too much."

"A little table talk between hands is fine," he said. "But not when you're supposed to be concentrating on your cards."

Peg noticed that several other members of the group appeared to agree. She made a note to keep chitchat to a minimum once she sat down.

"Last but not least," said a melodious voice.

A striking woman separated herself from the crowd. Dark hair fell in soft waves to her shoulders and artfully applied makeup accentuated the angular planes of her face. Even Peg, who took as little interest in clothing as she could possibly manage, could tell that hers was couture.

"I'm Paige Greene, and I'm here with my husband, Reg. We live in Belle Haven. Reggie used to work in Manhattan but he's retired now. I run a thriving real estate business in Greenwich." Paige's smile was bright and sparkly. "Maybe you've seen my commercials?"

"I'm afraid not," Peg said. "I've lived in the same house since the nineteen-seventies. It's been a very long time since I was in the market for real estate."

"More than forty years." A calculating look flickered in Paige's eyes. "In Greenwich?"

Peg nodded. "Back country."

"You and I should talk. If you're thinking about downsizing—"

Carrie's sudden laughter sounded forced. "Now, Paige, let's give Peg and Rose a chance to settle in before you start trying to sell their houses out from under them."

"Hear, hear!" said a male voice from the other side of the room.

Paige started to scowl, then quickly wiped her expression clean. "I apologize for being overly enthusiastic. But you all know how much I love my job."

Reggie Greene had broad shoulders, a full head of hair, and coffee-brown eyes. He looked down at his wife indulgently. "Let's turn that enthusiasm toward your cards this afternoon. Okay, honey?"

"Yes, dear."

"Perfect!" Carrie clapped her hands again. "Now let's sit down and play bridge."

Chapter 6

After that pronouncement, it still look a few minutes to get everything coordinated. Though she and Peg had only been members of the bridge club for fifteen minutes, Rose was already beginning to realize that organization wasn't the group's strong suit.

Carrie started things off by drawing name slips out of a small, lacquered box to see which pairs would compete against each other in the first round of play. Each group of four would complete a rubber of bridge. When everyone was finished, there would be a short break before the players were remixed into new combinations for a second rubber.

Carrie and Lacey looked pleased to be paired with John and Violet Severson. Stanley and Mick sat down at the second table with Sue and Bennett. The Grover sisters would play with Paige and Reggie Greene. That left Rose and Peg with Jerry and Mae Watkins.

"This is going to be fun," Mae said happily as her husband shuffled the cards before the first deal. She picked up the second deck and shuffled that one too. "We always enjoy coming to bridge club, but it'll be more interesting getting to play with new people. Right, Jerry?"

"Right, Mae." He nodded and handed the deck to Rose so she could cut the cards.

Mae peeked over at Rose from beneath lowered lashes. "Carrie said the two of you were good. But I hope you're not Life Masters, or anything like that. Because Jerry and I are just a couple of amateurs."

"Not even close," Rose assured her. "In fact, Peg hasn't played bridge in a number of years. So I'm hoping that she and I won't have a hard time keeping up with you and Jerry."

"I'm sure you'll do just fine." Jerry dealt the cards into four neat piles.

Looking at the stiff set of Peg's shoulders as she picked up her cards and arranged her hand, Rose wished she shared Jerry's confidence. She hoped she hadn't given too much credit to Peg's seemingly effortless ability to rise to any occasion. Now the dratted woman was frowning in concentration. Surely Peg wasn't having trouble counting her points.

Rose had considered getting together with Peg to run through a few practice hands before coming today. But she hadn't wanted to take a chance that meeting in person might ruin their fragile détente before they could even make it this far. Now she could only hope that hadn't been a mistake.

Jerry gazed down at his cards, considered for a few seconds then said, "Pass."

Rose's hand looked fairly useless. She also passed.

Mae was beaming at her cards. The woman clearly didn't have a poker face. "One club." She opened.

Then it was Peg's turn. She bid one diamond.

Rose tried to read her partner's body language. Was that a strong opening bid or a weak one? Beyond the basic prep work they'd done over the phone, Rose had no idea what to expect from Peg. The woman had always been a wild card in more ways than one. To make matters worse, diamonds were Rose's weakest suit.

When Jerry supported his partner's bid by raising it to two clubs, Rose was forced to pass again. Peg stared at her across the table. She didn't look pleased.

On the other hand, Peg seldom looked pleased when Rose was around. So that was nothing new.

After Mae raised Jerry's bid to three clubs, Peg frowned and passed too.

Mae was the declarer; she would play the hand. Rose and Peg would defend. Sitting to Mae's left, Peg placed the first card faceup on the table. The ten of spades. Jerry was the dummy. He laid down his hand so they could all see what cards he had.

Based on the information she now possessed, Rose thought the bid of three clubs looked like a slam dunk for her opponents. It didn't take long for her to be proven right. Playing quickly and decisively, Mae not only made her contract, she also picked up an extra trick. Jerry, who'd appointed himself scorekeeper, dutifully wrote down the result.

Rose picked up the preshuffled deck, let Mae cut it, and then took her turn to deal the cards. After several more games rapidly went by, Mae and Jerry succeeded in winning the rubber handily. The husband-and-wife team had controlled most of the bidding and the play.

Just amateurs indeed, Rose thought.

She and Peg had only won the contract once when Peg prodded Rose to an overly optimistic four spade bid. Rose thought she'd played well enough, but she'd still fallen short by two tricks.

Maybe this partnership hadn't been her best idea.

"Tell us about yourselves," Mae invited while the four of them were waiting for the other tables to finish playing. "The rest of us have been together for so long it almost feels like we're family now. We have nothing new to learn about each other. Peg, what are your other interests besides playing bridge?"

"Dogs." Peg had been looking glum after their quick defeat. Now, offered the chance to talk about her favorite subject, she quickly perked up again. "I breed and show Standard Poodles. I'm also a dog show judge."

"Mae and I watch the Westminster dog show on TV," Jerry said.

Peg smiled. "I judged the Non-Sporting Group there two years ago."

"Poodles are the poufy looking dogs, right?" asked Mae.

Rose knew Peg wouldn't be pleased by that description. She considered jumping in before her partner could snap back a retort. But to her surprise, Peg's reply was unexpectedly restrained.

"The poufy part is just hair," she said. "Underneath is a dog with great intelligence and an innate desire to please. The breed was originally developed to be a retrieving dog, and there are many sportsmen who still use them in that capacity. There's no better companion than a Poodle."

"I never knew any of that." Jerry sounded surprised.

Rose figured he'd probably never met anyone who'd given that much thought to Poodles before. Come to think of it, neither had she.

"Don't encourage her, or Peg will talk your ear off," Rose said lightly. "She never talks about anything but dogs if she can help it."

She slipped Peg a quick wink to show she meant no offence. To her surprise, Peg winked back. Until that moment, Rose would have thought Peg didn't have a lighthearted bone in her entire body.

"What about you and Jerry?" Peg asked Mae. "How long have you been married?"

"Coming up on thirty-five years," Mae replied. "And we have four wonderful children."

"Three girls and a boy," Jerry said proudly. "It took us four tries until Jerry Jr. came along but he was worth the wait."

One by one, the matches around them ended. Carrie got out her box and reshuffled the players. After a break for people to stretch their legs and refill their coffee cups, play resumed.

Once they'd taken their new seats, Rose and Peg's second rubber proceeded much the same way their first one had. This time they were paired with Florence and Franny. The sisters bid and played with the serene assurance of partners who could almost read each other's minds. By contrast, Rose and Peg bumbled through the bidding and performed only slightly better during the play.

At least this time they managed to get some points on the score pad. Peg made a contract of three hearts. Then Florence bid a small slam in spades and just missed making it when her finesse of Rose's king of diamonds failed. Those minor triumphs were small consolation in the face of a second, stinging defeat, however.

"I don't like this game anymore," Peg said under her breath as she pushed her chair away from the table and stood up. "I used to love playing bridge. I can't imagine what's changed."

"Fifty years," Rose said. "That's what's changed. You're out of practice."

"Which is why you should be sure to return next week," Violet Severson offered from the next table over. "Everybody makes mistakes when they haven't played in a while. And trust me, nobody here minds being handed a few easy wins while you take the time to sharpen up your game. Bridge is like riding a bicycle. That muscle memory will come right back."

Rose wasn't so sure of that. Especially since, in this case, the muscle involved was the one between Peg's ears. Peg seemed encouraged by Violet's words, however, so that was probably a good thing.

The scorecards were turned in, and the points were tallied. Paige and Reggie Greene were announced as the day's top scorers. Everyone applauded. Reggie grinned, and Paige took a small bow. All the club members looked as though they'd had a good time.

On the way out of the community center, Rose thanked Carrie for inviting her and Peg to attend the meeting. Though she hadn't consulted with Peg, she promised that they would return the following week. Then she hurried to catch up to Peg who had already reached the parking lot.

"I wouldn't mind sitting down over a cup of coffee and holding a postmortem before we head

71

home," Rose said before Peg could climb into her minivan.

Peg considered, then nodded. "I know just the place. There's a lovely little café in the middle of town. Get your car and follow me."

Ten minutes later, Rose and Peg were settled at a small table in a cozy tearoom just off Sound Beach Avenue. At just before five o'clock, the place was nearly empty. Peg had chosen a seat with a view out the front window. She ordered a pot of Earl Grey tea and an extra-large slice of whatever kind of cake the kitchen recommended.

Rose sat down opposite her and asked for a cup of coffee. During the years she'd spent living in a hut in Honduras—where cream and sugar had seemed like unimaginable luxuries—she'd grown accustomed to drinking it black. As Rose took her first hot sip, an enormous piece of coconut cake was delivered to the table.

Peg's eyes lit up. She immediately reached for her fork.

"That will ruin your dinner," Rose commented.

Peg cut off a wedge of cake and slipped it in her mouth. She chewed blissfully, then swallowed. "More likely this will be my dinner."

Oh. Rose hadn't considered that.

When Rose got home, she and Peter would cook something for dinner—chicken and pasta dishes were their current favorites—then sit down at the table and eat together. Peg lived alone. She had no one to cook with, or to cook for. Unless you counted all those Poodles, which Rose most definitely did not.

"This coconut frosting is sublime." Peg paused briefly to savor it. "I might even order another piece."

"You should do that," Rose blurted.

Peg gave her an odd look as she continued to shovel cake into her mouth.

"You know. If it makes you happy."

Peg stopped chewing. "Why, Rose, I didn't think you cared."

Did she? All at once Rose wasn't sure. The ambivalence made her feel decidedly annoyed.

"Don't get used to it." Rose lifted her cup to her lips and gulped down too much hot coffee at once. She sucked in a breath as her throat burned. Rose waited until the pain passed, then said, "I thought our first bridge session went well enough."

"Did you really?" Peg peered at her across the table. "I thought it was a near disaster."

Rose sputtered out a laugh. If nothing else, Peg could be counted on for honesty.

"Perhaps a small disaster," she admitted. "Our bidding felt like a wrestling match."

"That's because you kept refusing to support my no trump bids."

"Just because you're afraid to commit to a suit

doesn't mean you need to play every hand in no trump."

"Every hand?" Peg snorted. "I only played one. And the bid was three hearts. If it had been three no trump, it would have made game."

"If the bid had been three no trump, you would have gone down."

"Would not," said Peg.

"Would too," Rose retorted.

At the same time, both women became aware that they sounded like a pair of bickering five-year-olds. As one, they stopped talking. Rose watched in approval as Peg paused to have more cake. That should improve her mood.

She waited until Peg's mouth was full, then said, "We need to do better next time."

"Next time?" As if Peg couldn't talk around a simple piece of cake. "You want to do that again?"

"Of course. Don't you?"

Peg stopped and thought for a minute. "Actually, yes, I suppose I do," she admitted. "Despite our failures, I was surprised by how quickly the time flew by. I had fun."

"We'll need to make some changes going forward, however," Rose said firmly. "For one thing, you spent more time watching the other players than you did looking at your cards."

Peg shrugged. "I was in a room full of people I'd never met before. They were more interesting than some of the hands I was dealt."

"And you like to snoop," Rose pointed out.

"You say that like it's a bad thing."

"It's not a good one."

Peg lifted a hand to call over the waitress. After requesting another slice of cake, she said to Rose, "I'm perfectly capable of doing two things at once, you know. I never once played the wrong card."

Rose wisely kept mum about that. She watched as a veritable brick of cake was set down in front of Peg, who promptly dug in with relish. The woman must have the metabolism of a racehorse.

"Paige and Reggie were signaling each other under the table," Peg mentioned when she next came up for air. "Not entirely surprising, I suppose. Paige struck me as the kind of woman who doesn't like to lose."

"What?" Rose gasped.

"You didn't notice?" Peg sounded smug.

Rose shook her head.

"Their feet were intertwined beneath the table."

"Maybe they were feeling affectionate."

"No." Peg considered. "That wasn't it. For one thing, they both kept their shoes on. And for another, their toes appeared to be tapping out some kind of code."

Rose was stuck on the first part of what Peg said. "What do their shoes have to do with anything?"

"Surely you're not that naive." Peg smiled so

the words wouldn't feel too much like an insult.

Rose just stared at her. Sadly, she had no idea what one might attempt to do underneath a table, with or without shoes. Maybe she really was that naive.

"And besides," said Peg, "they won, didn't they?"

"Paige and Reggie?" Now Rose was trying to remember what kind of shoes the couple had been wearing. In case that made a difference.

"Of course Paige and Reggie. That's who we were talking about, isn't it?"

Rose nodded. Conversations with Peg were never easy. Even when she thought she knew what they were about. And right now, she wasn't sure if she had a clue.

Peg polished off her cake, then nabbed the check before it even reached the table. "My treat."

"Thank you." Rose dug in her purse to leave a tip on the table. "Next time it's on me."

The two women parted ways at the door. They both had minivans, but the vehicles were parked in different directions. It wasn't until Rose had climbed in her front seat and fastened her seat belt that a sudden thought struck her. For perhaps the first time in her life, she'd managed to hold an entire conversation with Peg where neither one of them was angry at the end.

Imagine that.

Chapter 7

Peg's puppy, Joker, was entered in a dog show the following weekend. She devoted the next few days to getting him ready.

With her schedule so crowded with judging assignments, it was hard for Peg to find a chance to get one of her own Poodles into the ring. That difficulty was compounded by the fact that just about everyone in the dog show world knew who she was. Even when Peg would have preferred to keep a low profile, her reputation preceded her.

Some judges, even experienced ones, quaked when they saw her walk through their in-gates. Then they handed her the win because they couldn't take the pressure of having to decide for themselves whether or not Peg's Poodle was actually the best one in front of them. She hated that.

Before she had a judge's license, Peg had spent years as an avid exhibitor. She loved the competition and the camaraderie at the shows. She enjoyed spending time in the grooming tent with other handlers as they prepared their Poodles for the ring. Conversations flowed and lifelong friendships were forged among a group of people for whom nothing was better than talking about Poodles, except perhaps living and competing with them.

Peg knew she could never return to those bygone days when she'd been just another exhibitor. All she wanted now was for her dogs to be judged fairly and without the deference some people thought she was due. For that reason, she'd made Saturday's entry under Henry Stillman.

Henry was a good man and an even better judge. He was older than Peg and had been a member of the dog community even longer. He and Peg's late husband, Max, had been close friends for years.

Henry wouldn't be intimidated by Peg's presence in his ring. Indeed, he would have laughed at the very idea. If Joker were to live up to his name and misbehave during the judging, Henry was likely to pat Peg on the head and send her to the back of the line. Which was exactly the attitude Peg wanted from a judge. Well, perhaps not the head-patting part, but that was just Henry.

Friday morning, Peg was in her grooming room, located in the basement of her house. The space was small, but perfectly appointed. One wall was lined with shelves of brushes, combs, clippers, and a dozen other tools of the trade. A raised bathtub made bathing easier. Two rows of track lighting on the ceiling lit even the darkest corners. Everything Peg needed was within easy reach.

Joker's face, his feet, and the base of his tail had already been clipped short. Now it was time to give the puppy a bath, then blow dry his coat. At ten months of age, Joker had already grown a tremendous amount of hair. The process would take three to four hours to complete.

Joker stood quietly for his bath, then waited for Peg to lift him out of the tub and onto a rubber-matted grooming table. She draped a towel loosely over the big dog's body, then stepped away to let him have a good shake. Next, she laid the puppy down on his side on the table. Meticulous brushing would straighten the hair while it was being dried by a stream of warm air from a large, freestanding blow dryer.

Peg was about to turn on the dryer when her phone rang. The device was sitting on a nearby counter. She glanced over at it and frowned. Time was of the essence now. If Joker's hair was allowed to dry naturally, it would kink and curl. Then she'd have to wet the puppy down and start over.

"Darn it." Peg knew better than to pause. Nevertheless, curiosity got the better of her. She gave Joker a reassuring pat, put down her pin brush, and stepped over to have a look.

It was Rose. Of course. Who else would be calling her at the worst possible time?

Peg looked back at Joker. The puppy's tail thumped up and down on the tabletop in reply.

He hadn't yet fallen asleep. That would happen once she turned on the blower.

"Good boy." Peg reached for the phone. "I'll be right with you."

"Are you busy?" Rose asked when Peg connected.

"Yes, very much so. There's a dog show tomorrow."

There was a pause, as if Rose was trying to figure out why a dog show tomorrow should impact Peg's schedule today. Apparently she failed.

"Another one," she said. From her tone, they might as well have been discussing flu shots. "How lucky for you."

"Indeed. So if you don't mind, I don't have time to chat."

"Then I'll be brief. I bought you a book. I ordered it online and had it overnighted to you."

"A book?" Peg was surprised. She loved to read. And she certainly hadn't expected that. "History? Biography? Perhaps a good thriller?"

"It's called *Bridge for Beginners*."

"Oh." Peg wasn't a beginner; she was just rusty. Did she really need to point that out?

"I know you're not a beginner," Rose said. Apparently she'd sensed that objection coming. "But even you have to admit that your skills need a bit of refreshing."

"I read several articles on my computer."

"Did they help?" Rose asked drily.

They both knew the answer to that.

"It's a very good book. I've read it myself. And it occurred to me that if we both utilize the same resources, you and I might have an easier time bidding and playing together. What do you think?"

"You might have a point," Peg conceded, brightening.

Homework. She'd always been good at that.

"Now that we know what to expect, next week we can be better prepared. I don't know about you, but I would like to win at least one game."

"Two would be even better," said Peg.

"So we just have to get you over the hump."

Peg's sunny mood vanished. "What hump?"

"Admit it, Peg. Your whole life you've been good at everything you turned your hand to. Things come easily to you, usually without a lot of effort on your part. A long time ago, bridge was easy for you too. And now you didn't bother to put in the work because you just assumed it would be easy again."

Peg made a sound under her breath. Luckily it wasn't quite a word. Otherwise it would have been a rude one.

"I heard that," Rose said. "And you can grumble all you like. It won't make a difference. The real reason you're irritated isn't because I bought you a book. It's because you hate making mistakes."

"Everybody hates making mistakes," Peg snapped.

"Yes, we do. But then most of us try again. Having learned something, we attempt to do better the second time."

Peg lifted the phone and stared at it in annoyance. She could outargue just about anyone. People who couldn't be subdued by her superior debating skills usually ran out of stamina and ceded defeat before Peg was ready to give in.

Not Rose. She didn't know when to quit.

"The book will be there tomorrow," Rose said. "Just read it, okay?"

Tomorrow Peg and Joker would be attending a lovely dog show in Westchester County. That would be a much better use of her time than spending the day sitting at home reading a book for beginners.

Once again Rose was ready for her objection. "The next bridge club meeting isn't until Tuesday. You have until then to take a look. There'll be plenty of time after you're finished with your dog show."

Peg was shaping a sharp retort when Rose ended the connection.

"Of all the nerve," she said.

Joker lifted his head to gaze at her.

"Not you." Peg reached over and gave him another pat. "You're perfect."

The puppy sent her an adoring look. He knew that.

Peg didn't have to touch the Poodle's coat to know that it had already begun to air dry. The long black hairs were rounding into curls.

Peg growled under her breath. That was Rose's fault too. She wet down the hair with a spray bottle, picked up her brush, and got back to work.

Chapter 8

When Peter and Rose returned from Central America in February, they had opened the Gallagher House, a refuge for women in need of shelter. The building was located in a somewhat shabby area of downtown Stamford. It was narrow, three stories tall, and situated on a tiny piece of land, from which the traffic on the nearby Connecticut Turnpike was clearly audible.

Formerly a residence, the place had been a rental property for years. It wasn't in good repair when Peter and Rose took possession, and they'd been working on rectifying that ever since. Already they'd replaced the furnace and some of the wood siding. When Peter wasn't busy with his other duties, he spent much of his free time tinkering with a host of plumbing problems. He and Rose were hopeful that before winter came, their budget would stretch to a new roof.

In the short time the shelter had been open, it quickly became apparent there was a need for the services it provided. In addition to offering women—and sometimes their children—a place to stay, the Gallagher House also supplied access to counseling, as well as legal and medical aid. Though the shelter's population changed from day to day, there always seemed to be at least a couple of women in residence.

Early Friday afternoon, Peter and Rose drove to the Gallagher House together. Peter had counseling sessions scheduled throughout the rest of the day. Rose had packed the back of their minivan with supplies for her newest idea to enhance the quality of life for the shelter's inhabitants.

More than a dozen small tomato plants were sitting in seed-starting trays, ready to be replanted in the small backyard behind the building. At the moment, the space was little more than a bare patch of hard packed dirt with a few scraggly clumps of grass. Rose couldn't wait to make the outdoor area more appealing.

A novice gardener at best, Rose had been looking forward to tackling her first horticultural project. Until the conversation with Peg that morning had dampened her good mood. Again.

Peter was behind the wheel for the short drive between their home and the shelter. Traffic on Hope Street should have been moving. Instead, they were barely crawling along. Rose was tempted to reach over and honk the horn when a rental truck pulled out into their lane without warning. Unfortunately, thinking about her sister-in-law often had that effect on her.

"Peg is going to drive me batty," she announced. Peter had already heard about the earlier conversation.

He glanced at her across the front seat. "I don't doubt it. But in this case, you bear some of the blame. Maybe you shouldn't have bought her a book for beginners."

Rose turned to face him. "Peg needs a book for beginners. Or near-beginners, anyway. I probably should have been listening more closely when she said she hadn't played bridge in years."

"I believe you said decades."

"I was hoping to get some sympathy," she grumbled.

"You don't need sympathy. What you need is patience. You've always said that Peg was a highly intelligent woman."

"I have *not!*"

"But you've thought it," Peter said. "Haven't you?"

"Maybe," Rose admitted.

"You're a smart woman too."

"I should hope so. I married you."

"You see? That's proof right there. I also happen to also know that you're not nearly as meek as you would like people to think."

"Of course not. Despite what I was taught, I've never believed that the meek will inherit the earth." She paused, then asked, "Did you?"

"No, not really. But in my previous profession, it didn't do to question those teachings." Peter nodded in her direction. "Yours either, for that matter."

"True. But what does this have to do with Peg?"

"Peg isn't just smart, she's strong."

"She's a bully," Rose muttered.

"So stand up to her."

"I tried that once. Look what it got me." She shifted her eyes away. Traffic was starting to move again. Rose gazed at the passing scenery—currently an auto repair shop—as though it was interesting. "Forty years of animosity."

"I said stand up to Peg, not kick her when she's down," Peter replied mildly. "You need to find a happy medium."

"There's no such thing when it comes to Peg. As far as she's concerned, it's her way or the highway."

"Maybe she's not the only one," said Peter.

Peter parked the minivan along the sidewalk in front of the shelter. They hadn't expected there to be so much traffic in the middle of the day, and now he was running late. Rose knew his first appointment was scheduled to begin in five minutes.

Even so, Peter stopped to open the sliding door on the side of the van. "I'll help you take this stuff around back."

"No, you go on inside. It'll be fine. I'll just make a few trips."

Normally Rose would have been delighted to have his help. But now she was annoyed with him for telling her the truth. Even worse, she was annoyed at herself for needing to hear it.

"You're sure?" Peter hesitated.

"Go." She frowned and flapped a hand at him.

Thankfully that did it. Now Rose could sulk in peace.

Except that no sooner had Peter hopped up the steps and disappeared through the front door than it opened again and Maura Nettles came striding out. Maura was the Gallagher House's live-in housekeeper. Thirty-eight years old with a sturdy body and a no-nonsense attitude about life, Maura had never met a problem she wasn't willing to tackle head-on. Except for her cheating, battering, soon-to-be ex-husband.

Maura had shown up at the shelter in April with a black eye and a duffel bag holding a change of clothing. She'd insisted she only needed a place to stay for the night. One night had turned into two, and then three. Under Rose's care Maura had begun to heal, both inside and out. She'd also listened to Peter's wise counsel and realized that she needed to make some significant changes to her life.

By the end of the week, Maura had a new job as the shelter's resident housekeeper and occasional cook, taking over responsibilities that Rose had been delighted to delegate. When the Donovans vacated the basement apartment to move to Springdale, Maura packed up her belongings and moved downstairs. Two months later, Rose couldn't remember how they'd ever managed without her.

Now Maura stood on the porch and looked down at Rose. "I heard you need some help out here."

"I thought I was managing just fine," Rose replied. "But since you've come out, I wouldn't mind having an extra pair of hands. Can you help me carry some tomato plants around back?"

"Sure." Maura came skipping down the steps. "What are you going to do with them back there?"

"I decided to brighten things up by planting a garden. I figured I might as well grow something useful."

"In the backyard?" Maura looked dubious. The steps that led down to the basement apartment were at the back of the house. Maura was well aware how barren the meager plot of earth was.

"Sure. Anyway, it's worth a try."

Maura surveyed the two full seed trays sitting in the back of the open van. "That's a lot of tomato plants you've got there."

"Sixteen," said Rose.

"Sixteen?" Maura laughed. "If you plant all those, we'll be drowning in tomatoes by August."

"I doubt it. This is my first attempt at growing anything. So I'm counting on at least a fifty percent mortality rate."

The door to the Gallagher House opened again and another woman emerged. She took a look around, then started toward them down the steps. Ivy had long legs, curly brown hair, and freckles everywhere. She'd been staying at the shelter for the last week, using the place as transitional housing while she worked on putting the pieces of her life back together.

Rose threw up her hands. "What's going on? Why is everyone coming outside?"

It was bad enough that she barely knew how to plant these seedlings. Why did there have to be witnesses to her incompetence?

"Peter said you might need help." Ivy strolled over and took a look inside the minivan. "Whoa, that's a lot of tomatoes."

"That's what I told her," Maura said. "She thinks half of them are going to die."

"Why would they do that?"

"Because I have no idea what I'm doing," Rose told her.

"Tomatoes are easy, as long as you treat them right." Ivy took another look around the interior of the van. There were two big bags in the rear. "I see you brought fertilizer."

"And mulch," said Rose.

"Add some sun and water and you're all set." Ivy sounded happy.

"Have you seen the backyard?" Maura asked her. "It's like a wasteland back there."

Ivy just shrugged. "I once grew chickpeas in a shoebox."

Rose and Maura shared a look. "Why did you do that?"

"Because my daddy said I couldn't, and I wanted to prove him wrong."

"And did you?" asked Rose.

"Of course." Ivy grinned. "Otherwise I wouldn't tell the story. I grew up on a farm in Iowa. I know all about crops. A piddly little garden will be a cinch. Are you sure you only want to do tomatoes?"

Rose nodded. "Considering I have zero experience, I figured I should start small and work my way up."

Maura grinned. "If this works, next year you can branch out to cucumbers. And maybe lettuce. By the time we're done with you, you'll be the salad queen of Digby Avenue."

Ivy reached into the minivan and hauled out the heavy bag of fertilizer. Rose thought she would need help with it, but Ivy handled the bulky bag as though it was weightless. Maura grabbed one seed tray of the small, leafy plants. Rose picked up the other one. They'd have to come back for the mulch and the gardening tools.

"Don't you worry about a thing," Ivy said with confidence as she led the way around the building. "I got this."

Chapter 9

The sun rose early in June and so did Peg. Saturday was a dog show day, and she was anxious to get on the road.

Not that there was any real need to hurry. Standard Poodles weren't due to be judged until noon, and the park in northern Westchester County where the show was being held was a mere forty minutes away. Peg routinely traveled much farther than that to get to the shows she judged. This one felt as though it was right around the corner.

At the showground, two parallel rows of six show rings had been set up in the middle of a large, grassy field. A tent covered the wide aisle between them. A second tent was placed nearby for grooming. There—in a space crowded with stacked crates and grooming tables—exhibitors would make their final preparations before taking their dogs into the ring. Peg couldn't wait to get settled in amidst the company of her fellow dog lovers.

She pulled her minivan into the unloading area beside the tent, rolled down the windows, then got out to have a look around. It wasn't yet nine o'clock, but the grooming area was already crowded. Professional handlers with their large strings of dogs would have been on-site since dawn. Their many grooming tables were aligned in neat rows; their generators created a buzz in the air. Everywhere Peg looked, people were already hard at work.

Over to the right, several Miniature Poodles were out on tabletops. Standards wouldn't be judged for several hours, but Minis were due in the ring earlier. She grabbed her folding table and the tack box that held her grooming supplies from the back of the minivan and headed that way.

Almost immediately, Peg saw two of her favorite people. Professional handler Crawford Langley and his longtime assistant and now husband, Terry Denunzio, were both at their setup. The two men were working side by side on a pair of silver Minis.

Automatically, Peg assessed the two Poodles as she approached. A dog and bitch, they were probably littermates. Their bodies were quite similar, though the dog had the prettier head. The bitch had better hair and feet. She would need to see them move before . . .

Before what? Peg nearly laughed. She wasn't judging today. Her opinion of the pair didn't matter.

She lifted her gaze to the people standing behind the Minis and saw that Crawford was smiling. He probably knew exactly what she'd been thinking.

"Morning, Peg," he said. "You're here early."

Crawford had been in the sport of dogs for decades. He'd risen to the top of the game early in his career and worked hard through the years to retain that lofty position. Now in his sixties, he had no intention of retiring anytime soon. Crawford had sharp gray eyes and impeccable hearing. He didn't miss much.

"I know," Peg replied happily. "I couldn't wait. I get so few chances to show a dog now, that I wanted to savor the whole experience."

"Savoring dog shows." Terry sighed from the next table over. "I remember those days."

In many ways Crawford and Terry were opposites. Crawford was older and more reserved. Terry, who hadn't yet turned forty, was brash, flippant, and always entertaining. Crawford conducted himself with calm and dignity. Terry invariably had the best gossip and the best jokes on the showground. Despite their differences, the pair had been happy together for years.

"You remember them because they were just last week," Crawford said.

"Maybe." Terry tucked a stray blond curl behind his ear. "Watching you win Best in Show with Harley was definitely worth savoring."

Harley was Crawford's top winning specials dog, Champion Hotspur Harlequin. He was a gorgeous Standard Poodle. Peg had put him up herself when Crawford shown the dog under her.

95

Terry was busy unwrapping his Mini's long ear hair, but now he set the task aside and reached out to take the grooming table from beneath Peg's arm. "I'll set that up and get you situated." He grabbed the tack box in his other hand. "Where's your puppy—still in the car?"

Peg nodded. It was a pleasant change to have someone else take charge.

"Go park your minivan. By the time you get back, you'll be good to go."

"Thank you, Terry. I appreciate that."

"Don't thank him yet," Crawford told her. "With Terry, there's always a price."

"Oh?" Peg propped her hands on her hips. She was a good two inches taller than Terry, which meant she could stare down her nose at him. "And what do you want this time?"

"News, of course." He flashed her a cheeky grin. "Melanie, Sam, and the two munchkins have been cooped up in that RV for nearly two weeks now. How is the road trip proceeding? Are they having the time of their lives, or are they minutes away from wanting to kill each other? I need the whole scoop, especially the parts Melanie doesn't want anyone to know."

"I'll start by telling you not to refer to Davey as a munchkin," Peg said. "He'll be sixteen in the fall. At that age, children are very much aware of their own consequence. He might take a swing at you."

"I'm not worried." Terry grinned. "If it comes to that, I can take him."

"Sure, you can," Crawford said with a laugh. "I've seen Harley out-wrestle you when it's time for his bath."

"Harley has four legs," Terry pointed out in his own defense. "You never know which direction he might kick you from next."

Peg went to park her minivan before returning to the tent with Joker. As she drove toward the lot at the other end of the field, she realized how odd it felt to be at a dog show without Melanie, Sam, and the boys. She and Melanie had been going to shows together since Davey was in preschool. The theft of Peg's best Standard Poodle had initially brought the two women together, and solving that mystery had forged a friendship between them that deepened through the years.

Peg knew Melanie and Sam had to be having a great time on their trip. She was sure that Davey and Kevin would be keeping them busy. Still, it was too bad that she had little more news to share with Terry than the contents of one meager postcard.

Peg returned to the grooming tent with Joker dancing on the end of his leash. There, she discovered that Terry had set up her table and placed her tack box within easy reach on a nearby stack of crates. Now he was next door in his own setup, using a knitting needle to part the long hair

97

on his Mini's head. The silky strands would then be gathered into the numerous small ponytails to build the dog's towering show ring topknot.

"Thank you, Terry. You're a marvel." Peg hopped Joker up onto the table and let him sit down. With plenty of time before judging, she didn't need to begin grooming the puppy right away.

"Yes, I know." Terry couldn't help preening. "I'm a man of many talents. Just ask Crawford."

"Please don't." Crawford's Mini already had her topknot in. He was using hair spray to layer her profuse coat into place. The handler looked over at Terry and tapped his watch.

"I've heard about your hidden talents," Peg said. "I know you're a great cook. And that you cut Melanie's hair. You don't happen to play bridge by any chance, do you?"

"Bridge?" Terry glanced up. "Isn't that a game for old people?"

Peg glared at him. "You may want to rethink that answer."

"Right. What I meant to say is, no, I never learned how. I'm pretty good at Scrabble though. And Monopoly. Why?"

"It seems I've joined a bridge club."

Crawford glanced over with interest. "With whom? Surely not Melanie."

"No, my partner is my sister-in-law, Rose Donovan. The whole thing was her idea."

"The ex-nun," Terry said.

Peg was surprised. "How do you know that?"

"From Melanie, of course. She tells everybody everything."

She did? Peg had always assumed she was Melanie's favorite confidante. Could she have been wrong about that? Perhaps she was simply one of many. What a terrible thought.

"An ex-nun," said Crawford. "You don't hear that every day."

"That's not all," Terry told him. "The ex-nun is married to an ex-priest."

Crawford's brow rose. "This is getting more interesting by the moment."

"All of that is in the past now," Peg told him. "Currently Rose and Peter lead a perfectly normal life."

"Nobody believes that for a minute," Terry said. "You're all related to Melanie, who has a shocking tendency to get involved in solving mysteries. By definition, that means none of you lead a normal life." He stopped and grinned. "Which is what I like best about the whole lot of you."

"Mini dogs in ten minutes," said Crawford. He glanced across the grassy expanse toward the show rings. "Perhaps we can discuss Melanie's peculiar proclivities another time?"

Peg didn't know why they would want to do that. It wasn't a particularly interesting topic.

She'd been hoping they might be able to discuss bridge. And that either Terry or Crawford would have something useful to say on the subject. But somehow they'd gotten sidetracked and now that didn't seem to be happening.

While Terry got busy with a can of hairspray, Peg strolled over to the Poodle ring to pick up their armbands and check if the ring was running on time. Which, of course, it was. Because Henry Stillman was judging, and he wouldn't have it any other way.

Crawford won the points in dogs with his silver Mini, while his Mini bitch placed third in a class of four. Henry always had been a sucker for a pretty face. Having seen this result, Peg wondered if Joker's head would be pleasing enough for him. Maybe not. It would depend on what the competition looked like.

When the Mini judging was finished, they all went to the grooming tent to work on their Standard Poodles. Peg took out her brushes and a long comb, then hooked a spray bottle of water over the lip of the tabletop. Her fingers moved quickly, making the first part in the puppy's dense coat so she could brush through the hair. Line brushing was busy work. Peg's hands knew just what to do, leaving her thoughts free to wander.

"Melanie and Sam," Terry reminded her from the next setup, where he was brushing Crawford's white puppy. "Tell us all about their trip."

"I hardly know a thing," Peg admitted. "I've only received a single postcard. It said they were on their way to Graceland."

Crawford looked up from the Standard lying on his table. "I wouldn't have figured those two for Elvis fans."

"I gather Kevin is the driving force behind that decision."

"I always knew I liked that kid," Terry said.

"When will they be back?" asked Crawford. "That's the important question."

"Yes," Terry chimed in. "Things have been pretty dull around here without them."

"Knowing the kind of trouble Melanie gets herself mixed up in," said Peg, "perhaps we should all thank our lucky stars for that."

Terry snorted under his breath. Like they all didn't know that Peg could be twice as much trouble as her niece.

She cast a glance his way. "Excuse me?"

Terry shrugged innocently.

"It takes a brave man to make fun of a woman who has access to sharp scissors and a knitting needle," Peg mentioned.

"Or a foolish one," Crawford replied. "I'll thank you not to injure my assistant, Peg. At least not today. There's a supported entry in Bichons this afternoon. We have four entered, including a bitch that desperately needs the major."

"In that case, I'll stand down," Peg said. "Far

be it from me to get in the way of your major. You've had a narrow escape, young man."

"Yes, ma'am," Terry replied.

"Watch your language," she retorted. "You call me *ma'am* again and I will take out that needle and poke you with it."

"I'd like to see you try."

Peg, who had ears like a fox, pretended not to hear him. Time was passing now. They all needed to keep moving.

Peg had entered Joker in the Bred-by-Exhibitor class. She was the puppy's breeder, and she was proud to advertise that fact. She and Joker were standing at ringside, ready to go, when the first Standard Poodle class was called into the ring.

There were two entries in the Puppy Dog class. Both were black, and both were being shown by professional handlers. Peg watched the first go-round critically, then picked the puppy in the rear as the easy winner.

Evaluating the pair, then making the decision was automatic. For the past five years, she'd spent the majority of her time at dog shows judging rather than exhibiting. She was accustomed to being the person in charge of the ring, the one whose opinion mattered. It was surprisingly difficult to step away—even for a day—from a role that had come to feel like second nature to her.

Peg and Joker were next to be judged, a single

entry in their class. Henry kept a carefully blank expression on his face as he approached the puppy to examine him for the first time. Old friends or not, it was very bad form to acknowledge a prior relationship while inside the ring.

With no competition, Joker won the class handily. Peg accepted the blue ribbon and Henry's congratulations with a smile, then walked the puppy out of the ring to await their next turn. As the Open class was judged, she took out her comb and made repairs to Joker's topknot and ears.

Normally at this point, Melanie and her family would be standing at ringside with her. Davey would be helping out. Kevin would inevitably be getting in the way. Melanie would be attempting to control her younger son. Sam would be a small island of calm amidst the chaos, observing the activity in the show ring and offering Peg insights on the competition.

Lord, how she missed all that.

Peg looked up when she heard her number called. The Open class was over, and a big white dog had won. She returned Joker to the ring. They took their place in the middle of the line between the Open dog and the Puppy class winner. Henry took a brief look at his entrants then sent them gaiting around the ring together.

Joker was doing everything right. Peg couldn't have been more pleased with him. But she could also see that the Open class winner in front of them was a *nice* dog. His head was a smidge more handsome than Joker's too. Darn it.

She wasn't surprised when the white Standard Poodle was named Winners Dog. A few minutes later, Peg smiled as Henry handed her the striped ribbon for Reserve Winners. Joker didn't win anything for being second best. Nevertheless, he'd shown well and Peg had enjoyed being back in the show ring.

"He's a handsome puppy," Henry said jovially. "You'll get 'em next time."

It was the mantra of every dog show exhibitor, everywhere.

"I hope so," Peg replied.

Chapter 10

It seemed like no time at all before it was Tuesday again.

When Rose arrived at the community center, Peg's maroon minivan was already parked in the lot across the street. Rose looked at it and sighed. Then she pulled her silver minivan in beside it. Today, they hadn't intended to go inside together. It figured that Peg would arrive early.

Rose locked her van, then paused to look both ways before crossing the street. She hoped Peg had found some time to read the bridge book. Or at least to skim through it.

Rose hadn't intended for the gift to be an insult. More like a bit of encouragement for Peg to improve her game. Couldn't she see how that would be a good thing for both of them?

The chill of the building's air-conditioning hit Rose as soon as she opened the front door. The previous week she'd been trying not to shiver by the time the meeting ended. Today she'd followed Peg's example and brought a light sweater with her.

Rose grimaced at the thought. Heaven forbid she learn something useful from Peg. Then abruptly she stopped walking. Her grimace turned into a frown. Although . . . if she was being totally fair, wasn't she expecting Peg to learn—or at least relearn—something on her behalf?

Dammit. It was annoying to have to view the issue from both sides. Peter would probably laugh if he could hear her thoughts now. Or maybe he'd say, "I told you so." Either way, it left Rose with some thinking to do.

As she started moving again, she made a quick decision. Win or lose today, she wouldn't grumble about the outcome. And she wouldn't even bring up that stupid book. Despite their lack of success, she and Peg had both had fun the previous week. That should be their goal for this bridge session too.

The meeting room was half-full when Rose entered. Bennett and Sue were already there, as were Carrie and the Grover sisters. Peg, who'd helped herself to an enormous cookie, was part of a small group consisting of John and Violet Severson and Stan Peters.

Since they hadn't played bridge with either the Seversons or Stan and his partner, Mick, the week before, Rose and Peg barely had a chance to talk to any of them. Rose was looking forward to getting to know all her fellow club members. She grabbed a cup of coffee and headed that way.

"I'm glad you made it," Peg said as she approached. "After our losses last week, I was afraid you might be planning to stand me up."

"The thought never even crossed my mind."

Rose smiled and greeted the others in the group. "I hope I haven't interrupted your conversation. What were you talking about?"

"Dogs," Peg said, before anyone else had a chance to speak up.

Rose should have known. Peg was an educated and well-traveled woman. So why were dogs the only thing she could seem to discuss?

"It turns out that Peg and I have a friend in common." Violet's hand was wrapped around a plastic water bottle. Rose noted that the woman's manicured nails had been painted a shade of purple that matched her name. "Rina and I went to school together oh-so-many years ago. And now she breeds Dandie Dinmonts."

Rose started to laugh. Then she realized Violet was serious. "Dandie Dinmonts? That's a thing?"

"No," Peg corrected her. "That's a breed. And Rina and I both belong to the Belle Haven Kennel Club."

"How's that for a coincidence?" asked Violet.

John patted his wife's shoulder affectionately. He had white, even teeth and a wonderful smile. "Perhaps it's not entirely unexpected. Rina always did seem like the sporty type. When we were younger, she was a terror on the tennis court."

"She was," Violet agreed. "As I recall, you never could return her serve, even after you got that graphite tennis racket."

107

Stan was on Rose's right. He was following the conversation, but judging by the expression on his face, he was entirely out of his depth. She knew just how he felt. She'd never returned a tennis serve in her life, with or without a graphite racket.

"I'm sorry we didn't have a chance to talk last week," Rose said, turning to face him. "I know you mentioned that you're retired, Stan. What did you do before that?"

"Umm . . ." he said, as if she'd caught him by surprise. And maybe she had. Stan hadn't said a word since she'd joined the group. "IT, mostly."

Rose was still out of her depth. "That's something to do with computers, right?"

"In a manner of speaking." Stan had a rather stern face, but now that they were on a familiar subject, he seemed to relax. "Basically, information technology is all about finding ways of applying technology to solve organizational problems on a broad scale."

"How wonderful for you," Rose said. "You must be very smart."

Peg made a derisive sound under her breath. Rose ignored her, which was just what she deserved. Peg probably didn't understand what Stan was talking about either.

"Stan is smarter than I am," John said with a self-deprecating laugh. "Thankfully, when I was running my advertising company, I had people working for me who knew how to do all that stuff."

The Seversons went to help themselves to refreshments. Stan wandered away. Rose frowned at Peg, who was still munching happily on her cookie. It looked like chocolate fudge and was nearly the size of a Frisbee.

"Aren't you going to ask me if I read your book?" Peg inquired now that they'd been left alone.

A few people were still missing, including the Watkinses and Carrie's partner, Lacey. Everyone else seemed content to continue socializing while they waited for the stragglers to appear.

"No." Rose gazed around the room, looking for another group to join. "I decided I'm over it."

"Over what?"

"Trying to tell you what to do."

"Really?"

Rose turned back to her. "Really. We're here to enjoy ourselves, so it doesn't matter whether we win or lose."

Peg's gaze sharpened. "It matters to me. And for your information, I read your blasted book last night."

Rose heaved a sigh. Peg was the most contrary woman she'd ever met. Really, there was just no pleasing her.

"I'm going to go talk to Sue and Bennett," Rose said. They were another couple she hadn't spent any time with the week before. They were standing near the card tables with Carrie. "Come with me or not," she added ungraciously. "Your choice."

Not only did Peg opt to cross the room with Rose, she also decided to lead the way. That was just typical. Rose didn't care if she was following. She didn't need to be in front for everyone in the room to know which player in their partnership was the one in charge.

"Your ears must have been burning, Rose," Carrie said as they approached. "We were just talking about you."

"Oh?" She slid in beside her friend. "Something good, I hope."

"Something wonderful, actually. I was telling Sue and Bennett how proud I was to know someone who works as hard as you do for the cause of women's health and welfare."

"Thank you." Rose reached over and gave her friend a hug. "That's a lovely thing to say."

"Carrie told us you and your husband are operating a shelter for battered women in Stamford," Bennett said. Large, metallic framed glasses gave him a pensive expression. As he leaned in to talk to her, Rose saw the strands of gray mixed in his ginger brown hair.

"Yes. We opened the Gallagher House in February. Right away, it became apparent there was a real need for its services."

"Watch your language, honey." Sue shot the

group an apologetic look. She was a small woman with fluttery hands. "You don't want to offend Rose. I don't think *battered women* is the PC term anymore."

"Questions and comments about what we do could never be offensive," Rose said seriously. "Peter and I are much less concerned about terminology than we are about getting results. The women who come to us for shelter are those who've found themselves in difficult situations, usually victims of domestic violence. They hope to find a place where they can feel safe and find solace, and Peter and I do everything we can to provide that for them."

"You see?" Carrie grasped her hands together in front of her chest. Light from above glinted off her many rings. "Isn't Rose just the best?"

"No argument from me," Bennett replied. "I assume the Gallagher House is a charitable organization?"

Rose nodded.

"Because I would be happy to send you a donation."

"That would be very welcome," Rose said. "Thank you."

"No," Sue interjected firmly. "Thank *you*. For seeing a need and stepping in to do something about it. Not everyone would do that. And I have no intention of being outdone by Bennett. I'd like to make a donation too."

"That's very generous of both of you." Rose smiled.

Peg looked back and forth between Sue and Bennett. "You two make a wonderful couple. You're very much in sync with each other. How long have you been engaged?"

"Just since spring." Sue held out her left hand so Rose and Peg could admire the sapphire and diamond ring on her third finger. "Bennett and I met last year at a Christmas party. We're planning to get married this year on Christmas Eve."

"That sounds so romantic," Carrie said with a sigh.

Lacey Duvall entered the room. Stan's partner, Mick Doran, came hurrying in behind her, completing the company. Lacey paid no attention to him. Instead, she immediately focused on Carrie. Pushing a pair of glasses up on top of her head, Lacey came over to join their group.

"Sorry I'm late," she said. "Traffic on the Post Road was murder. Did I miss anything important?"

"We were talking about Rose's women's shelter and the wonderful work she and her husband are doing," Carrie informed her.

"Oh, right. I heard about that." Lacey didn't sound particularly impressed. "Well done you."

"We were also talking about Sue and Bennett's upcoming wedding," Rose added.

Lacey spared the couple a small smile. "Good luck with that."

Sue looked shocked by the comment, but Bennett just laughed. "Just because you've been divorced three times doesn't mean everybody else makes the same mistakes."

Carrie stepped forward, deliberately inserting her body between Lacey and Bennett who were still glaring at each other. Her bulk forced them both to move back. She frowned in exasperation, then turned to face the room.

"Now that everybody's here," she said, "let's all settle down and play some bridge."

Chapter 11

Peg and Rose drew Paige and Reggie as their opponents for the first rubber. "I wonder if they'll be playing footsie under the table again," Peg said to Rose as they went over to take their seats.

Rose quickly shushed her. "It's no secret how poorly we played last week. They probably won't feel the need."

"Nevertheless, it occurs to me that my long legs may serve a useful purpose today. Perhaps I'll stretch them out across the space between us."

Rose stared at her. "You wouldn't."

"Of course I would. Don't worry. I'll make it look entirely natural. I would hate for them to think their little games have gone unnoticed."

"You just can't help yourself, can you?"

Peg stopped walking. "What do you mean?"

"Everywhere you go, you're always looking for a way to stir up trouble."

Peg frowned. Even now, when they seemed to have formed a tentative alliance, was that *still* what Rose thought of her? At this rate, the two of them would never be able to form a partnership that worked across a bridge table. No matter how many books Peg read.

"Fine," she said. "I'll keep my feet to myself."

Rose had stopped walking too. After all, what

choice did she have? She turned back to face Peg and sighed.

"I suppose it's not the worst idea you ever had," she admitted. "Actually, it might be kind of funny. As long as you're sure you can pull it off."

"You're kidding, right?"

No, Rose hadn't been kidding. Not in the slightest.

"Just make sure you don't kick me," she added. "We don't want Paige and Reggie to think that we're hatching plots of our own."

Peg dealt the first hand. She had fourteen points including two aces, but no dominant suit. The hand begged for a one no trump bid. Except that Peg had already irritated her partner once today. And considering the complaints she'd had to listen to the week before, Peg knew that a no trump bid would only compound their issues. Plus one no trump implied she had more points than she actually did.

"One club," she said unhappily. Just queen high, it was her only four-card suit.

Reggie, on her left, bid one diamond. Rose supported Peg's clubs, but Paige demonstrated a higher level of enthusiasm for her husband's diamonds. Reggie ended up winning the contract in four diamonds, and making it. That put eighty points below the line on the Greenes' side of the score sheet. It wasn't enough for game, but it gave Peg and Rose's opponents a significant head start.

As Reggie dealt the second hand, Peg gasped suddenly. She leaned down and reached a hand beneath the table.

Paige turned to her in concern. "Is everything all right?"

"Yes." Peg winced. "Just a sudden cramp in my calf. I'm sure it'll be fine if I just stretch out my leg. Don't mind me. Please, let's play on."

Rose's eyes were twinkling when she won the bid in four spades. Peg was suppressing a laugh too. She laid down her hand as dummy, pleased to be able to show her partner four supporting spades. Rose needed to make ten tricks; she ended up making eleven.

Peg and Rose slapped palms across the table. They'd finally won their first game.

"That was nicely bid and played," said Reggie.

"Thank you," Rose replied, sneaking a glance at Peg. "I'm glad things went our way."

Paige and Reggie won the second game. As Rose dealt to start the next hand, Paige turned to Peg and said, "After we met last week, I couldn't resist looking up your house. What a lovely piece of property."

Peg swallowed the first retort that came to mind, then said, "Thank you. I enjoy living there."

Paige leaned closer, as if she were imparting confidential information. Her dark hair fell forward around her face, framing eyes that were a brilliant shade of green. *Probably contact lenses,* Peg decided.

"I'd be happy to stop by and do an appraisal for you," Paige said. "You might be surprised by the number I come up with. People who've lived in one place for a long time are often unaware of how much the value of their home has appreciated over the years."

"That would only matter to me if I were planning to sell though," Peg said innocently. "Right?"

"Well, of course. But it never hurts to be informed about the possibilities. And if you ever do decide to sell . . ."

"I'll know just who to call." Peg smiled sweetly. On the other side of the table, Rose suppressed a chuckle.

"Paige, pick up your cards," Reggie said impatiently. "We're all waiting for you."

"Yes, dear." Paige's tone was sharp enough to cut glass. She snatched up the pile of cards in front of her and quickly sorted them. "Was that fast enough for you?"

"Not really." Reggie was staring down at his own hand. He didn't bother to look up at his wife.

Peg fanned out the cards in her hand. Several faces stared up at her. That was always a good sign. She counted her points, then leaned back in her chair and stretched out her long legs.

Rose looked across at her and said, "One no trump."

And just like that, they were back in business.

Twenty minutes later, Peg and Rose had taken their first rubber. Sure, there'd been plenty of luck involved. First, because they'd been dealt good cards. And second, because Reggie and Paige were obviously still irritated with one another. The couple had flung down their cards and glared across the table as if each of them couldn't wait for their partner to lose.

Even so, to Peg and Rose it felt like a win.

"Stop gloating," Rose said to Peg as they went to the refreshment table during the break. "You look ridiculously pleased with yourself."

"I'm pleased with both of us." As Rose refilled her coffee cup, Peg gazed around the room.

Sue and Bennett had just completed their rubber with Jerry and Mae Watkins. All four players stood up together. Mae and Sue were engrossed in a conversation. Peg watched as Jerry dug a hand in his pocket, pulled out several folded bills, then surreptitiously palmed them to Bennett.

Bennett quickly fisted his hand over the money. Within seconds, it had disappeared from sight. The hand-over took place so quickly and so quietly that Peg doubted anyone else had even noticed. Certainly Sue and Mae seemed oblivious.

That was interesting.

For their second rubber, Peg and Rose were partnered with Stan and Mick. The two women were still basking in the glow from their first win. It didn't take long, however, for their new opponents to put them back in their place. From the moment they picked up their cards until they admitted defeat thirty minutes later, Peg and Rose never stood a chance.

Peg felt she was doing well when she was able to predict how the game would play out two or three tricks ahead. Compared to Mick, however, she was a rank beginner.

The man said little, and stared a lot. His eyes never left the table while the cards were in play. Within seconds of the dummy being laid down, it was clear that Mick already knew how every card in the deck would be played. If Peg hadn't been losing to him so badly, it would have been a pleasure just to watch him think.

The foursome had played just two hands. Stan and Mick bid to game both times. Then Mick had made the execution of both wins look simple. Being defeated that easily was almost depressing. Even worse, Mick's card play had been so swift, Peg wasn't even entirely sure how he'd accomplished everything he'd done.

Had Mick really trumped his own ace when he'd needed transportation from the dummy to his hand? Or had she imagined that?

"You're wasted playing bridge with us," Peg said to Mick as he gathered up the tricks neatly laid in front of him and shuffled them back into the remaining deck. "You should be in Las Vegas, or wherever it is that people go to play professional bridge."

Mick just shrugged. Today he was wearing a loud Hawaiian shirt tucked into a pair of wrinkled khakis. A faded red ball cap was pulled low over his eyes. He had the weathered skin of a man who'd spent the majority of his life outdoors. Peg wished he would look up so she could see his expression better.

"Mick's not much of a talker," said Stan. "That's why we get along so well. He and I are both strong, silent types."

"I can see that." Peg smiled.

"I can talk," Mick said. His voice was low and gritty. "I just prefer waiting until I have something useful to say."

"Six hearts sounded pretty useful to me," Rose muttered.

Stan barked out a laugh. "Me, too, now that you mention it."

Peg turned to Mick. "Where did you learn how to play the game so well?"

"I first learned bridge when I was in the army. Vietnam. Downtimes, we played plenty there. When I got back stateside, I just kept playing every chance I had. Keeps me sharp, you know?"

Peg nodded. Now that she belonged to a bridge club, she was wishing she'd kept up with her game too.

"How did you and Stan come to be partners?" Rose asked.

"Funny story," Stan answered for him. "My BMW broke down. When I took it to the dealership in Greenwich, Mick was the mechanic who fixed it for me. That was many years ago. I've had five cars since that one, and they all run like tops."

"That's because I keep them in shape for you," Mick pointed out.

"Just like I keep your computer and your internet connection solid," Stan said. "What about you ladies? How did the two of you meet?"

Rose and Peg looked at each other. There was no easy answer to that. Peg decided to give Stan and Mick the short version.

"We're sisters-in-law," she said. "I was married to Rose's older brother Max."

"Was." Stan nodded. "Divorced?"

"Widowed."

"I'm sorry," he said.

"Thank you. Me too," Peg replied. "Max was a fine man."

"He must have liked dogs," Mick said. "I heard you took part in that big dog show that's on TV."

Peg remembered that she'd briefly mentioned Westminster to Mae and Jerry the week before. Apparently news traveled through this group with alacrity. She made a mental note to keep that in mind.

"He most certainly did," she confirmed.

The players around them were finishing their second rubbers and totaling their scores. Franny Grover stood up and stretched. Florence went from table to table, gathering up the score sheets before handing them to Carrie.

Now that play had ended, several people pulled out their phones. Peg picked up the empty cups from their table and carried them to the trash container beside the refreshments. All the chocolate cookies were gone, but there were a few oatmeal raisin ones left on the platter. She contemplated nabbing one for the drive home.

As Peg reached out her hand, she realized that Rose was watching her from across the room. Peg pointed to the cookies, then to Rose. *Do you want one?*

Rose started to shake her head, then paused. Instead she lifted her hands and mimed breaking something in half. The thought that she might be a bad influence on her sister-in-law briefly crossed Peg's mind. She pushed it away, and selected the largest of the remaining cookies to share.

Peg delivered half the cookie to Rose, then made her way over to Carrie. The woman had just announced Stan and Mick as the day's winners. Couples were beginning to file out of the room. Carrie was gathering up the decks of cards and placing them in their boxes. She looked up as Peg approached.

"So what do you think of our little bridge club?" she asked.

"Rose and I are definitely enjoying ourselves. You have an interesting group of people here and I think my game is starting to improve already."

"Good for you. That's the point." Carrie swept another deck up off the card table. "We're all just here to have a good time."

"Not all of us," said Peg.

Carrie stopped what she was doing. "Oh?"

"Bennett appears to be gambling on the results of the games."

Carrie didn't look surprised. Instead she just laughed. "I don't doubt that he is. I've never caught him at it myself, but Bennett was kicked out of his country club for running a betting pool on their golf scramble. It makes sense that our games would be an irresistible attraction for him."

"Doesn't that bother you?"

"It would bother me more if I thought anyone was being hurt by his actions. Or if Bennett would be easy to replace. Don't forget—if he goes, Sue does too. Then we'd be down a couple again." Carrie shrugged. "My job is to ensure that everything runs smoothly. Despite his little peccadillos, Bennett's still an asset to the club. He's great fun to have around and he's always been popular with the ladies. So I don't see the harm in looking the other way."

Peg nodded. It wasn't her decision.

"Do you suppose Sue knows?" she asked.

"I wouldn't have any idea about that." Carrie's tone sharpened. "Sue appears to be madly in love with Bennett, and the two of them are happy together. What she does or doesn't know about him is none of my business. I certainly wouldn't mention it to her."

Peg sensed Rose's presence behind her a moment before her arm was grasped from behind. "Time for us to go," Rose said in a fake cheery voice. She yanked Peg away. "Thank you for everything, Carrie. We'll see you next week."

Rose didn't release Peg until the two women were out the door and halfway down the hall. She was back in Mother Superior mode. Rather than picking an argument, Peg decided just to ride it out.

"I couldn't hear what you were saying but it was clearly upsetting to Carrie," Rose said once they were outside. "What was that all about?"

Peg related the conversation. By the time she was finished, Rose was frowning.

"Not again," she said. "This is just like when you decided that Paige and Reggie were cheating. You don't have to snoop into everything, you know. Would it kill you, just once, to leave well enough alone?"

Peg was stung by the criticism. "I only

125

mentioned Bennett's behavior in case Carrie wasn't aware of it."

"Which it turned out she was," Rose pointed out. "Has it ever crossed your mind that since I'm the one who brought you into the club, your behavior reflects on me too?"

Actually it hadn't.

"Next week, quit looking around at what everyone else is doing. Just keep your eyes on your own cards, okay?"

"I can do that," Peg said. It would require willpower on her part, but she supposed she could muster some up if that's what it took to placate Rose.

"See that you do."

They'd reached the parking lot. Rose slammed the door to her minivan for emphasis before driving away.

Peg assumed the matter had been resolved to Rose's satisfaction. So she was surprised when her phone vibrated on her nightstand early the following morning and Rose's name appeared. Seeing the phone was one thing, however. Reaching it was another.

Coral was lying like a deadweight across Peg's legs. Hope was sharing her pillow. Joker, who'd jumped up when the phone began to buzz, was standing on the edge of the bed, leaning over to sniff the device cautiously.

"Everybody out of my way," said Peg.

Hope and Coral opened their eyes. Joker wagged his tail. It wasn't the most useful effort the three Poodles could have made. Peg maneuvered herself out from beneath the covers and grabbed the phone.

"What now?" she barked.

"Stan Peters is dead," said Rose.

Chapter 12

"What?" Rose heard Peg shriek. A moment ago, she'd sounded sleepy. Now she was wide awake.

Rose had finally succeeded in surprising Peg for a change. Too bad it had to happen under these circumstances.

"How?" Peg demanded. "When?"

"Last night. Stan was shot to death in his home. It's on the local news. Turn on your TV."

"I'm still in bed."

"Well, get up," Rose said. That was obviously the next step, wasn't it?

"That'll take too long. Tell me what happened."

"I don't know much more than I already told you. Stan was shot. Nobody saw or heard anything unusual. The police are investigating."

"What police?" asked Peg.

Seriously? How was Rose supposed to know that?

"The ones on television," she said. The answer sounded dumb, even to her.

Rose glanced over at the small TV on her kitchen counter. Of course the reporter had moved on to another story. There was nothing new to be learned from the picture on the screen.

"No, I mean which police department?" Peg was saying. "Where did Stan live?"

"Apparently somewhere near Bulls Head. You know, where High Ridge Road and Long Ridge come together?"

"Good," Peg said with satisfaction. "Stamford."

"Yes, Stamford," Rose repeated. "Why is that good? No, wait. Do I want to know the answer to that?"

"Probably not," Peg replied. Then her tone softened. "What a terrible shame. Stan seemed like a nice man."

"Yes, he did," Rose agreed. "This feels so bizarre. We were just talking to Stan yesterday. You hear about violence in the news, but you never imagine it will touch someone you know. We barely even had a chance to get to know him. I can't believe we wasted time talking about his car, when we could have asked about important things, like his family."

"That's because we thought there would be plenty of other opportunities to talk about those things," Peg said unhappily. "Mick must have known Stan better than anyone else at the bridge club. We should contact him in a day or two to see where we should send our condolences."

"Good idea," Rose agreed. She heard the sound of a crash on the other end of the line. "What was *that?*"

"Joker just jumped off the bed. He clipped the nightstand and knocked over a clock. He's a puppy who just woke up, so he needs to go outside to pee."

Of course it would have been one of Peg's Poodles.

"That's more information than I need," Rose said crisply. "Go take care of your puppy, and we'll touch base later."

Rose disconnected the call and put her phone down on the counter. There was a bowl, a carton of eggs, and bottle of milk sitting beside it. Rose had been about to make breakfast when she'd turned on the TV to catch up on the news from overnight.

It had been utterly shocking to hear the reporter talking about someone she knew. Rose's immediate response had been to call Peg. Now she couldn't decide if that was a good thing or a bad thing.

It was certainly a first.

"Problem?" Peter came walking into the kitchen, wearing a polo shirt and cargo shorts. His hair was wet from the shower, and rather than shoes, he had slippers on his feet. He still looked great to Rose. "It sounded as though you were talking to Peg."

"Yes, there's a problem." Rose sighed. "And for once it isn't Peg's fault."

Peter helped himself to an orange from the bowl on the table and waited for her to continue.

"A member of the bridge club that she and I joined was killed last night in his home."

131

Peter put down the piece of fruit. He quickly crossed the room, wrapped his arms around his wife, and gathered her close in a hug. "I am so sorry to hear that. How disturbing that must have felt. Did the two of you know the man?"

"Yes." Rose nodded her head against his shoulder. "His name was Stan Peters. Peg and I were just talking to him yesterday afternoon. He seemed like a nice guy. Around our age, retired. He used to work in IT. His bridge partner was a car mechanic who'd once fixed his car."

Peter reared back and looked at her. "It sounds as though you knew a fair amount about him."

"Not the things that matter," Rose said sadly. "We didn't ask if Stan was married, or if he had children. We don't know where he grew up or went to school. All we knew were the few random facts he'd chosen to tell us."

"The bridge club is a new activity for you and Peg. So you must have just met Stan." Peter's tone was soothing. "That's how people get to know one another, by sharing a little bit about themselves, and then a little bit more. Nobody opens up all at once."

"I know. But I still feel bad that I didn't make more of an effort when I had the chance." Rose stepped back out of her husband's embrace. The breakfast supplies were still sitting on the counter. "I was about to make us scrambled eggs. Now I'm not hungry anymore."

"I'll just have an orange," Peter said. "I wanted to get over to the shelter early this morning anyway. I've got plenty of paperwork to do."

"Do you mind if I drop you off and take the van?" asked Rose. "I have some errands to run. And then I might stop by and see Peg."

"Sure, that's fine," Peter told her. "Whatever you need to do."

It was nearly ten-thirty by the time Rose made it to north Greenwich. She hoped Peg was out of bed by now. And that she wasn't off doing some Poodle thing (Rose had no idea what that might be) with her multiple dogs.

Rose hadn't bothered to call ahead. It was a beautiful June day. The sun was shining in a cerulean blue sky, and the warmth of late spring had not yet given way to July's humid heat. Rose was delighted to have an excuse to trade the congested area of Stamford where she lived and worked for the rolling pastures, leafy lots, and stonewall lined roads that typified back country Greenwich.

Peg's house with its two chimneys and wide front porch wasn't set back from the road nearly as far as those of her neighbors. In winter, it was visible from the small lane that led to it. Now, however, the view from the road was blocked by an abundance of summer greenery. Rose rolled down her window and enjoyed the scent of the cultivated wildflowers that bloomed along the edges of the front yard.

Her minivan had barely rolled to a stop in front of Peg's garage before the door to the house opened. Three big, black, hairy dogs came racing down the steps and across the driveway. Watching their approach, Rose was glad she hadn't gotten out of the van yet. Indeed, it occurred to her that maybe she should rethink getting out at all. Now the giant Poodles were circling her van with all the savage glee of marauders intent upon storming a defenseless village.

Rose knew just how those villagers might have felt.

Peg wasn't helping matters any. Instead of coming to Rose's aid, she remained standing on the porch with her arms crossed over her chest, waiting to see what would happen next. For a long minute neither woman made the first move.

Then, finally, Peg started down the steps. She was laughing as she drew near. "You might as well get out. It's either that or sit there all morning. They won't eat you."

Rose peered out her open window dubiously. The three Poodles were lined up beside her door. Their mouths were open and their pink tongues were hanging out. Rose could see that all three dogs had a full set of big teeth.

"Are you sure about that?"

Peg shrugged. "They haven't devoured anyone yet."

"Will they jump on me?"

"Do you want them to?"

Rose's head snapped up. "No, of course not. Why would anyone want that?"

"They're just trying to be friendly."

Peg walked over to the trio and patted her chest. The Poodle closest to her—the one with hair that was banded into numerous silly-looking ponytails, Rose noted—sprang upward, making a four-footed leap in the air. Peg caught the dog easily in her arms. The Poodle's pomponned tail whipped back and forth in a frenzy of happiness.

When his tongue came out to lick Peg's chin, Rose gave an involuntary shudder. Nevertheless, her fingers dropped down to grasp the door handle. At least with one of those monsters secured in Peg's arms, Rose's odds were improving. Now she was only outnumbered two to one.

Rose opened the door and stepped out onto the driveway. She closed her eyes and braced for the inevitable onslaught. It didn't come. Ten seconds later, she opened one eye and gazed downward. Two Poodle faces stared up at her curiously. They had soft, dark eyes and poufy topknots on their heads. Both their tails were waving in the air.

"I told you so," Peg said. She popped the Poodle out of her arms and back down to the ground. "Are you ready to go inside?"

In response, the trio of dogs spun around and raced back toward the house. They scrambled up the steps together and disappeared through the open doorway. Stunned, Rose watched them leave.

Then she turned to Peg. "What just happened?"

"The Poodles thought I was talking to them."

"They thought . . ." Rose stopped and shook her head. "You're making fun of me, aren't you?"

"I wouldn't dream of it."

"You're telling me that those Poodles understand what you say?"

"Of course they do," Peg replied. "That part's not even up for debate. Otherwise, what would be the point of talking to them?"

"Next you'll be telling me they answer back."

"Sometimes," Peg allowed. "Even usually. But not always."

" 'Not always.' " Rose smirked. "What happens when they ignore you?"

"Nothing. We all go on with our day. Sometimes the Poodles have better things to do than listen to me chatter."

Tell me about it, thought Rose.

Once they were inside the house, Peg led the way to her kitchen. Rose followed behind. The three Poodles formed an honor guard on either side of them. Reaching the room, Rose paused in the doorway. Compared to her cramped kitchen with its dim lighting and old fashioned appliances, Peg's kitchen was a thing of beauty.

The room was bright and airy, lit by a large window that filled nearly half of one wall. Wide counters offered plenty of space to work and Peg's Sub-Zero refrigerator was huge. A long butcher block table filled the middle of the room.

The Poodles immediately went trotting to the water bowls on the floor near the back door. Just as quickly, Peg strode over to a white bakery box that was sitting on a counter. She opened a cabinet above the box and took out two plates.

"I have cake," Peg announced.

As if that was a surprise. Peg always seemed to have cake at her house. The woman's fondness for sweets was near-legendary. Despite that, she didn't weigh a ton and still had all her real teeth. Rose wasn't so lucky.

"No, thank you," she said.

Peg was already sliding the cake out of the box. Its frosting was a creamy shade of mocha and there were dark chocolate tuiles on top. "No? Really?"

"Really," Rose replied with less conviction than she'd mustered a moment ago. The cake really did look good.

She pulled out a chair and sat down at the table. A Poodle with a graying muzzle and a shiny black nose came over to say hello. Rose reached out a tentative hand. The Poodle sniffed it delicately.

"That's Hope," said Peg. "She's the old lady of the house."

"I thought that was you," Rose replied tartly.

"Point taken." Peg laughed. "I suppose it's both of us."

Rose saw that Peg had cut two slices of cake and put them on plates. She got out a pair of forks, then carried everything over to the table. Peg put one plate down in front of her own seat, and the other in the middle of the table between them.

"I hope that's not for me," said Rose.

Peg shrugged. "If you don't want it, I'll eat it."

"It's not up to you to rearrange the whole world to your satisfaction. You need to learn how to take 'no' for an answer."

Peg sat down across from her. "And you need to learn that abstaining from things that give people pleasure doesn't somehow make you better than everyone else."

"That's not what I'm doing."

"Isn't it?" Peg helped herself to a large bite of cake, swallowed happily, then licked every bit of frosting off the fork before going back for another piece.

"I don't like cake," Rose growled.

"Nonsense. Everybody likes cake."

"Sugar makes my teeth hurt."

Peg considered that. It gave her time to eat more cake. "You had half a cookie yesterday."

"That was different. It was oatmeal and had raisins."

"I see," said Peg. "So almost like eating a salad, then."

"Precisely." A smile played around Rose's lips. She eyed the piece of cake in the middle of the table, then pulled her gaze away and got down to business. "Carrie called while I was on my way here. Bridge club is suspended for at least a week, and probably longer. I think she was in shock over what happened."

"I don't blame her," Peg replied. "I'm feeling rather shocked myself and we barely knew Stan."

"I haven't been able to think about anything else since I heard the news," Rose said. "Shooting someone in his own home is a horrible, but also a very purposeful, act. What are your thoughts?"

Peg stared at her. "I don't have any thoughts."

"Don't be ridiculous. You always have thoughts. Whenever something goes wrong, you can't wait to get in the middle of it."

"That's not me, that's Melanie."

"Oh please." Rose scoffed. "Everyone knows you're the one prodding her to get involved."

"Not last time," Peg pointed out. "That was all you."

Beatrice Gallagher, benefactress of the Gallagher House, had been killed in March. Rose and Melanie had ended up working together to help the police solve the crime.

"Maybe," Rose admitted. "To tell the truth, the investigation turned out to be rather interesting.

I confess to being better able to understand your motives after it was over."

"I don't have motives," Peg told her. "I just happen to be a curious person."

"Someone who notices things that other people might not."

Peg nodded. Her mouth was filled with cake.

"Like Paige and Reggie cheating at bridge."

"Precisely."

"And Bennett's gambling. By the way, you didn't tell me whether he was taking bets on the outcome of his own games or everyone else's."

"I don't know," Peg said. "I hadn't figured that part out yet."

Rose blew out an annoyed breath. "Joining a bridge club was supposed to be an innocent pastime. That was all very disappointing to hear."

"I knew you'd think so. After all, cheating goes against your commandments."

"The Church's commandments," Rose corrected automatically. Then she stopped to think. After all her years in the convent, she considered herself to be quite conversant with the Ten Commandments' dictates. But now Peg had her stumped.

"Which commandment are you talking about?"

"Number seven."

Rose quickly ran through the list in her mind. "Thou shalt not commit adultery?" she sputtered. "That's a different kind of cheating entirely."

"So? With this group, it's beginning to seem as though almost anything might be possible. Maybe that's happening too."

Yet another sobering thought. Rose sighed. Then she reached for the piece of cake in the middle of the table and pulled it toward her. She'd start with a nibble and see how that went.

"Peg," she said. "You have a very devious mind."

"I'm well aware of that." Peg smiled complacently. "It's one of my best qualities."

Chapter 13

Suddenly Joker and Coral both jumped up. The two Poodles had been asleep on the cool kitchen floor. Now they were on their feet. Hope was slower to rise but within seconds she, too, was standing and facing the hallway that led to the front door. All three dogs had their ears pricked.

Joker was first to take off running. Coral and Hope followed. The Poodles quickly disappeared from sight. Then they began to make noise. Joker's deep throated, big-dog bark sounded surprisingly menacing. Hope's hoarse growl provided an undertone to the excitement.

"Good dogs," Peg said.

Rose had turned in her chair to stare after them. "What's all that about?"

"It's my canine early warning system."

"Warning of what?" Rose glanced back to see that Peg was on her feet too. Of course she would act in unison with her dogs.

"Visitors. They're telling me someone's here."

"*I'm* here," Rose said unnecessarily.

Peg slanted her a look. "Yes, and you were announced earlier. This is someone new."

"Oh. Are you expecting anyone?"

Peg was making her way around the table. "I

wasn't even expecting you. This day is turning out to be full of surprises."

Peg left Rose sitting in the kitchen and strode to the front door. The Poodles would have jumped up as soon as a car turned in the driveway. By now, her next guest should be making his or her way up the steps. The three big Poodles were dancing on their hind legs in front of the door.

Peg hoped whoever it was liked dogs more than Rose did.

She grasped the knob and drew the door open. A man was standing outside on her porch, his hand raised as if he'd been about to knock.

He was shorter than Peg and at least a decade younger. His body was thick through the middle, and looked as though it had been designed for power rather than speed. Dark, bushy eyebrows framed his deliberate gaze.

The Poodles went dashing past Peg to eddy around the man's legs. He looked down at them and sighed. Gingerly, he patted the top of Coral's head with the tips of his fingers. She wriggled her whole body happily in response. The man didn't look impressed.

"Hello, Rodney," Peg said. "What an unexpected pleasure."

"Hello, Mrs. Turnbull. I'm afraid I'm here on official business today, so if you don't mind, it's Detective Sturgill."

"Yes, of course. Please come in."

144

The detective stepped past her. Peg called the Poodles inside and closed the door behind them. "My sister-in-law and I are having cake in the kitchen," she told him. "You're welcome to join us."

"What kind of cake?" Sturgill asked as they walked that way.

"Mocha. It's delicious."

"St. Moritz?" He named a bakery in downtown Greenwich.

"Indeed," Peg replied.

Rose was on her feet, waiting for them, when they entered the kitchen. Peg made the introductions.

"Rose, please meet Detective Rodney Sturgill of the Stamford Police Department. Detective, this is my sister-in-law, Rose Donovan."

The two of them stared at each other for several seconds. There was a pause before either one spoke.

Then Rose said in a clipped voice, "Detective Sturgill and I have already met."

"That's right," he said.

Peg had started toward the cabinet on the far side of the room. Now she stopped and turned around. "Really? When?"

"Last winter," Sturgill said. "When Beatrice Gallagher died."

"The detective viewed me as a suspect in her death."

"Of course." Peg should have remembered that Rodney had been involved in that investigation.

"Mrs. Gallagher's son told us things that pointed us in your direction," Sturgill said to Rose.

"He lied to you," she replied tartly.

"Nevertheless, it's my duty to check out all leads and suspicious people."

Rose's brow rose. "You think of me as a suspicious person then?"

"Not at the moment, no."

"You're sure of that? After all, here you are."

"Actually, I came by today to talk to Mrs. Turnbull," Sturgill told her.

"Peg," she corrected him.

The detective nodded. "I had no idea I'd find you here, too."

Rose supposed that made sense. She was still frowning, however. "I imagine you'll want to talk to me as well."

"Both of you were among the last people to see Stanley Peters alive," Sturgill pointed out. "I need to ask you a few questions."

"We understand," Peg interjected. "And we'll be happy to answer your questions. Won't we, Rose?"

Peg didn't wait for an answer. Instead she stepped between the pair. These two people definitely needed cake. She pointed toward chairs on either side of the table. "Sit, please."

146

Detective Sturgill complied. After a brief hesitation, Rose did too. Now they were facing each other. Peg could only hope the heavy wooden table was wide enough to keep them apart.

She picked up the mocha cake and brought it over. Then she went back for another plate and more utensils. Peg was pleased to see that Rose had done some nibbling around the edges of her cake. That was a start. She cut off another big piece and handed it to the detective.

Sturgill accepted it from her and dug in eagerly. "Thank you. This looks great."

Peg checked on the Poodles, who'd gone back to snoozing on the kitchen floor. Then she returned to her own seat. Despite Sturgill's assertion that he only wanted to ask questions, Rose still looked uncomfortable. Her hands were primly folded together in front of her and her gaze seemed to be directed somewhere near the ceiling.

Peg decided it was too bad Melanie wasn't here. She'd have inevitably found a way to draw Sturgill's attention away from Rose. Plus, Melanie could always be counted on to eat cake.

Searching for a neutral topic while her two guests studiously ignored each other, she said, "Melanie must have been the person who introduced the two of you."

"She was," Rose confirmed.

Detective Sturgill looked up. "Don't tell me Melanie is a member of the bridge club too? I didn't see her name on the list."

"No, she and her family are in a rented RV, taking an extended driving tour of the heartlands and points west," Peg informed him.

"Good place for her," he commented. "Under the circumstances."

"Yes, the circumstances," Peg said. "What can you tell us about them?"

Sturgill shot her a peeved look. Peg knew what that meant. It was one thing to eat her cake. It was another to fall for her machinations. The detective wasn't about to allow himself to be lulled into complacency where his investigation was concerned.

"This isn't about what I can tell you," he said. "It's about the information you might have for me."

Peg nodded. There'd be time to ask her own questions later. "What do you want to know?"

"How did you meet Stanley Peters?"

"Rose got the idea that she and I should join a bridge club together."

Sturgill looked back and forth between the two women as if he was assessing the likelihood of that partnership working out. Perceptive man.

"Stan and his partner, Mick Doran, were two of the other players in the club," Peg added.

"How long had you known him?"

"Barely more than a week," Rose put in. "We went to our first meeting last Tuesday and our second one yesterday. Or to put it another way, our acquaintance spanned approximately five hours—taking into account that each of the two bridge sessions lasted about half that long. Peg and I barely knew Stan. We'd have no idea why anyone would want to harm him."

Rose paused, then added deliberately, "And of course, having just met the man, neither Peg nor I possess anything resembling a motive."

Sturgill frowned and put down his fork. "I'd feel better if you would relax, Mrs. Donovan. I'm not accusing either of you of anything. Right now, I'm simply gathering background information."

Rose sat back in her chair. She folded her arms over her chest. She didn't look convinced.

"Go on," said Peg.

"You probably chatted with Mr. Peters a bit over the bridge table, right? You were new to the club, wanted to get to know the other players?"

"We did," Peg said, thinking back. "Both before and after the games. Stan wasn't a big talker. He referred to himself as the strong, silent type."

"He mentioned information technology," Rose said.

"What about it?" Sturgill turned to her with interest.

"Apparently that was Stan's career before he

retired. He started explaining about what IT entailed, but none of the rest of us understood much of what he was saying."

"So I guess you didn't learn anything about his personal life?"

Peg and Rose both shook their heads.

"Not really," said Peg. "Just that he drove a BMW. That came up because it was how he met his partner, Mick."

Sturgill nodded. "We'll be talking to him too. Actually, we're talking to all the members of your bridge club."

"How did you even know about the bridge club?" Peg asked. "And that Stan was a member?"

"Mr. Peters had an events calendar on his desk. Tuesday afternoons were marked off for playing bridge. On one of his notations, a woman named Carrie Maynard was listed as a contact. We spoke with her and got everybody's names."

"Carrie sounded devastated when I spoke to her earlier," said Rose. "From what we'd been told, most of the couples had been playing together for a very long time. She said they felt almost like a family."

"That paints a nice homey picture," Sturgill allowed. "But families have problems, too, Mrs. Donovan."

"Yes," Rose acknowledged. "But Stan obviously also had a life outside the club. Is there a reason to suspect that what happened to him is related to one of the other players?"

"Right now, we're checking everything and looking into all aspects of Mr. Peters' life. The reason your bridge club is getting the first look is because that appears to be the last place he went before he was killed."

Rose shuddered at the thought.

"From what we know, he spent yesterday afternoon playing cards with you ladies and your friends. Then he got in his car and drove straight home. Over the next several hours, he drank two beers, fixed himself a little dinner, then sat down in front of the television set.

"At approximately nine o'clock last night, someone entered his home and shot him twice. A neighbor heard the sound of the gunshots and called the police. Mr. Peters was already dead when the first responders arrived on the scene."

"Was there any sign of a break-in?" Peg asked.

"No."

"Robbery?"

"Not as far as we've been able to determine." Sturgill looked at the two women. "And the only reason I'm telling you that much is because the media already has that information."

The detective's cake was only half-eaten. He went back for another big bite.

"Was Stan married?" asked Peg.

"Not that we're aware of." He spoke around a full mouth.

"Did he have a girlfriend?"

"Seemingly no. Not currently, at any rate. We're still checking through his contacts."

"How about an ex-wife?"

Sturgill swallowed, then glared at her.

"What?" said Peg. "How can any of this be confidential? There are probably reporters looking into all these things right now. News outlets will have the answers by this afternoon. You'd only be saving me the time it takes to look them up."

"Frankly, I'm wondering why I should want to save you any time. Apparently you weren't interested enough to delve into the guy's personal life when he was alive and could have answered your questions himself," Sturgill pointed out. "So why are you so curious now?"

"When Stan was alive, I didn't want to pry," said Peg.

"And now?"

"Now he's dead. I should hope I don't have to point out what a huge difference that makes."

"Don't get any ideas, Peg."

"Excuse me?"

Detective Sturgill pushed back his chair and stood up. "You know what I mean."

"Do I?" Peg rose to her feet as well. "Just to be sure, why don't you explain it to me?"

"Just because Stanley Peters was an acquaintance of yours doesn't mean you need to get mixed up in things that are none of your business." He turned and started toward the hallway that led to the front door. "You know the old saying. 'Curiosity killed the cat.' "

"Then it's a good thing I have a houseful of dogs," Peg snapped.

She skirted around the table and went after him. Her hasty departure meant that all three Poodles jumped up and ran out of the kitchen too.

Rose was left sitting by herself at the table. She picked up her fork and nicked off another tiny sliver of cake. She could understand why Peg loved the stuff. It really was delicious.

Rose heard the door open and then, seconds later, slam shut again. Four sets of footsteps returned her way.

"I thought you and Detective Sturgill were supposed to be friends," she said when Peg appeared in the doorway.

"I did too." Peg sounded grumpy.

"You're curious about what happened to Stan, aren't you?"

"Of course I'm curious. One minute he was alive and well and beating us at bridge. Then the next, he was gone. Who wouldn't want to get to the bottom of that?"

Rose nodded. Then smiled.

For once, she and Peg were on the same page.

Chapter 14

Rose had met Carrie Maynard four years earlier when they both enrolled in an adult education course in Spanish. Rose had been preparing for her upcoming mission to Honduras. Carrie was seeking to broaden her horizons. The two women were both the oldest and the most diligent students in the class. They'd hit it off immediately.

Six months later, both women ended the course with a passable grasp of the language and a new friend. Carrie was in her sixties, twice divorced, active in her community, and always open to exploring new opportunities. She was proud of the fact that the bridge club she'd founded was still going strong in its eighteenth year with many of its original members.

Carrie lived in an older cottage in Riverside, a coastal neighborhood tucked between Cos Cob and Old Greenwich. The Mianus River was visible from the small widow's walk on top of her roof. Rose had reconnected with Carrie when she returned to Connecticut, and she'd visited her friend's home several times since. Carrie had never invited her up to the roof, however. And thank God for that.

Rose had left Peg's house twenty minutes

earlier. Thoughtfully—or ironically, Rose wasn't quite sure which—Peg had packed her a to-go box filled with mocha cake. Rose tossed the box on the passenger seat, then called Carrie to see if she wanted company. When Carrie gratefully agreed, Rose drove straight there.

Carrie's compact, two story bungalow had weathered siding and sparkling multipaned windows. Its roof was shaded by an enormous oak tree that dated from the middle of the previous century. Rose parked her minivan in the short gravel driveway. From there it was just a few steps to Carrie's front door.

Seconds after Rose rang the doorbell, the rustic wood-paneled door opened. Carrie was dressed in blue jeans with a stretchy tunic top pulled down over her hips. Her makeup was smeared and her eyes were rimmed in red. Rose had never seen her friend without her glittering jewelry, but now Carrie's fingers and throat were bare of any adornment. She appeared to be taking Stan's death harder than Rose had expected.

"My dear friend Rose!" Carrie's voice lifted to a high treble tone as she opened her arms to gather Rose into a hug. "I'm so glad you've come."

She pulled Rose inside and shut the door. The entry led directly into a cozy living room with a stone fireplace and plump, tweed-covered furniture. There was a tall, multiplatform cat tree in one corner. Rose saw an inquisitive face peeping out from one of the enclosed perches. Though it was sunny outside, the room's linen curtains were partially closed, blocking out much of the day's light.

Carrie waved Rose toward a love seat, then sank down in an upholstered chair across from it. She leaned her head back against the bolster and stared upward with one hand pressed dramatically against her forehead.

"This is the worst day of my life," Carrie announced.

"I'm so sorry," Rose said. "I hadn't realized that you and Stan were that close."

"We weren't. I mean, not really. At least not anymore." Carrie struggled to sit upright in the cushioned chair. "But it was the shock of finding out that he'd been murdered. You know?"

Rose nodded.

"I never expected something like that to happen to a friend of mine. This is Connecticut, for Pete's sake. Nobody around here even owns a gun."

"I know you spoke with Detective Sturgill," Rose said. "What did you learn from him? Do the police have any suspects?"

"Learn from him?" Carrie snorted. "Not a blessed thing. That policeman was more tight-lipped than my first husband. All he wanted to do was ask questions. When was the last time I saw Stan? Were we on good terms? Could I think of anyone who had a grudge against him, or might have wanted to hurt him?"

"And could you?" Rose asked.

"Of course not. I certainly wouldn't associate with someone who was capable of committing murder."

Rose thought Carrie might be surprised to know how easy it was to be mistaken about that. Recent events in her life had certainly rearranged her own thinking on the matter.

"How did Stan come to be a member of your bridge club?" she asked. "Was he there from the beginning?"

"Just about. The idea to get a group together started because several of us were members of the Lakeview Country Club. Nice place, but some of its customs were stuck in the Dark Ages. Like there was a room called the men's grill where all the men went to drink, watch sports on TV, and play cards."

Rose frowned. "A room for men only?"

"Yup. It was basically a bar with dark paneling, round tables, and brass fixtures. The place looked like something you'd see in a British period movie. No women were allowed."

Rose was still frowning. Perhaps it was a good thing she'd never had the means or the desire to join a country club. "Was there a women's grill too?"

"No. Other than that, Lakeview had a 'mixed'

grill for families. Men, women, and children. When the women wanted some peace and quiet to sit around and play cards, they had to get together in the ladies' locker room."

"That's ridiculous," Rose said.

"I know. Right? Segregating the sexes is an archaic idea. Plus, some of the more dedicated bridge players at the club were men. So why shouldn't we all be able to play cards in the same place?"

"That sounds perfectly sensible to me."

"Thankfully, it made sense to other people too. But then the club wouldn't let us use one of their rooms for our meetings." Carrie rolled her eyes. "I guess they didn't want other members getting any ideas about starting their own rebellions against rules they didn't like."

The two women smiled together.

"So I found us a place at the community center and we all went over there. Lacey was in the group from the beginning because she and I are partners. Then the Seversons hopped on board. So did Florence and Franny." Carrie pursed her lips as she thought back. "Once we had a few couples who wanted to play, they asked around among their friends to see if any of them wanted to join us. Someone brought Stan along, I think it might have been Jerry Watkins. And obviously when Stan joined, we got Mick too."

"Mick's an interesting guy," Rose said.

"You think so?"

"He plays bridge better than anyone I've ever seen."

Carrie shrugged. "He's too quiet."

The cat jumped down gracefully from her tree house. She was mostly gray with white on her face and paws. She padded over to the love seat and twined herself around Rose's legs. Rose reached down to give her a pat. Now that she and Peter were settled in one place for a while, she was thinking about getting a kitty of her own.

"Quiet," Rose said, looking up again. "Why does that matter?"

"Oh, you know. We're a pretty convivial group. Our meetings are as much about socializing as they are about playing bridge. But Mick never seems to have much to say. It's hard to even get him involved in a conversation."

"Stan didn't seem like a big talker either," Rose commented.

"No, but Stan had other things going for him." Carrie waggled her eyebrows suggestively.

Rose stared at her friend, nonplussed. Did that mean what she thought it did?

Carrie tipped her head to one side and grinned like a cat who'd been in the cream.

Rose still felt dubious. She ventured a guess anyway. "You had a thing with Stan?"

"A *thing*." Carrie laughed. "Stan and I were

160

consenting adults. We might as well call it what it was. He and I had a hot and heavy affair."

"When?" Rose nearly shrieked. "Like recently? How come I didn't know about it?"

"Good gracious, no. Not now. There was no reason for you to know about something that was over and done with years ago. Like ten, maybe. Stan and I were both younger then."

Well, yes. Rose bit back a laugh. Presumably they'd been ten years younger. She pictured the tall, slender man with his thinning hair and serious demeanor. Stan was no George Clooney. Even in his prime, she couldn't imagine he'd have been a handsome man.

"I know what you're thinking," said Carrie.

"You do?" Rose certainly hoped not.

"Maybe Stan wasn't the best looking man in the room. But he had it up here." Carrie tapped her forefinger on the side of her head.

"He was smart?"

"Yes, he was smart," said Carrie. "But that's not what I meant. Stan was kind. He was an all-around nice guy. He cared about people. That was what made him so appealing."

Rose swallowed heavily at the thought. Obviously not everyone had shared Carrie's opinion.

"So what happened?" she asked. "Who ended things between you?"

"It was a mutual decision. The affair was fun

while it lasted, but after a while we both knew that it had run its course. By that time Paige and Reggie had joined the club—they weren't among the early members—and Stan had begun to look around again."

" 'Look around,' " Rose repeated. This wasn't the easiest conversation for her to follow. "You mean he was interested in Paige?"

Carrie smirked. "Are you kidding me? It wasn't just Stan. When the Greenes became part of the group, *all* the guys were interested in Paige."

Rose had no problem imagining that. The sleek, dark haired woman barely looked like the same species as the other women in the bridge club.

"But Paige is married," she said. Pointing that out made Rose feel like she was twelve years old. Or a former nun.

Carrie's shoulders rose and fell in an eloquent shrug.

All at once, Rose realized that maybe she was supposed to have understood Carrie's comment about group socializing in a different way than she initially had. She couldn't decide whether to be fascinated or repulsed by the thought.

"Umm . . . okay," Rose said slowly. She certainly didn't want to appear judgmental. On the other hand, she had next to no experience acting hip and sophisticated. "How did Paige feel about that?"

"She didn't care," Carrie said with a chuckle.

"All that woman is interested in is building her brand and selling top dollar real estate. She was happy to flirt with the guys in the beginning—when she thought it might net her a sale or at least some good connections. It took some time, but eventually everyone got everyone else's true motivations figured out. Things finally settled down then and we all just went back to playing bridge."

Just playing bridge. Suddenly Rose was afraid she'd never be able to think about the game the same way again.

The cat jumped up and landed lightly on the cushion beside her. She lay down like a sphinx and tucked in her two front paws.

"That's Stella," Carrie said. "She likes it if you scratch under her chin."

Rose was happy to comply. Stella's fur was as soft as silk. The cat closed her blue eyes and began to purr. Her tail wrapped around her body. Carrie watched the interaction with a smile on her face.

"Peg and I never had a chance to get to know Stan," Rose said. "Obviously you knew him quite well. Tell me about him."

"Sure. What do you want to know?"

"Anything interesting. Was he ever married? Does he have any kids?"

"Yes, to the first question, and no to the second," Carrie replied. "At one time, Stan was married to a woman named Bethany. They wanted to have children, but it never happened for them."

Rose rubbed the side of Stella's head with her finger. The cat leaned into the caress. "Where is Bethany now? Are she and Stan divorced?"

"Unfortunately, no," Carrie told her. "Stan was a widower. Bethany died in a terrible car crash. On a dark night, in the pouring rain, a drunk driver crossed two lanes of traffic and hit her car head-on. She was killed instantly. It happened a long time ago. At least twenty years, I think."

"That's so sad," Rose said. No wonder Stan had always looked somber. She couldn't imagine ever being able to get over a tragedy like that.

Carrie nodded. "Stan said that he and Bethany were soul mates. And that after she died, his life fell to pieces. It took him a long time to get it put back together. He was determined to never risk his heart like that again."

"That poor man," said Rose.

"I know." Carrie sighed. "I always felt sorry for him. Even when we were together. Stan probably would have been horrified if he'd known that. He didn't want anyone's pity."

"What about his family? Did Stan have brothers or sisters? Is there someone to plan a service for him?"

Carrie considered the question before replying. "Lacey might step in. If she does, I'll offer to help out."

"Lacey?" Rose said, surprised. "Why her?"

"I guess I left out that part earlier."

"Don't tell me she was involved with Stan too?"

"No, nothing like that," Carrie said. "She and Stan were related after a fashion. Stan's wife, Bethany, was Lacey's half-sister."

Chapter 15

The morning after she heard the news about Stan, Peg was back at work. She'd be spending her day the way she spent so much of her life: at a dog show. This time, she was judging again. And it was raining.

"Yuck," said Joe Klein, who was stewarding for her. "I hate it when it rains on dog show days."

In his forties, smart, and passionate about his Schipperkes, Joe was an officer of the show hosting kennel club. The man was usually a dapper dresser. Today it was hard to tell. Like Peg, he'd made sure to come well prepared for the inclement weather.

They were both wearing waterproof raincoats and tall rubber boots. Joe had on a waxed cotton safari hat. Peg's head was covered by a vinyl rain hat with a wide brim. It was bright yellow, chosen so she could be seen from afar even on a gloomy day.

Joe had already informed her that she looked like the fisherman who sold seafood on TV. Now he was busy setting up the judge's table. Peg was standing nearby, peering out from beneath the lip of the tent that covered only a small portion of the ring. Judging would start in just a few minutes.

Her assignment included most of the non-sporting breeds and some of the toys. She couldn't have asked for a better selection of breeds. Now, however, looking at the puddles that were already forming in the uncovered area of her grass ring, Peg couldn't help but sigh.

This wasn't just a light drizzle. Rain was driving down from the cloud-covered sky in sheets. These conditions would make everyone's job tougher.

Exhibitors with long-haired breeds who'd spent hours grooming their dogs to perfection, would see all their hard work undone as soon as Peg sent everyone out into the rain to gait around the ring. Smooth-coated breeds, especially the smaller ones, would have issues as well. No dog showed its best while dodging puddles and being buffeted by rain from above.

The alternative would be for Peg to judge her assignment in the small covered area of her ring. However that space was cramped, narrow, and semi-dark. It was barely acceptable for evaluating the dogs standing still. It would offer no opportunity for her to adequately access their movement.

No, that wasn't happening on Peg's watch. Despite the weather, everyone would simply have to buckle down and get on with it. Like she intended to do.

"Ready?" Joe asked her. He'd been handing out armbands to the Boston Terrier exhibitors who were gathered outside the ring.

"Ready," Peg replied. She pushed back the low brim of her hat and turned to face the incoming class with a cheerful smile. On a day like this, it felt like the least she could do.

Midmorning, Peg was pleased with how things were proceeding. Dog show exhibitors were a hardy breed. So far, there'd been few absentees and almost no audible grumbling from handlers when she'd motioned them and their dogs out into the weather.

The fact that Peg followed them out from under the tent and watched their performance while standing in the rain herself, probably had something to do with that. Or perhaps her hearing wasn't as good as it used to be.

She stopped to take a quick water break while a class of four Cavalier King Charles Spaniels took a surprising amount of time to get themselves arranged in a line. It appeared that no one wanted to be in front. Their reluctance seemed silly to Peg. They were all going to end up getting wet eventually.

As she began to judge the class, Peg saw a movement by the in-gate out of the corner of her eye. A woman motioned Joe over to the opening and said something to him. Joe glanced briefly at Peg, then nodded. The woman was encased in plastic rain garb from head to toe, but Peg didn't have any problem recognizing Rina Jacobs.

She and Rina belonged to the same kennel club.

But it was summer and everyone was busy, and Peg and Rina hadn't seen each other in several months. She'd just been talking about Rina the other day, however. And now here she was. That couldn't be a coincidence.

Peg finished judging her Cavaliers in record time. She might have felt guilty about that except with this weather, nobody appeared to mind spending less time in the ring than they normally would have. While her first class of Toy Fox Terriers came into the ring, hopping and bouncing in the wet grass, Peg walked over to where Joe was standing.

Rain had been blowing underneath the tent all morning. The jaunty bow tie Joe was wearing under his slicker was damp and droopy. Water dripped from the brim of his hat down onto the catalog he held open in his hands. Nevertheless, Joe greeted her with a smile.

"Rina Jacobs," she said.

Joe nodded. "She was just here. You must have eyes in the back of your head."

"I do," Peg replied crisply. "And don't you forget it. What did she want?"

"She said she needed to talk to you."

Peg's brow rose. "In the middle of judging?"

"No, it wasn't urgent. Rina just wanted me to give you a message to find her at some point before you left the showground."

"Maybe during my lunch break," Peg mused.

170

"What time are Dandies being judged today?"

Joe flipped to the judging schedule in the front of the book. "Two o'clock. Ring six."

"Perfect. I'll track her down while I'm supposed to be eating."

An hour and a half later, Peg found Rina huddled under the grooming tent with the several hundred other exhibitors. Most were trying to look like they were having a good time. Some were succeeding better than others. A group of terrier handlers were set up in the middle of the tent. Peg spotted Rina right away.

Rina was shorter than Peg, and slender enough to be called skinny. She had smokey brown eyes and an infectious laugh. When Peg approached, Rina was sitting on her grooming table, peering at a dog magazine through reading glasses that were perched on the end of her nose. The large, rounded head of a Dandie Dinmont was visible inside the stacked crate behind her.

"I shouldn't really be fraternizing under here," Peg said. "Do you want to take a walk with me?"

Rina looked up, slapped the magazine shut, and hopped down off the tabletop. "Out there?" She pointed. "In *that?*"

"Joe said you needed to talk to me."

"I do." She looked at her watch to check the time. "I just wasn't picturing doing it in the middle of a monsoon."

Peg considered their options. "The judges'

parking lot isn't far away. How about if we go sit in my van?"

"It's a deal." Rina tucked away her glasses, pulled on her raincoat, and stuck the matching hat on her head. "Lead the way."

Soon they were settled across from each other on the minivan's two front seats. Rina took off her rain hat and shook out her hair like a dog. Peg rolled her window down halfway to let in some air. Rivulets of water ran down their boots and pooled on the floor mats.

"What's up?" Peg asked. "Please don't tell me there's trouble brewing at Belle Haven."

Peg was a past president of their mutual kennel club, Rina was the current secretary. Like all dog clubs, theirs was subject to occasional bouts of discord and infighting, but as far as Peg knew things had been mostly calm lately.

"No, nothing like that. I had an unexpected phone call yesterday."

"About?"

"You, actually. It was from John Severson."

"How interesting." Peg reached down into the pocket beside her seat. "I have two energy bars, a fig and a raspberry. Which one do you want?"

Rina extended her hand. "I'll take the raspberry."

Good choice. Peg preferred the fig bar. She tore the wrapper open.

"You know John and his wife, Violet, right?" Rina asked.

"We've met, although I wouldn't say that I know either of them well. I recently joined a bridge club that the Seversons belong to."

"That's the club that the man who was murdered in Stamford was also a member of, right?"

Peg wasn't surprised Rina knew about that. A murder in lower Fairfield County was inevitably big news.

"Right," she said. "Why did John call you?"

"It was very odd. Apparently, he wanted to ask a bunch of questions about you. Like how long you and I had known each other, and what kind of person you are."

Peg straightened in her seat. "I hope you told him it was none of his business."

"Not right away." Rina frowned. "Because I was still trying to figure out what was going on. The Seversons and I frequent some of the same social events, but it's not like we're close friends. Let's just say, John has never felt the need to call me about anything before. So I asked him why he wanted to know."

"And?"

"John explained a bit about your bridge club. He described it as a group of people who, for the most part, had known each other and played together for years. He said that one of the longtime couples had recently moved away and two new players had taken their place."

173

Peg nodded. "That was me and my sister-in-law, Rose."

"I gathered that," Rina replied. "John told me he was concerned because after everything running smoothly within the club for all those years, as soon as the new people joined, one of the other players had turned up dead. That's when your name came up."

Peg had been munching contentedly on her fig bar. Now, suddenly, it felt like it was stuck in her throat. "And he thought that was *my* fault?"

"Something like that," Rina said with a smile.

"You think that's funny?"

"Little bit." Rina tried to arrange her features into a more serious expression and failed utterly. "Those people might have just met you, Peg, but you and I have been friends forever. Face it, even on a good day you can be more trouble than a sack of cats."

Peg wished she could argue the point. But she hadn't told a single lie yet today and she wasn't about to start now.

"I hope you didn't tell John that," she said instead.

"No, of course not. In fact, I gave you a glowing recommendation. I told John that you're smart and perceptive, and probably a darn good bridge player. And that his group should be honored to have you as a member."

"I wouldn't go quite that far," Peg said.

Rina just shrugged. She looked quite pleased with herself.

Peg took another bite of her fig bar. She chewed it slowly as she considered what Rina had told her. Something didn't add up.

"Granted Rose and I are new to the club," she said. "But that hardly seems reason enough for someone to be suspicious of us."

"Apparently there was something else."

"Now what?" Peg scowled. This conversation was one surprise after another. And none of them were good. "As far as the club's bridge games are concerned, I've been a veritable model of decorum."

"How about when you're not playing?"

Peg shook her head. She had no idea what Rina was talking about.

"John said that you'd gone to the club's director to complain about the behavior of one of the other players."

"Oh."

Well, she had done that. And once again, it hadn't taken any time at all for the news to spread. Peg probably should have realized that even something she'd thought was said in confidence wouldn't remain a secret for long in that tight-knit group.

"Bennett was placing bets on the outcome of the games," Peg said in her defense. "And another couple was cheating."

Come to think of it, she hadn't even mentioned that to Carrie. Which as it turned out was probably a good thing.

Rina chuckled. "And I thought dog shows were tough. Bridge is supposed to be a genteel game, isn't it?"

"I guess that depends on who you're playing with." Peg slid her hand down into the seat pocket again, hoping to find another fruit bar. She fished around for a few seconds and came up empty. Darn it.

Peg turned back to Rina. "If John Severson thinks he has the right to be keeping tabs on me, then turnabout should be fair play. What can you tell me about him and his wife?"

Rina looked like she was wishing Peg had found more fig bars too. "Normally I wouldn't be any more inclined to gossip about John and Violet than I was to do the same about you. But since . . . you know . . ."

"Stan Peters is dead and John suspects I might be responsible?" Peg said drily.

"Yes, that." She frowned. "I figure you should probably know who you're dealing with. The Seversons have money. Seemingly plenty of it. And both of them are very aware of their own consequence."

Peg nodded. That confirmed her own initial impression of the couple.

"Before John retired, he was president of some

176

large corporation. Violet often talks about how nice it is to have him around the house now. John says it's great he has a chance to get involved in projects that he never had time for before. They both imply that his retirement was voluntary."

"And you don't think it was?"

Rina shrugged. "You know how people love to talk. When there's dirt about someone, they can't wait to share it. I've heard whispers that maybe John didn't choose to retire. That he was forced out of his company due to some impropriety."

"Well that's an interesting turn of events," Peg said cheerfully. It sounded as though John didn't have much right to complain about her behavior. "What kind of impropriety are you talking about? Financial? Ethical?" She paused, then added, "Sexual?"

"It could be any of those. I don't know all the details. And it's not like I can ask."

"Why not?" Peg demanded.

"Apparently because I'm not you." Rina grinned at the thought, then quickly sobered again. "Anyway, I just thought you should know what you're up against."

"So a man who was accused of malfeasance is now going out of his way to do the same to me," Peg mused. "It still seems odd, considering that John and I barely know each other. It makes me wonder why he would even bother. Unless . . ."

Rina was checking her watch. She and Peg both

needed to get back to work. Now she looked up. "Unless what?"

"Maybe John has something to hide himself. And he's hoping that the best defense is a good offense."

Chapter 16

The next morning Rose was sitting outside in the small patch of scrubby ground that served as the Gallagher House's backyard, staring at sixteen tomato plants, when the building's door opened behind her. Maura stuck her head out.

"There's a woman here to see you," she said. "And she's got a"—her voice lowered to an inaudible whisper—"with her."

"A what?" Rose stood up and turned around.

Immediately her question was answered. Peg was stepping around the housekeeper to come through the doorway. A big black Poodle followed at her heels.

"A dog," Maura said, louder this time. Her eyes were wide as she followed the pair's progress down the steps. "Maybe the biggest Poodle in the world."

"Hope is a Standard Poodle," Peg told her. "They're all big. Thank you for showing me where I could find Rose. I'll take it from here."

Maura's eyes flickered to Rose, who nodded. "Maura, this is my sister-in-law, Peg Turnbull. For some reason, she often takes a dog with her when she goes places."

"The reason is simple," Peg said. "Dogs are

179

social animals. They enjoy outings, and I enjoy their company." She waved in Maura's direction. "Nice to meet you."

"And you as well," Maura replied. She went back inside and closed the door.

"You know," Rose mentioned, "cat owners don't feel obliged to take their cats with them everywhere."

"That's because no one really likes cats." Peg glanced around as Hope began to sniff along the perimeter fence. The entire space would have fit inside a good-sized dog pen.

"I like cats."

"Do you have one?"

"Well . . . no," Rose sputtered.

"I rest my case."

There was a second lawn chair folded up and leaning against the back of the house. Peg went to get it. She set it up beside Rose's chair.

"I hope I haven't interrupted anything," she said. "What are you doing sitting out here by yourself?"

"Watching my tomato plants grow," Rose admitted unhappily.

"Is that what they are?" Peg peered downward at the neat double row of small green shoots. "It's hard to tell. How long ago did you plant them?"

"It's been a week. And they still look pretty much the same."

"Maybe you need to water them."

"No, that's not it. Ivy says I'm already drowning them."

Peg looked up. "And Ivy is?"

"A farmer's daughter."

"Ahh, she should know then. Maybe your problem is too much water."

Rose nodded. She'd considered the same thing. Still having planted the seedlings herself it was hard not to want to nurture them in some way. Doing nothing more than waiting for the small plants to grow made her feel like she was incompetent to oversee their care. Which it was beginning to look like she might be.

Peg walked over and sat down. Hope was already finished exploring the small area. She came over and lay down in the shade beside Peg's chair.

"That's your older dog, isn't it?" Rose could tell by the graying muzzle.

"Yes." Peg's hand dropped down to scratch the Poodle's ears. "Her name is Hope."

Rose already knew that. But she noted the gentle reminder. "Does she need anything? A dish of water? A dog biscuit?"

Peg shaded her eyes as she looked over at Rose. "Do you have a dog biscuit?"

"No, but I'd imagine I can find a cookie in the pantry."

"Thank you for offering, but she's fine. Come and sit down."

Rose complied. Where Peg was concerned that was usually the safest course of action. Besides, she still had no idea why Peg was here.

"This is your first visit to Gallagher House, isn't it?" she said.

"Yes, it is. I would have come to see what you were up to sooner, but you never invited me."

"I would have invited you if I thought you'd show up."

"Pish," said Peg. "You didn't invite me precisely because you were afraid I *would* show up."

"Perhaps there's a small amount of truth to that." Rose smiled.

After a few seconds, Peg did too. "Hope and I walked in the front door and came straight out the back, so I didn't have a chance to see much of anything inside. How many women do you have staying here?"

"There are five at the moment. But our population is pretty fluid. Depending on need, it changes from day to day. And sometimes night to night."

Peg stared at the back of the house. Like the others on the street, it was tall and narrow. "You must be just about full, then."

"Actually, no. There's more room inside the house than you might think. We have three bedrooms on the second floor, with an additional bedroom and half bath on the third. And of course, we can double up when we need to. There's also a small basement apartment."

"That's where you and Peter were living in the spring."

Rose nodded. Peg had been paying more attention than she'd realized. Perhaps Melanie had been keeping her informed.

"Maura lives there now. She keeps house for us and does some of the cooking. She's also on-site twenty-four/seven in case someone needs to unlock the door in the middle of the night."

Peg looked thoughtful. Apparently that need hadn't occurred to her.

Rose watched as Peg lifted a hand and began to fan her face. "Can I get you a cold drink?"

"No, I'm not thirsty. Just a bit warm. I find the summer heat bothers me more now than it did when I was younger. Do you feel the same?"

"I might if Peter and I hadn't spent the past couple of years in Honduras. After that, summer in Connecticut feels almost cool." Rose was still waiting for Peg to tell her why she'd come.

"I judged a dog show yesterday," Peg said.

"Did you?" Rose was surprised. "I had no idea they still went on when it was raining."

"Dog shows happen in all kinds of weather. I once judged in the snow. And another time under a hurricane watch. At least yesterday's downpour kept it cooler than it might have been. I ran into

Rina Jacobs at the show." Peg paused to amend her thought. "Actually, she sought me out."

"Rina," Rose repeated. "Why does that name sound familiar?"

"Because the Seversons and I were talking about her at the bridge club meeting on Tuesday."

"That's right. She's the lady with the Dandie Do Nots."

"Dinmonts," Peg corrected.

"Whatever."

"It turns out that John had contacted her to ask questions about me. He thinks there's something suspicious about the fact that Stan was murdered not long after you and I joined the bridge club."

"Suspicious, how?" Rose asked. Then she realized what Peg meant and frowned. "He thinks *we* might have had something to do with it?"

"Apparently so."

"That's absurd," Rose snapped. She wondered why Peg didn't sound as aggrieved as she suddenly felt. "It's also backward logic. If we were planning to kill someone, why would we form a very public relationship with that person right before we did the deed?"

"I didn't say John's thought process had merit," Peg replied mildly. "Only that he seems to believe it. And to be perfectly honest, I think he's more suspicious of me than you."

Rose relaxed fractionally. "Okay. That makes more sense."

"It does?"

"Of course. Everyone knows I would never hurt someone. Whereas you . . ."

"Yes?" Peg said ominously.

"Have a reputation for being tough as nails when the occasion calls for it. And don't even bother trying to look perplexed because I'm not buying it. You know it's true. Not only that, but you enjoy intimidating people."

"Some people deserve to be intimidated," Peg muttered.

"I never said they didn't. But face it, Peg. You're not soft and cuddly. More like stern and uncompromising."

"You make me sound like I'm some kind of Gorgon."

If the shoe fits, thought Rose.

"Confession time?" she said aloud.

Peg nodded.

"That's how I pictured you when we first met."

"Remind me of when that was. I seem to have put it out of my mind."

Rose sincerely doubted that. Nevertheless, she did as requested. "I was a novice then. I was preparing to become a nun but I hadn't yet taken my vows. Max brought you to the convent so we could meet."

"It's coming back to me now." Peg's lips flattened. "As I recall, that was when you accused me of trying to usurp your place in the family.

A place that, for all intents and purposes, you'd already willingly vacated."

"You're right. I did say that," Rose replied quietly. "Because that was how it felt to me at the time. I was so young when I entered the convent that I'd had no real experience of adult life. I was content with the choice I'd made. Contentment seemed like enough to me at the time."

Peg waited in silence for Rose to continue.

"I'm not trying to excuse my behavior. Only to explain it. Max was my adored older brother. Seeing him with you and realizing how happy the two of you were together, it felt like a punch in the gut. I was barely more than a child. And for the first time I was confronted with the reality of how much I had given up. In that moment, I was consumed by jealousy."

"So you decided to make yourself feel better by lashing out at me."

Rose shook her head. "Believe me, there was no decision involved on my part. At least not a conscious one. I know I behaved horribly. Later I went to confession."

"*Later,* you could have apologized to me," Peg said sharply.

Rose exhaled a sigh. Peg wasn't going to make this easy for her. Not that she'd ever expected her to.

"Yes, I could have. And I should have. I know I'm making a mess of this, but that's what I'm trying to do now. I want you to know how sorry I am. Not just for that awful day, but also for everything else that followed. You didn't deserve that. I was very wrong to have said the things I did."

A minute passed in silence. It felt like a very long time.

Finally, Peg spoke. "Thank you for that. Since we appear to be clearing the air, I should admit that it's not as though I was entirely blameless. Perhaps I reveled in the fact that I had everything I'd ever wanted, while your life seemed to me to be . . . something less."

Rose opened her mouth to comment. Peg held up a staying hand. She wasn't going to allow herself to be interrupted.

"I'm well aware that's not how you viewed your vocation," she said. "You felt that dedicating your life to God was like offering a treasured gift. I should have found your choice honorable. Instead, it was incomprehensible to me. I'm afraid I scoffed at what I couldn't understand. For that, and for some of the mutual nastiness that has followed throughout the years, I owe you an apology too."

Rose swallowed heavily. She hadn't foreseen that response. In all the years she'd known Peg, the woman had never demonstrated anything other than an unswerving conviction in the infallibility of her own path.

Suddenly Rose felt as though an entirely different person was sitting beside her. One whom she might enjoy getting to know better.

"Well?" Peg prompted.

"Apology accepted," Rose replied. "Assuming you do the same."

"Yes." Peg sounded thoughtful. "I do. Now that we've put that behind us, let's move on, shall we?"

Rose nodded.

"I refuse to believe that you've simply been sitting here watching tomatoes. Therefore I'm going to assume I'm not the only one who has continued to ponder the circumstances surrounding Stan's unfortunate and unexpected demise."

Just like that, Peg was trying to take charge again. Rose should have known that their moment of shared harmony was too good to last. On the other hand, Peg's assumption was correct.

"I spoke with Carrie," she said. "She's obviously the person who's known everyone in the bridge club the longest."

"What an excellent idea." Peg settled back in her chair to listen. "Did she have anything useful to say?"

"Quite a lot, actually."

"Please continue. I'm all ears."

Rose enjoyed being the one with answers for a change. "For one thing, she and Stan had once had a rather torrid affair."

Peg choked on a surprised laugh. Then she looked over at Rose. "I thought you were kidding. You're not, are you?"

"No. And there's more. Stan was a widower. He was married to a woman named Bethany who was killed in a car crash caused by a drunk driver."

"How long ago?" asked Peg.

"Years." Rose considered. "I don't remember exactly how many. Even more interesting, Bethany was Lacey Duvall's half-sister."

"The same Lacey who is Carrie's bridge partner?"

"Precisely."

"My, you are a font of information," Peg said admiringly. "I'm afraid what I have to offer seems paltry by comparison."

"Aside from the fact that John Severson suspects you're capable of killing someone?"

"Yes, besides that." Peg wasn't amused. "The rest of what I've learned may or may not be germane, but it's information that we didn't previously possess. According to Rina, John didn't retire from his high-level corporate post voluntarily. He was forced out for some kind of unspecified misbehavior."

"So the pot was calling the kettle black," Rose mused.

"Other than that I object to being referred to as a kettle, yes. I'm beginning to suspect there may be more to our little bridge club than initially meets the eye."

Rose nodded in agreement.

"Detective Sturgill assured us that his department would be looking into all aspects of Stan's life," Peg continued. "But it occurs to me that you and I already have an 'in' with the other club members. They may reveal things to us that they wouldn't tell strangers, especially not official ones."

Peg had a point. Rose nodded again.

"Admit it, Rose. You wouldn't have gone to see Carrie if you didn't want answers too."

Rose was quite certain she'd already admitted that. But now that she thought back, maybe she hadn't done so aloud. A day or two earlier, she might not have trusted Peg that much. But things felt different now. *Rose* felt different now, more open to exploring possibilities she hadn't previously considered.

Could she and Peg work together as a team? Their first partnership, at the bridge table, had met with only moderate success. Would they be able to do better in this situation, where there was so much more riding on the outcome?

Rose truly didn't know the answer to that. She only knew that she wanted to try. She looked over at Peg and smiled.

"The first thing we need to do is make a plan," she said.

Chapter 17

A plan? Peg thought. Of course they needed a plan. That would not be a problem. She woke up every morning with her head swimming with plans. Then it was just a matter of sorting through them and deciding which ones were the most useful.

Abruptly it occurred to Peg that this time the decision wouldn't be hers alone to make. Rose would also have a say in their upcoming choices. The thought was unsettling. Peg was accustomed to running her own life without having to cede even a modicum of control to anyone else.

Hopefully this new arrangement wouldn't be too unwieldy.

Were she and Rose really going to be able to chart a joint course toward a mutual goal? Peg wasn't sure about that yet. It would obviously require some compromise on her part. Or maybe, what would actually be required was Peg's acceptance of the fact that neither one of them was always right or always wrong.

Except that Rose had insisted that she liked cats. She was definitely wrong about that.

Peg leaned over the side of her chair and trailed a hand down Hope's warm back. The Poodle opened her eyes and lifted her head.

"Good girl." Peg patted her knee. "Come on up."

Hope stood up and stretched. She took a few seconds to ponder the invitation. Usually there was plenty of room in Peg's lap. But today her seat in the folding chair made for cramped quarters.

"Don't worry about that," Peg told the Poodle. "You'll fit just fine."

"Two things," said Rose, who was watching the interaction. "First, you're reasoning with Hope as if she can follow your logic."

Peg spared her a glance. "She can."

"What makes you think that?"

"Because she responds to my suggestions," Peg said as if it were obvious. "Didn't we talk about this the other day?"

"Yes, but I thought you meant that your dogs understood basic commands."

"They do. And more. Is that a problem?"

"Not for me." In the interest of their newfound harmony, Rose decided to play along. "Has Hope answered you yet?"

"She's still thinking about it," Peg replied. "What's the second thing?"

"What do you want her to do?"

Peg patted the tops of her knees again. Hope leaned back briefly, then sprang in the air and landed lightly in Peg's lap. There was a moment of juggling as Peg balanced the big Poodle until she found her footing. Then Hope turned around in place and lay down across Peg's thighs.

"That," Peg said with satisfaction. Her fingers tunneled through Hope's thick coat. The Poodle's tail thumped up and down happily.

"A few minutes ago, you were complaining about the heat. That's not going to help."

Peg shrugged. "I'll manage. Besides, I always think better with my hands on a dog."

Peg didn't just have her hands on Hope. Much of her body had disappeared behind and underneath the big fuzzy animal.

"Maybe you should think about getting one of those itty-bitty breeds that you can tuck inside a purse," Rose said.

Before Peg could reply, the door to the house opened. Maura walked outside, carrying a tray with a flower-sprigged pitcher and two tall glasses. Ice cubes clinked against the sides of the pitcher as she made her way carefully down the steps.

When she reached the ground, Maura looked up and saw Peg. Her eyes widened. "Yikes! What happened to you? Do you need help?"

"That would have been my first guess too." Rose laughed. "But no. Peg thinks she's comfortable like that."

"I *know* I'm comfortable," Peg corrected her. "Have you brought us something cold to drink? What a perfectly lovely idea."

Maura handed the tray to Rose, then went to

grab a small wooden crate that could serve as a table. "You know you'd be cooler without a big black dog in your lap," she said to Peg.

"But not nearly as content."

"It's no use arguing with her," Rose said to Maura. "Peg's a stubborn woman, and never more so than when she's wrong."

Maura shoved the crate into place between them. She retrieved the tray from Rose and set it down on top. "There's iced tea with lemon in the pitcher. But we also have lemonade and sodas in the fridge. And cold water, of course."

"Iced tea is perfect for me," said Peg.

"Me, too," Rose agreed. She reached over and poured them each a glass. "Maura, would you like to get another chair and join us?"

"That depends," Maura said. "What are you talking about?"

"We were discussing past history," Peg told her. "But thank goodness we're done with that. Now we've moved on to murder. Rose and I need a plan."

Maura's gaze flew to Rose. Clearly she was wondering if Peg was serious. Rose just shrugged.

"Thanks, but no thanks." Maura crossed the small yard in three quick steps and disappeared inside.

"Now you've scared her away," said Rose. "That wasn't nice."

"I had no idea she'd scare so easily." Peg gazed in the direction Maura had gone. "I hope you're made of stronger stuff."

"I once faced down a knife-wielding bandit in Tegucigalpa. Is that strong enough for you?"

"It certainly is." Peg swung back to face Rose. "I'm impressed."

"Then I probably shouldn't admit that he was ten years old."

"Even so. Knives can be dangerous in any hands."

"So can guns," Rose replied. "Which brings us back to the topic at hand. I think the first thing we should do is get to know our fellow bridge club members better."

"I couldn't agree more," Peg said. "Let's divvy up the list and go visiting."

"I'll take Jerry and Mae Watkins." Rose paused for a sip of cold tea. "And you can have Mick Doran."

"Don't try to make it sound as though you're doing me a favor," Peg replied. "The man hardly ever opens his mouth. We both know he'll be the hardest one to get to share anything."

"Which is precisely why I gave him to you. Besides, he's potentially also the most interesting person, considering that he was Stan's partner."

Peg nodded. She would concede that.

"I'd better take John and Violet Severson. It sounds as though they already don't like you,"

Rose said. "Hopefully I'll have a better chance of getting them to open up."

Peg ignored the dig. She was feathering her fingers absently through the silky hair on Hope's ears. "Since you have the Watkinses and the Seversons, I'll take Sue and Bennett, Paige and Reggie Greene, and the Grover sisters. And you can add Carrie's partner, Lacey, to your list."

Rose considered their two assignments. "Why do you get to talk to more people than I do?"

"Because I move faster than you do." Surely Peg didn't have to point that out? "Plus, I have plenty of experience getting people to do things they don't want to do."

"Huh," said Rose. She didn't sound impressed. "Don't forget what I said earlier about intimidating people. We'll be asking the other club members for their help, so don't go all Scary Peg on them. Think about trying a diplomatic approach for once."

For a moment, Peg felt insulted. As if she needed instructions on how to talk to people! Then her brain caught up with her emotions and she conceded that Rose might be right. Plus, the idea that there was a scary version of herself lurking beneath the surface and waiting to be unleashed, felt a little bit like a compliment.

"You have the opposite problem," she said to Rose. "You're too soft. If you expect to get useful answers from people, you need to toughen up."

"The soft approach works for me. Look at all the information I got from Carrie."

"Carrie's your friend. Of course she would tell you things." Peg reached around Hope to get to her glass. She downed half its contents in a single long swallow. "Speaking of information, do we know how to get in touch with all these people?"

"We do." Rose pulled out her phone. "When I was first talking to Carrie about joining the bridge club, she sent me a copy of the roster. Names, addresses, and phone numbers."

"Perfect," Peg replied. "Email it to me, please. I don't know about you, but I'm ready to get started."

Peg took Hope home, ate a quick lunch, then set out for Port Chester, a town in New York just across the Connecticut border. Mick hadn't listed his home address on the club's roster. Instead, he'd supplied his place of business: Doran's Auto Works. The car repair shop was located in the thriving commercial district along Route 1.

A small sign beside the road told Peg that she'd found the right place. There was a tall chain link fence, its gate now open, surrounding a long, low building and the crowded parking lot in front of it. All three garage doors were open in the summer heat, presumably to let in air.

Two of the bays were empty. In the third, a car was up on a lift. A man who wasn't Mick was standing beneath the car, looking upward into its undercarriage. Next to the first bay was a closed door whose hand-lettered sign indicated that it led to the office.

Despite the number of vehicles parked outside, there didn't appear to be much activity going on. Peg hadn't wanted to call ahead in case Mick tried to put her off. Now she hoped she hadn't made the trip in vain.

Peg drove to the end of the lot and wedged her minivan between a mint condition Porsche and an older Mercedes that looked as though it might have already driven its last mile. *Vintage.* Just like her. Except that Peg still had plenty of mileage left in her chassis.

She got out and strode across the lot. The dark macadam radiated heat up through the soles of her shoes. Peg stopped just outside the occupied bay.

"Excuse me?"

The man hadn't looked her way when she'd driven past him. Now it took a minute for him to stop what he was doing and glance over. "Help you?"

"I hope so. I'm looking for Mick Doran."

The man crooked a thumb over his shoulder. "Check the office."

"Thank you," Peg said, but he'd already gone back to work. She hoped she'd receive a more enthusiastic reception from the owner.

Peg walked across the front of the building and rapped sharply on the office door. She opened it without waiting for a reply.

The room was medium in size and darker than the day outside since its only source of light was the grimy windows that lined the back wall. At first glance, every available surface in the office appeared to be cluttered with something. Peg saw a tall stack of car manuals, a rusted muffler, and numerous engine parts whose function she couldn't begin to guess.

Mick was seated behind a metal desk that faced the doorway. A computer was open in front of him, but he wasn't looking at it. Instead, Mick was frowning as he spoke to someone on the phone.

His brow rose in surprise when he saw the identity of his visitor. He rose to his feet and motioned for her to come inside and shut the door. Peg quickly realized why. It was at least ten degrees cooler in the office than outside.

"Yes, Mrs. Harris," Mick said into the phone. He held up a finger to indicate to Peg that he'd only be a minute. "I know, Mrs. Harris. I did tell you that your car might be ready today. But unfortunately, we're still waiting for a part."

Mick was dressed in a T-shirt with his company logo printed across the front. The best thing Peg could say for his frayed cargo shorts and battered sneakers was that they looked well broken in.

Today was the first time she had seen Mick without his ball cap. It turned out that he was mostly bald.

While Mick wrapped up his call, Peg cleared a pile of old magazines from the seat of an office chair. She sat down and folded her hands in her lap to wait. Now that she was settled in, Mick would have a harder time getting rid of her—if indeed that was his reaction to her visit.

"Yes, ma'am, I will call you as soon as the part arrives and let you know when you can pick up your Ferrari . . . yes, sorry, your son's Ferrari."

Mick disconnected the call, then threw the phone onto a rag sitting on a nearby shelf. "God save me from rich old women," he muttered under his breath.

"Problem?" Peg inquired sweetly.

"No more than usual." When Mick turned to face her, he was smiling. "If something's wrong with your minivan, I'm afraid I won't be able to help you. We only work on foreign cars. I'd be happy to recommend someone, however."

"Thank you, but that won't be necessary." Peg gazed at him thoughtfully. "How do you know I drive a minivan?"

"I always check out people's cars." Mick folded his arms over his chest and leaned back against the lip of his desk. "Occupational hazard, I suppose. You can tell a lot about a person by the vehicle they choose to drive."

"Really?" Peg was intrigued. "What does my minivan tell you about me?"

"That you're a practical person. One who cares more about carrying capability and good mileage than impressing your neighbors. If I had to guess, I'd say that you value safety over speed. And that you probably need the extra room for carting your dogs around."

"Well done," said Peg. "You're right on all counts but one."

"What'd I miss?"

"I've been known to have a lead foot on the gas pedal."

Mick's brow rose. "You got me there. I wouldn't have figured you for a woman who likes to take chances."

"And again," said Peg, "you would have been wrong."

It was interesting how the usually taciturn Mick became positively chatty when given the opportunity to talk about his favorite topic. Now that the conversation had some momentum, Peg could only hope that a change of subject wouldn't cause him to clam up.

"If it isn't car troubles," Mick said, "what can I do for you?"

"I'd like to talk to you about Stan."

Immediately his expression clouded over. "Stan was a good guy. He didn't deserve that."

"I quite agree." Peg nodded. "No one does. I

201

was wondering if you had any ideas about why someone might have wanted to harm him."

"Me? Why would I know something like that?"

"Based on our conversation the other day, I'd have thought you were one of Stan's best friends."

"You're right about that," Mick agreed. "He and I go way back."

"The two of you met when he came to you for a car repair. Isn't that what he told us?"

"Yes. I was working at Precision Motors in Greenwich then. Stan had a BMW with a lousy electrical system."

"And you fixed it for him."

Unexpectedly Mick smiled. "Not right away. First I told him the car was a lemon and he should turn it back in to the dealer. Faulty wiring like that, you fix one problem and it just crops up somewhere else. You could spend your whole life troubleshooting. Stan didn't want to hear it though, so he kept bringing it back in and I kept working on it. Eventually I got that car running like a champ."

Peg shifted back in her chair. She wished Mick would take a seat too. As long as he was on his feet, she had the feeling he might decide to rush her out the door at any moment. It was probably a good thing that they were still talking about cars.

"And you and Stan became friends in the meantime," she said.

"We did," Mick confirmed. "We've been friends ever since. Maybe more than friends. Stan's the reason I have my own garage now. Over the years, he sent so much business my way that it became feasible for me to go out on my own. Best thing that ever happened to me."

Mick shook his head. "I'll never be able to repay him for that."

"I understand that Stan was married when he was younger. Was Bethany alive when you and he met?"

"Nah. He told me plenty about her though." He paused to pull in a deep breath. "And about what happened. Whenever Stan talked about her, it was clear how much he still missed her. The biggest regret of his life was that he and Bethany never had kids. He wanted that more than anything."

"He wasn't tempted to marry again?" Peg asked.

"Apparently not. It's not like Stan was a monk or anything. He dated plenty. But after Bethany, I guess none of the other women were special enough."

Carrie, of the so-called torrid affair, probably wouldn't be happy to hear that. The thought reminded Peg of something else.

"Bethany was Lacey's half-sister," she commented.

"Lacey?" Mick's gaze shot up. "You mean Lacey Duvall?"

"Yes."

"That's news to me. I had no idea."

"Why does that surprise you?" Peg asked.

"I guess because Stan and Lacey never seemed particularly friendly with each other. There are plenty of different personalities in that group—but the reason we're all there is to play cards. So it's not like everyone has to get along like gangbusters. But now that you mention that Stan and Lacey had a connection like that . . ." Mick's voice trailed away. "I guess I would have expected something different."

Me too, thought Peg.

"I'm sorry you lost your bridge partner," she said.

Mick sighed. "I'm sorry I lost my best friend."

Chapter 18

An hour after Peg left, Rose popped her head into the small office in the Gallagher House that she and Peter shared. The room had originally served as storage space, so its dimensions were limited. It held only a desk, a file cabinet, a straight back chair, and a shiny green rubber plant that added a welcome pop of color to the otherwise drab decor.

Peter was working at the desk. When Rose entered the room she could see that he was frowning at something on his computer screen.

"Am I interrupting?" she asked.

"No. Never." He looked up at her. "I'm reading about political unrest in Central America, so I'm happy to take a break. What's up?"

"Mae Watkins, from the bridge club, invited me to her house for a late lunch with her and Jerry. So I was wondering if you need the van this afternoon?"

"No, I have plenty to keep me busy here." Peter's eyes twinkled as he leaned back in his chair. "A last minute lunch invitation from people you scarcely know. How very lucky for you."

Of course he was fishing for information. Rose would have done the same if their roles were reversed.

"Indeed," she said primly.

"Does this have anything to do with your visit with Carrie the other day?"

Rose nodded.

"And Peg this morning?"

Rose smiled. "Not much gets past you, does it?"

"Certainly not when it's happening right under my nose," Peter said. "Are you going to tell me what's going on?"

"Peg and I talked. You were right about my needing to apologize to her. So I did."

"Good for you. That was well done. Did Peg accept your apology?"

"She did more than that," Rose said. "She apologized to me, too."

"And to think, I didn't feel the earth move earlier. I must not have been paying attention." Peter stood up and held out his hand.

Rose looked down at it. "You want to shake my hand?"

"That sounds like a rather remarkable achievement. The least you deserve is a handshake."

"Keep thinking." Rose cast him a look. "I'm sure you can do better."

Peter chuckled. His gaze went to the open office door and the home's main hallway outside it. "Not under the current circumstances, I'm afraid. But if you hold that thought until tonight, I'm sure something suitable can be arranged."

"It's a deal," said Rose.

"Now let's get back to that lunch of yours. Tell me what's really going on."

"Peg and I have formed an alliance," she announced dramatically.

"A second one?" Peter's brow rose. "Because merely being bridge partners wasn't enough togetherness for you? And here I thought the news coming out of Central America was exciting."

Rose supposed she deserved that. She loved Peter dearly. He was the first person to give her credit when it was due. But he was the last person to appreciate her love of theatrics. After all the years of tamping down her emotions in the convent, Rose enjoyed letting them show now.

"The police are investigating Stan Peters' death," she said.

"As well they should."

"Peg and I are going to help."

"I see." Peter sat back down in his chair. "Did the police ask for your help?"

"Not in so many words."

"Do they want your help?"

"They would if they stopped and thought about it," Rose said firmly. "After all, Peg has quite a bit of investigative experience. And I have some, too."

"Only because Melanie dragged you along last winter when she cornered Beatrice Gallagher's killer."

Rose chose to ignore that comment. "Plus," she pointed out, "Peg and I know the members of the bridge club better than anyone else who's looking into what happened to Stan."

"Well enough to get yourself invited to lunch, you mean."

"Exactly. I'm just going to do what Melanie does in these situations. I'll merely ask the Watkinses a few questions."

"What will you do if you don't like their answers?" Peter asked curiously.

Rose paused. She didn't know. She hadn't yet thought that far ahead.

"I suppose I'll cross that bridge when I come to it," she said finally.

Under the circumstances, the metaphor seemed surprisingly apt.

Mae and Jerry Watkins lived in an L-shaped ranch house in a comfortably upscale neighborhood in the nearby town of Cos Cob. The home had a long, low roofline, plenty of windows, and a brick patio out back.

Mae answered the door with a big smile on her face. She was wearing a floaty pink tunic top with white cropped pants. Her hair was a mixture of gray and blond. It curled around a pair of braided gold hoops that hung from her earlobes.

"Isn't this a lovely surprise," Mae said. "When you called to ask if we could get together for a little chat, the timing couldn't have been better." Her voice lowered to a confiding tone. "With our children grown and out of the house, sometimes Jerry and I get a little tired of each other's company. You know what I mean?"

"I can imagine," Rose replied. "Though I never had any children myself."

"You poor thing." Mae ushered her into a home whose open floor plan was spacious and airy. "Children are such a blessing." She motioned toward a collection of framed family photos on a glass-topped table. "Addy's our oldest, then Britt, then Cindy. Jerry Jr. is the baby of the family. He didn't come along until five years after all the others. We call him J.J. now and he's in college, so he's not much of a baby anymore."

Mae giggled happily and kept moving. Rose barely had time to even glance at the photographs. They were crossing a wide space that was a combination living and dining area. A sliding glass door in the rear wall led to a terrace that was partially shaded by a rose covered pergola.

"It's such a nice day, I thought we'd eat outside," Mae said. "I'd just finished making a big batch of gazpacho when you called. Like I said, perfect timing. I got out some baguettes and toasted cheese on top of them. I hope that will do?"

"That sounds wonderful," Rose replied. She was just happy to have a chance to get a word in. "Will Jerry be joining us?"

"He'd better," Mae said with mock severity. "Otherwise he'll have to go hungry." She slid open the door and waited for Rose to step through before turning back to the house and yelling, "Jerry! Lunch!"

An outdoor dining table was set with brightly colored woven place mats that held matching plates and soup bowls. There was a tureen of gazpacho and a platter of grilled baguettes in the middle of the table. A nearby serving tray held both a pitcher of ice water and a cooler of beer.

"That man," Mae muttered. "If he thinks I'm going to go fetch him, he'd better think again. I told him we were having company."

"I can hear you," Jerry said as he came walking out of a side hallway. He moved with surprising agility for a man his size. "Could be the whole neighborhood can hear you, Mae."

"Don't be silly." She flapped a hand in the air. "Nobody's listening to us."

"Hello, Rose." Jerry flashed her a smile. "I hope I didn't keep you waiting long."

"Not at all." Rose returned the smile as the three of them pulled out their chairs and sat down. "Thank you for inviting me to lunch. This looks delicious."

"Mae knows how to set out a spread all right." Jerry slid a linen napkin onto his lap and helped himself to a cold beer. He popped off the bottle cap and took a swallow. "She knows I married her for her cooking."

"I don't know any such thing," Mae said, but her cheeks went pink with pleasure. She was ladling the soup into bowls and passing them around. "I married Jerry because he was the smartest man I'd ever met."

He grinned. "That, and because I put her boss out of business, which meant she lost her job." Jerry snagged another bottle and offered it to Rose. "Beer?"

"No, thank you. I'm fine with water." She placed a toasted baguette on her plate as Jerry picked up the pitcher and filled both women's glasses. "If you don't mind my asking, how did you put Mae's boss out of business?"

"Jerry's an entrepreneur," Mae said proudly.

"Was," he corrected her around a mouthful of food. "I hardly keep my hand in at all anymore."

"Which is why we get to play bridge now," Mae added. "Because Jerry isn't working every minute of the day."

As they began to eat, Rose was feeling rather pleased of herself. She suspected that Peg's interrogation technique involved jumping down people's throats and demanding answers. Whereas she was going to do a much better job by starting slowly, making sure everyone was relaxed, and giving them a chance to talk about themselves first.

"An entrepreneur," she said pleasantly. "What exactly does that mean?"

"My job was to find companies with good ideas and decent value that were underperforming in their markets," Jerry told her. "When everything went according to plan, I would swoop in and take over a controlling interest, then turn them around and make them profitable. My partners called me the money man. Deal after deal, I just about always came through for them."

"How very interesting," Rose commented. "I don't know much about the world of business. What would happen when things didn't go according to plan?"

Jerry had a big, booming laugh. "The less said about those occasions, the better."

"Thankfully they were few and far between," Mae said. "How do like the gazpacho, Rose?"

"It's wonderful," Rose replied honestly. She was thinking about asking Mae for the recipe before she left.

"Can you guess my secret ingredient?"

Rose took another spoonful and let the flavors roll over her tongue. "Tarragon?"

"Nope. But you can keep guessing."

"Mae, let Rose eat in peace," Jerry said. "You know she didn't drop by today to talk about the food." His gaze swung Rose's way. "I assume you're here because of what happened to Stan."

"I am," she admitted. "His death was so sudden,

and so unexpected. Even though I hadn't had a chance to get to know him well, I still feel like I'm trying to understand how such a thing could have happened."

"I feel the same way," Mae agreed.

"When Carrie was introducing Peg and me to everyone in the bridge club, you mentioned that you and Stan had met in high school," Rose said to Jerry. "After all these years, you must have known him better than just about anyone."

"You were paying attention," he said with an approving nod. "Most people only listen when they're the ones doing the talking. Reggie, Stan, and I all graduated from Greenwich High School. Reg and I were the same year. Stan was in the class behind us. But we were teenage boys, so it was a given that we were all into sports. Our paths crossed on a couple of teams. I wouldn't have said that any of us were close friends—either back then or now. But we knew each well enough. And since none of us moved out of the area, we more or less stayed in touch over the years."

Mae was helping herself to more gazpacho. She paused and looked up. "You and Stan did a little business together once, didn't you, Jerry?"

"You're right, we did. That was a long time ago, though. Twenty years, at least. Professionally, our lives didn't intersect much. But once we were all retired and had extra time on our hands, that changed. Mostly because the bridge club brought the three of us back together."

"It sounds like that was a good thing," Rose said.

"It was. Especially because Stan brought Mick along as his partner. I learn something every time I watch that guy play." Jerry paused, then added, "But don't let Mick know I said that. Otherwise he'll probably start guarding his cards."

"I wonder how much more we'll see of Mick," Rose said quietly. "After all, he doesn't have a partner to play with anymore."

"Darn it." Mae sniffled. She looked like she might be blinking back tears. "I hate it when everything changes."

"Not everything, Mae." Jerry reached across the table and laid his hand on top of his wife's. Rose saw him squeeze her fingers gently. "You still have me."

"Thank goodness for that." Mae managed a wobbly smile.

Rose devoted herself to her food to give the couple a minute. When they'd resumed eating, she said, "I'm sure the police must have talked to you."

"They did," Mae confirmed. "They asked us all kinds of questions."

"Unfortunately, we weren't able to be much help," Jerry said. "It's not like Mae and I knew anything useful to tell them."

"Neither one of you was aware of any problems Stan might have been having?" Rose asked.

Mae and Jerry looked at each other. They both shook their heads.

"Anyone he'd complained about recently? Or that he was angry at?"

Mae shook her head again. Jerry just shrugged.

"That isn't the kind of thing we'd have been likely to know," he said. "Other than the bridge club, Mae and I mostly tend to socialize with other couples. With Stan being single, we didn't see him very often. It seemed like we just didn't have that much in common."

"What's with all the questions?" Mae asked, her head tipped to one side. "You're very curious about someone you barely knew."

Rose had been dreading that question. Unlike Peg, she wasn't good at making things up. She'd been hoping the subject wouldn't arise.

"It's not me," Rose blurted, without thinking. "It's my bridge partner, Peg."

Immediately she felt contrite—and also like a big chicken. It wasn't fair of her to place the blame on Peg when she was just as invested in their joint inquiry. Judging by the looks on Mae's and Jerry's faces, however, it was too late for Rose to backpedal now.

"What about her?" asked Jerry.

"Peg's like a cat, she's curious about everything," Rose said. "She always has to get to the bottom of things."

"Even a murder?" Mae sounded disbelieving.

"That doesn't sound like a good thing," Jerry said with a frown. "You'd better tell her to be careful."

Chapter 19

Peg arrived home from Port Chester to dogs who felt her absence from the house meant that they'd been seriously neglected. She tossed the mail onto a hall table, then dropped to her knees. The three big Poodles quickly swarmed around her.

"Of course you're bored," she told them. "You've been cooped up inside for much of the day. Who wants to go for a walk?"

Three black pompons waved in the air. The Poodles turned and raced for the back door. Peg braced a hand on the floor and slowly rose to her feet.

About to follow the dogs, she glanced at the pile of letters on the side table. The edge of a colorful postcard peeked out from the middle of the stack. Peg reached over and snatched it up. A picture of a line of mules making their way down the side of the Grand Canyon was on the front. She was already smiling before she turned the card over.

Peg had expected to hear from Melanie again, but this postcard was from fifteen-year-old Davey.

Greetings from Arizona! Mom wanted us to see the Grand Canyon on muleback

*but it turned out Kevin was too young. On
our way to Las Vegas next. Wish you were
here, ha, ha!*

Peg blinked once or twice; her eyes were
unexpectedly stinging. All at once, she found
herself wishing that she was there too. And
what an odd thought that was. Until this very
moment, it had never once crossed her mind that
she might want to travel across the United States
packed inside an RV with four other people and
numerous assorted dogs.

Yet now, curiously, the idea held a certain
appeal. Peg growled under her breath as she
tossed the postcard back on the table.

She was being ridiculous. She didn't want to be
on the other side of the country with them. She
wanted them to be here, in Connecticut, with
her. Peg missed the special kind of chaos that
swept through her life like a whirlwind whenever
Melanie, Sam, and the boys were around.

She turned and headed for the back door. Her
Poodles were waiting for her. Peg could hear
the sound of their feet tapping on the kitchen
floor.

It wasn't as if she didn't have plenty of other
friends. But mostly they were members of the dog
community, a far-flung group of people whom
she saw at shows and kennel club meetings.
When Peg wanted company on a moment's

notice, it was Melanie and family to whom she always turned. There was never a dull moment at that house. Which was just the way she liked things to be.

Melanie often called Peg nosy, but she was wrong about that. What Peg actually felt was a driving need to keep thinking, to keep *moving*. She wanted to be a busy person. She wanted to get up every morning with a sense of purpose and a long list of things to do.

Peg's steps slowed, then stopped all together. *She was not lonely.*

No, of course she wasn't. Who could possibly be lonely living in a house with three charming and entertaining Poodles? If Peg wanted someone to talk to, they were always right there. Ready to listen and sometimes to reply.

About to walk on, Peg had a sudden thought. She reached in a pocket and pulled out her phone. Maybe she should give Rose a call to see what she'd accomplished today.

Then Joker came skidding around the corner. The puppy's long topknot hair was banded into ponytails that swung wildly from side to side as he galloped past her, then circled back.

Hurry up! He might as well have shouted the words.

"You're right, I'm taking entirely too long." Peg tucked her phone back in her pocket. "Let's go have our walk, shall we?"

Peg had called Franny Grover when she and the Poodles returned from their walk. She was issued an invitation to visit the two sisters the following morning at their home in Shippan Point. Shippan was a narrow peninsula extending out into Long Island Sound to form Stamford's southernmost tip. Now Peg was carefully navigating its tight grid of residential streets.

Franny had instructed Peg to find their road, then drive until she saw water. At that point, she should look for a compact, single story house, painted pink with turquoise shutters. The directions were spot on. It helped that the bungalow was hard to miss.

Peg parked her minivan on the street out front. She was halfway up the short walk that led to the house when the front door opened. Franny—or perhaps Florence, Peg couldn't be entirely sure—was waiting for her in the doorway. The woman was wearing a shiny purple track suit. Despite the day's warmth, its jacket was zipped almost all the way up to her chin. She had flip flops on her feet and a bright slash of red lipstick across her lips.

"Florence and I have been waiting for you to show up," she said, helpfully identifying which sister she was. "We don't get many visitors these days. So this is a big event for us. Mind you don't step on Esmeralda now."

Peg's gaze dropped. Pressed up tight against

Franny's slender legs was a brown Toy Poodle. The small dog eyed Peg suspiciously. Then she lifted her lips and snarled.

"Hush," Peg said softly. She stooped down low and held out her hand. "Don't make a scene. You know perfectly well we're going to be best friends."

Esmeralda regarded Peg's outstretched fingers disdainfully. She made no attempt to come closer. After several seconds, she spun around and ran away down the narrow hallway. Peg sighed and levered herself up.

"Don't let it bother you," Franny said. "I know you're supposed to be some kind of special dog lady, but Essie doesn't like anyone."

"She'll like me," Peg replied, stepping inside.

"How do you know that?"

"Dogs do," she said.

Some people said Peg had a gift. The truth was, she simply adored dogs. All shapes, all sizes, all breeds. And they adored her back. It wasn't any more complicated than that.

"Come this way." Franny closed the front door and led her down a narrow hallway. "Florence is out back. We'll sit on the porch and watch the water go by while we talk."

Peg first walked past a small living room. It was followed by a dining room that was little more than an alcove. The home's kitchen was barely big enough for two people to stand side by side. Compared to the interior of the house, the outdoor porch was surprisingly expansive.

It ran along the entire rear of the house and was shaded from the strong summer sun by an extended roof. Two wicker chairs and a matching love seat were grouped around a low table. Whichever way Peg looked, the view of Long Island Sound was spectacular.

"Welcome." Florence was rocking gently in one of the wicker chairs. She lifted her hand in a wave. Her outfit matched her sister's in everything but color. Florence's track suit was neon blue. "Come on out and take a seat."

"This is absolutely lovely." Peg walked over to the wooden railing and inhaled deeply, breathing in the fresh sea air wafting in off the Sound. Waves slapped gently against a water wall at the end of the small yard.

"Our own little slice of heaven," Franny said happily. "Florence and I have lived in this house for more than fifty years."

Peg turned back to face them. "Are the two of you twins?"

"Heck, no." Florence laughed. "Though you're not the first person to ask. I'm the older sister. By a whole year."

"As if a year makes a difference at our age," Franny sniffed. "Besides, it isn't even a year. More like eleven months."

Esmeralda came running out the open door.

She cast a wary glance at Peg, then went straight to a dog bed near the rear wall of the house. The dog turned three circles before lying down. When she'd finished, she was facing the wall rather than the people.

Peg knew she should feel snubbed by the little Poodle. Instead she was intrigued. She'd always enjoyed a challenge.

"Peg says Esmeralda's going to be her best friend," Franny told her sister.

"Really?" Florence made no attempt to hide her surprise. "How's that going to happen?"

"Beats me. I told her Essie doesn't like anyone."

Florence turned to Peg. "That dog doesn't even like us and we're the ones who feed her."

"How long have you had her?" Peg asked.

The sisters looked at each other. "About a month?" Franny ventured.

That explained the matted hair between Esmeralda's legs and the topknot that nearly covered her eyes. "Has she always behaved that way?"

Florence nodded. "Ever since we brought her home. We got her from a rescue. As soon as they told us she'd come from a bad situation, we knew we had to help her."

Peg grimaced. As far as she was concerned, people who mistreated dogs should be horse-whipped. Essie wasn't just shy; she was a victim of abuse. That changed everything.

"Do you know how old she is?" Peg asked.

"The rescue lady said maybe two years. Or a little older. She told us Essie was skittish around people, but she just needed time."

"Time." Franny snorted. "It's been a month. It's not like Flo and I are going to live forever. We've had Poodles before, and they've always been great dogs. They loved us and we loved them. We assumed Essie would feel the same way."

Florence nodded in agreement.

"What have you done so far to make her feel comfortable in her new surroundings?" Peg asked.

"We bought her toys, but she doesn't play with them. We tried to take her for walks, but she freezes and doesn't want to move."

"The leash makes Essie scream," Franny said. "And that was hard on all of us. After a while, Florence and I decided maybe it would be less upsetting if we just left her alone."

"I see." Peg looked down at the little Poodle and sighed. "Do you mind if I sit on the floor while we talk?"

"On the floor?" Franny looked shocked. "Why would you want to do that?"

"Because Essie is a small dog and I'm a big person. That way I'll be closer to her level."

"If you say so." Florence didn't sound convinced.

She watched as Peg lowered herself onto the

weathered boards near Esmeralda's bed. The Poodle cocked an ear in Peg's direction, but didn't turn around. Peg crossed her legs and got comfortable. Essie issued a low growl.

"Shhh," Peg murmured. "Nobody's bothering you. I'm just sitting here."

"Now what?" asked Franny. One of the chairs was already facing in Peg's direction. She turned around the other one and sat down.

"Now we'll have a pleasant chat," Peg said. "If that's all right with you."

"I thought that's what we were doing." Florence grinned. "Though I'm guessing you didn't come here to talk about our dog."

"No, Peg came here to grill us about what we know about Stan Peters," Franny chimed in. "I knew you'd get around to us sooner or later. Carrie told us to be on the lookout."

"News travels fast in that bridge club," Peg commented.

"You know it."

"And there don't seem to be many secrets among the members."

"Right again," said Florence.

"So, that being the case, what was Stan Peters up to that made someone want to shoot him?" Peg asked.

"What makes you think we would know that?"

"Because people always underestimate older women," Peg said. "To a large segment of society, we're invisible. I'm guessing that both of you notice things other people pay no attention to. And that you probably know a good deal more than you let on. Am I right?"

"Could be you are." Franny chuckled, then glanced down at Esmeralda who was still facing the wall. "You may not be a dog whisperer, but it sounds like you've got people figured out pretty well."

Peg ignored the jab about her dog whispering skills and focused on the reason she'd come. "You two obviously knew Stan better than I did. What's your best guess about what happened to him?"

"He must have made somebody mad," Florence said. Franny nodded in agreement.

That didn't tell Peg anything new. "Who?"

There was a long pause while the two sisters seemed to engage in some kind of unspoken communication. Peg used the time to inch her fingers across the floor in Essie's direction. When the Poodle's head snapped around to see what she was doing, Peg stopped moving and relaxed back against the porch railing.

"Funny thing about that club," Franny said eventually. "You got a group of people who've known each other over a long period of time and who mostly get along pretty well. Maybe bridge wasn't always the only game that was being played."

Peg thought about Bennett taking bets, and Paige and Reggie cheating. She suspected, however, that wasn't what Franny was referring to.

"You haven't been around as long as some," Florence added.

Peg nodded encouragingly. Once again, she wasn't learning anything she didn't already know.

"The bridge club isn't just about playing cards. It's a social occasion, too. For some of us in the group, it's the highlight of our week. People tend to get friendly with one another." Florence paused then said meaningfully, "Sometimes more than friendly."

Oh. Peg considered that news for a moment. Rose had told her about Carrie and Stan. But maybe they weren't the only club members who'd been engaging in illicit activities?

"Just to clarify," she said. "Are you talking about a little innocent flirtation or—"

"Sex," Franny pronounced. "People were doing it. Oh, not Flo and me, more's the pity. Even when we were younger, we were still older than everyone else in the club. Nobody gave us a second look."

Florence sighed to convey her shared disappointment. "Some years, that club felt like a veritable Peyton Place."

"Are you talking about current behavior?" Peg

asked. "Or things that were happening in the past?"

"Mostly in the past, I guess," Franny said. "Things have calmed down now. It seems like everybody got it out of their systems, at least as far as the bridge club goes."

"And yet Stan was killed four days ago," Peg pointed out.

Florence shrugged. A second later, so did Franny.

The women looked like two halves of the same whole.

Franny was ready to change the subject. "So what are you going to do about Essie?" She nodded in the little dog's direction. "It doesn't look like you've fixed anything yet. She still doesn't like you any more than she likes us."

"These things take time," said Peg.

"It's already been weeks."

"That's not much time to undo years of abuse." Peg rose to her feet. "Especially when you don't possess the right tools to communicate your good intentions."

"What's that supposed to mean?" Florence frowned as she and her sister stood up too. "Franny and I have treated Essie like a member of the family. We didn't need any tools to do that. She should have figured out by now that we're not going to hurt her."

"And yet she hasn't."

Essie must have realized they were talking about her. She'd curled up into a tight ball and begun to tremble. Peg's heart clutched just looking at her.

"The two of you have done a fine job of keeping Essie safe," Peg said gently. "But with her past history, she needs more than that. Essie has to learn that people can be trusted. She needs to develop a whole set of life skills that you've been assuming she already knows."

"How's she going to do that?" asked Franny.

"With your permission," Peg said, "I'm going to teach her."

"When? You've been here half an hour and she hasn't learned a single new thing."

"If you'll let me, I'd like to take her home with me."

Franny immediately shook her head.

Florence considered the idea. "For how long?"

"A week, maybe two," Peg said. "We'll have to see how it goes."

"No way. You're not taking our dog away from us." Franny moved quickly to place herself between Peg and Essie. The Poodle jumped up, spun around, and bared her teeth.

"I wouldn't be taking her from you," Peg said calmly. "Merely borrowing her for a short period of time, after which the two of you and Essie should see a huge improvement in your relationship. Even when she's living with me,

Essie would still be your dog. You could come and visit her if you like."

"No—" Franny began.

"Yes." Florence talked over her. "We can't go on like this, Franny. It's not fair to us, or to Essie. She isn't happy here. If Peg thinks she can change that, we have to give her a chance to try."

"Just because you're the older sister, you always think you're in charge," Franny grumbled. Peg could see that she was wavering, however.

"I'm just trying to do what's best for all of us," Florence said. "Including Essie."

"And we can really come and see her?" Franny asked Peg.

"Of course. As soon as Essie has settled in, we'll be happy to have visitors."

"Then I guess it's all right." Franny started to lean down to pat the Poodle. When Essie curled her lip, she thought better of the idea and withdrew her hand.

"Excellent," said Peg. "Perhaps you have a towel I can wrap her up in for the trip?"

Florence hurried away to get one.

"I still don't like this idea," Franny muttered.

"And I don't like the idea that someone I just met managed to get himself murdered," Peg replied. "Hopefully this next week will prove to be enlightening on several fronts."

Chapter 20

That evening after dinner, Rose took her phone into the bedroom she shared with Peter and shut the door. Nearing the longest day of the year, it wasn't yet dark outside and she didn't bother to turn on a light. The room was small, square, and sparsely decorated. Most of its furniture had been rented along with the house.

Rose had been adding personal touches to the decor little by little. The lace curtains at the windows were new. So was the blue-and-white foulard print quilt on the queen sized bed. A shared collection of books and Peter's pre-Colombian art filled the shelves along one wall.

The house wasn't luxurious, but it was theirs, and it was beginning to feel like home. Rose sat down on the bed and kicked off her shoes. Leaning back against the headboard, she stretched out her legs and wiggled her toes. Even with the door closed, she could hear the hum of voices coming from the television in the living room.

Peter had discovered reality TV upon their return from Central America. Now the man was obsessed. Some of the shows he watched made Rose laugh. Others made her want to grind her teeth. But Peter studied each one with the rapt intensity of an anthropologist uncovering new and important data.

The only way she could talk on the phone when Peter's shows were on was to go somewhere else. Now that Rose was comfortable on the bed, she scrolled through her contacts to Peg's number and touched her fingertip to the screen to put through the connection.

"I have a confession to make," Rose said when Peg picked up.

There was a brief pause, then Peg replied, "Funny thing about that. I do, too."

Rose rolled her eyes. Trust Peg to feel the need to one-up her, even when it came to admitting to a transgression.

"You go first," said Peg.

"I'm afraid I used you as a scapegoat when I was talking to Jerry and Mae Watkins."

"That sounds interesting. Tell me more."

"I was trying to get information about Stan, and Mae asked me why I was so interested in someone I barely knew. I don't have your years of experience talking to suspects and ferreting out their secrets. I'm afraid I panicked and told them it was all your fault."

Peg sounded as though she might be laughing. "Go on."

"I said the only reason I was being so inquisitive was because you're relentlessly curious about everything."

"I *am* curious about everything," Peg agreed. "So I can't argue with that. And if blaming me enabled you to find out anything interesting, I'll gladly take responsibility. What did they say to that?"

"Jerry told me to warn you to be careful."

"Pish," said Peg. "It sounds as though he's been watching too many cop shows. But just in case, I will consider his warning noted."

"Now it's your turn to confess," Rose said.

"I went to see Franny and Florence Grover, and instead of information, I came home with a dog."

"A dog?" Now it was Rose's turn to laugh.

"A little brown Poodle."

"Of course it would be a Poodle."

"Her name is Esmeralda and I would have brought her home with me no matter what breed she was. She's a rescue dog who wasn't fitting into her new situation. I thought I could help."

"By rescuing her from them?"

"No, Essie is only here temporarily until I get her sorted out. She obviously had a bad beginning in life. It appears the poor girl never had a reason to put any faith in her human caretakers. She needs to start over and learn everything. Basically, she has no idea how to be a dog."

"You're pulling my leg, right?" Rose said. "Because I'm pretty sure that must be something dogs are born knowing."

"Not necessarily. Puppies are like children.

They learn by example and imitation. A puppy that's separated from its dam and littermates at a very young age so it can be shipped off to a pet store in time to arrive at the stage of maximum cuteness, misses out on much of its emotional development and socialization."

"I had no idea," Rose said. "So where is Esmeralda now?"

"She's in an exercise pen in my kitchen." Peg sounded pleased with herself. "She has a big fluffy bed, a couple of new toys, and three friendly Standard Poodles with whom to get acquainted."

"How's that going?" In spite of herself, Rose was curious.

"Better than I might have hoped for this stage of the game. Coral and Joker are probably a bit lively for Essie's tastes, but she and Hope are already on their way to becoming tentative friends."

"So that's good," Rose said. "Isn't it?"

She had no idea how Peg could tell whether dogs were friends or not. Could dogs even become friends? Rose didn't know the answer to that either—and she certainly wasn't about to ask. Doing so would be bound to lead to a long lecture from Peg on canine habits and personalities and all sorts of other dog things that Rose really wasn't interested in.

"Yes, that's a very good thing," Peg told her.

"Now that we've gotten that out of the way, tell me who you've spoken to and what you've learned in the last day and a half."

"Not a whole lot," Rose admitted. "Mostly only that Mae Watkins is quite a good cook, and that Reggie, Stan, and Jerry haven't remained particularly close since they all knew each other since high school. I hope you did better than that."

"I most certainly did. In addition to Franny and Florence, I also paid a visit to Mick Doran's car repair shop."

Rose reached over, grabbed a pillow, and wedged it behind her back. "He has his own place? I thought Stan said Mick worked for some foreign car dealer in Greenwich."

"He used to, but now he's out on his own. According to Mick, he couldn't have done it without Stan's help."

"That's interesting," Rose mused. "I assume you're talking about financial help?"

"That part wasn't entirely clear. Mick just said that Stan had sent a lot of business his way. But here's something else that's interesting. When I was there, the place didn't seem very busy. Two of the three garage bays were empty, and only one mechanic was working. It could be that Mick's repair shop is having money problems."

"What if those money problems were impacting Mick's ability to repay Stan's investment?" Rose asked.

"Which we're not even sure he made," Peg pointed out.

"I know that. I'm just thinking out loud."

"Another thing Mick mentioned is that Stan and Lacey didn't get along with each other."

"That seems odd." Rose lifted the phone away from her ear and switched it to the other side. "Stan was married to Lacey's half-sister."

"I know that and so do you, but Mick claimed that he had no idea."

"Odder still." Rose frowned as she considered the news. "If Mick was Stan's friend, not to mention his bridge partner, how could he not have been aware of that relationship?"

"Good question," said Peg. "But he seemed surprised when I told him about it."

Rose heard a crash in the background, then the sound of a door opening. Peg said, "Out! Outside, both of you!" Then the door slammed shut. A moment later, Peg was back. Rose could hear her breathing into the phone.

"What are you doing now?" she asked.

"Joker was being silly and he nearly knocked over the ex pen. So now he and Coral are out in the fenced yard and I'm about to open up the pen so Essie can come out and get to know me and Hope a little better."

Rose smiled to herself. Even mid-conversation, Peg could never sit still for a minute.

"Why?" asked Peg. "What are you doing?"

Rose was tempted to reply that she was busy talking on the phone, but the reproach would probably go right over Peg's head. Instead she said, "I'm sitting stretched out on a bed. There's a window nearby and I'm watching my lace curtains flutter in the evening breeze."

Peg remained silent for a moment, as if to let the difference between her activity and Rose's indolence sink in. Like maybe she thought Rose should feel bad that she wasn't driven to be constantly moving the way Peg was. Rose refused to care about that. She was content.

"Are you settled now?" she asked.

"More or less," Peg replied.

Considering the noises that were coming from the other end of the connection, Rose didn't even want to try to imagine what the *lesser* part of that equation might look like.

"Tell me about your visit with the Grover sisters," she said. "Leave out the part about the dog. We've already sufficiently covered that."

"The Toy Poodle is the most interesting part."

"Only to you," Rose replied firmly. "What did Franny and Florence have to stay about Stan?"

"Not a whole lot, unfortunately. Although they did have plenty to say about the extracurricular activities that have been taking place in the club over the years."

"I don't understand."

"As Franny so bluntly put it," Peg said with a laugh. "Sex."

"Sex," Rose repeated. She nearly choked on the word. "I told you about Carrie and Stan's affair. Were there others?"

It occurred to her that Carrie might have implied the same thing, although not in such graphic terms. Rose had done her best to put that part of their conversation out of her mind. Now she had no choice but to consider it.

"Apparently numerous people." Peg still sounded amused, as if she could picture Rose sitting there with her legs tightly crossed. "Although not all at once. At least I don't think so. I believe it was more like couples switching spouses, or maybe singles getting together. Things have quieted down now, but Franny said that at one point the bridge club was like Peyton Place."

Rose sat and stared at her own reflection in the mirror over the dresser on the opposite wall. She looked shocked, and maybe even a little pale. Rose knew Peg was waiting for a reply, but she couldn't think of a single thing to say.

"Oh, wait." Peg's snicker broke into her thoughts. "Do you know what Peyton Place is?"

That rude question broke the spell. "Of course I do. I was in the convent, not on the moon."

"Okay. I was just checking. You know, when I was talking to Carrie about Bennett's gambling, she mentioned that one of the reasons for keeping him around despite his bad habits was that he's popular with the ladies. So that supports what Franny and Florence told me."

Peg paused to take a breath. There wasn't time for Rose to say a thing, however. Within seconds, Peg was trying out another idea.

"Speaking of Carrie, what if—when her affair with Stan ended—he moved on to someone else, maybe another club member, and Carrie got jealous?"

"Stan did move on." Rose thought back. "Carrie said he became interested in Paige. She also told me that she was ready to end things, too, and that their parting was mutual."

Peg snorted. "As if anyone would believe that. That's how every rejected woman in history has ever described a breakup."

Rose had believed what Carrie said. It hadn't occurred to her not to. Then again, she had no real world experience with breakups. She was also lacking in girlfriends who'd gone through breakups. But if Peg said that was the case, she was probably right. Now she felt dumb for not having pressed Carrie further.

"Carrie's affair with Stan ended years ago," Rose pointed out.

"If she was telling the truth about that." Peg was ever the skeptic. "For all we know, it could

239

have ended last week. Under the circumstances, she'd hardly have been likely to admit that."

"I guess not," Rose agreed. "Here's something else I've been wondering about. How much money do you think Bennett can be making betting on bridge games? And what if Stan was involved with him in the gambling?"

"It's not always about the money," said Peg. "For people who are addicted to gambling, the rush of winning is the important part."

"Yes, I realize that. But speaking of winning, everyone in the club had to know that Mick was far and away the best player. So how did he and Stan ever lose even a single rubber?"

"Bad cards?"

"Sure, occasionally," Rose conceded. "But consider this. What if they were betting against themselves? Mick's a great player. Good enough to be able to control the outcome of many games. What if he and Stan were using his card playing ability to cash in?"

"We could take that idea a step further," Peg said. "What if Stan found out that Reggie and Paige were messing up their scheme by cheating under the table?"

Rose wasn't convinced. "That doesn't seem like something important enough to get him killed. In fact, it sounds pretty far-fetched."

"Every idea we've come up with sounds far-fetched," Peg grumbled. "We've got to do better."

Of course they had to do better. That wasn't even up for debate.

Rose swung her legs over the side of the bed and fished around on the floor for her shoes. Peter was probably wondering what had ever become of her. She and Peg had been talking for at least half an hour.

She only had one last question. "So . . . what would Melanie do at a time like this?"

"That's easy," Peg replied. "She'd come to me for advice and I'd help her figure things out."

"Then you should be doing the same for me," Rose said crisply.

"I'm working on it."

Abruptly the connection ended.

As Rose stood up, the bedroom door opened. Peter's show had to be just about over. She could hear the theme playing as the credits rolled.

Peter stuck his head in the room. "You're not fighting with Peg again, are you?"

"No, I think we're mostly past that now."

"Then what's the matter?" he asked. "You don't look happy."

Rose sighed. "Even when Peg and I are in agreement about things, talking to her is utterly exhausting."

Chapter 21

Peg called Paige Greene late the following morning. Paige was delighted to hear from her. When Peg suggested they get together, perhaps meeting in Greenwich for coffee, Paige announced that she was going to be in Peg's neighborhood anyway and would drop by. Would half an hour suit?

Peg disconnected the call and looked down at Hope who was lying at her feet. "Paige thinks I called her because she talked me into listing my house," she said.

Hope looked up at Peg and cocked her head, as if she were considering what to do about that problem.

"I didn't tell her she was wrong," Peg added.

Hope's tail swished from side to side. She liked that decision.

"It's not my fault Paige only sees people in terms of how she can use them to turn a profit."

The big Poodle sat up and placed one of her front paws on Peg's lap, a gesture of support. "Thank you for that," Peg said with a fond smile. "I knew you'd agree with me."

She had half an hour until Paige arrived. That wasn't much time. She could use it to straighten her house, but that didn't sound like much fun.

Besides, making an attempt to have everything look perfect might give Paige the wrong impression. So Peg did what she usually did when she couldn't decide on a plan. She took her dogs for a walk.

Twenty-nine minutes later, a sleek silver Lexus pulled into Peg's driveway. This time the Poodles didn't have to sound the alarm. Peg was waiting near the front door with them.

She watched as Paige stepped gracefully out of her car, then paused to take a long look around the property. Peg's house was cozy and extremely livable, but it was no showplace. Despite several renovations over the past hundred years, the home's early twentieth century roots were still plainly visible.

The land that surrounded the house, however, was magnificent. The border of the five acre property was lightly wooded to give Peg privacy from her neighbors. The remaining land was mostly lawn and rolling meadows where wildflowers bloomed at will. A fence encircled a level field behind the house, providing a safe space for the Poodles to run and play.

Two full minutes passed before Paige walked across the driveway to the house. By that time, Peg felt as though both she and her property had been examined and assessed, and that their value decided upon. It wasn't a pleasant sensation.

The heels of Paige's open-toed shoes clicked a

staccato beat up the front steps. She was wearing white slacks and a silk T-shirt. A green scarf that matched her eyes was tied jauntily around her neck. Paige was carrying both a purse and a leather satchel. Her manicure was perfect.

Peg was wearing the same blue jeans she'd put on that morning to clean the enclosed acre field with a poop scoop. She had sneakers on her feet and her gray hair was pulled back in a loose ponytail. She hadn't had a manicure in at least a decade. None of that mattered to Peg.

Paige would simply have to take her as she was.

Peg cautioned the Poodles to behave themselves. Then she opened the door as Paige strode across the front porch.

"Oh!" Paige issued a tinkling laugh. She'd been reaching for the doorbell. "You already knew I was here."

"I did," Peg said. "We were watching you look around."

"We?" Paige stepped inside.

Peg motioned toward the three large black dogs standing in the hallway with her. So far, Paige had ignored the trio of Poodles. Or maybe she hadn't noticed them. Now her eyes widened.

"Oh my," she said, as her hand flew up to cover her heart. "That's a lot of dogs."

"There's another one in the kitchen," Peg warned her. She headed that way. "Can I get you something to drink? Maybe a cup of coffee?"

Paige stepped carefully around the Poodle pack, making sure that her white slacks didn't come in contact with the dogs. She started to follow Peg, then cast a wary glance behind her. The Poodles were following her. Paige sped up.

"What are you having?" she asked.

"Earl Grey tea. But I have coffee too." Peg had a new coffee maker. She was always looking for opportunities to show it off.

"Tea is fine for me, too."

Paige reached the kitchen doorway and stopped abruptly. Esmeralda had been lying on her bed inside the exercise pen. Seeing a visitor, she jumped up and began to bark. That made the other Poodles go racing past Paige so they could add to the commotion.

Peg hushed the entire bunch with a stern look. Even so, it took several seconds for everything to settle down.

Paige gazed around before taking a seat at the butcher block table. "This is a wonderful room. I love that it's so bright and sunny. The big window really adds to its appeal."

Peg was busy at the stove. "Thank you. I like it."

"Why do you have that dog inside a cage?"

"She's still learning about life." Peg could have added volumes to that explanation. But considering her audience, a short answer seemed like the way to go. "For now, Essie feels safer having an enclosed space all to herself."

"When she grows up, will she be as big as the other ones?"

Peg was briefly stumped by the question. Then she realized what Paige meant. "Essie is already full grown. The black Poodles are the Standard variety. That's the largest size. Essie is a Toy Poodle. She'll never be any bigger than she is right now."

"That's too bad."

Peg got out two earthenware mugs and put tea bags inside them. Now she was just waiting for the water in the kettle to boil. "I'm sure Franny and Florence don't think so. They're the ones who adopted her. She's just the right size for them."

"Franny and Florence Grover?"

"Yes, Essie is their dog." The kettle began to sing. Peg poured the steaming water into the mugs, then glanced back over her shoulder. "Milk? Lemon? Sugar?"

"Just lemon, please. Fresh, if you have it." Paige was frowning. "Why do you have the Grover sisters' dog? It looks as though you already have plenty of your own."

"I'm helping them socialize her." Peg got a lemon out of the refrigerator, cut off several thick wedges, and put them on a plate. Then she made two trips to carry everything over to the table.

"I'm not surprised those women need help," Paige muttered as Peg sat down opposite her.

"Really? Why is that?"

"You must know what I mean. Franny and Florence are old and set in their ways. They don't have a clue about what the real world is like now. That house of theirs is hardly better than a hovel."

The harsh assessment made Peg's hackles rise. "But it has a gorgeous view."

"Well, sure. The location is stellar. Any land near the water is valuable. But if I was going to list the property, I'd have to describe the cottage as a tear-down. I offered to help Florence and Franny market the place and they wouldn't even entertain the idea."

"Probably because they're happy there," Peg said mildly.

"Happy." Paige snorted. "I'll tell you what makes people happy. Money, security, and the knowledge that they'll be taken care of in their old age."

Peg was pretty sure that the Grover sisters were already in their old age. And as far as she could tell, they were doing a fine job of taking care of themselves.

"Enough about them," Paige said. "Let's talk about you. Obviously I haven't seen much yet, but I can already tell you that your house has great potential. I ran some comps back at the office and I'm sure you'll be impressed by the numbers I've come up with."

Paige had yet to touch her tea. Instead she pulled a folder out of her bag and opened it on the table between them. Her smile widened and her demeanor grew more animated as she went on to deliver her pitch.

Peg nodded every so often but she was only half listening. Instead she sipped her tea, kept an eye on Joker, and wondered whether Paige's sparkling white teeth were capped. Five minutes later, the woman's ear-splitting squeal of delight abruptly dragged her back to the conversation.

"And do you *know* who your neighbors are?" Paige cried.

"Yes, I do." Peg assumed that wasn't a serious question.

"Proximity to people with name recognition is almost as good as being famous yourself!"

Peg didn't think so.

"Believe me, those are connections you can *exploit*. They're a significant selling point all on their own."

As if Peg would ever be tempted to use her neighbors that way. She held up a hand to pause the flow of eager words. "Let me stop you right there."

"Of course." Paige's smile was still dazzling. "Sometimes I let my enthusiasm run away with me. I should have asked if you have questions.

I'm sure you do. What would you like know? Feel free to ask me anything."

Oh, did Peg have questions. Unfortunately, they weren't going to be the ones that Paige was expecting.

"I appreciate the work you've done on my behalf," Peg said.

"I assure you it was my pleasure—"

"But as I mentioned at the bridge club, I'm not interested in selling right now."

Paige's smile dimmed a bit, but she pressed on gamely. "It doesn't have to be right now. Just let me know what time frame you're comfortable with. Three months? Six months? And of course the good news is that your property will only continue to appreciate in value in the meantime."

"Paige," Peg said quietly. The woman didn't appear to hear her.

"That's the joy of owning land in Greenwich!" she chirped happily.

"Paige," Peg said again, this time more forcefully.

"Yes?"

"I didn't invite you here today to talk about real estate."

Paige blinked several times. She looked utterly confused. "But," she said slowly, "what else is there?"

"Stan Peters' murder."

"I don't understand." Her frenetic activity

halted, Paige slumped back in her chair like a puppet whose strings had been cut. "That has nothing to do with me."

"How well did you know Stan?"

"Probably about as well as the other members of the club did. We played bridge together. That's all."

"Are you sure?" asked Peg.

"Of course I'm sure," Paige snapped. "I'm a married woman. Don't you dare imply anything else."

"It's interesting that's the conclusion you jumped to."

"Oh please. We're both adults. You know how men are." Her gaze flicked over Peg dismissively, as if she suspected that maybe Peg didn't.

Peg might have laughed at that, but she didn't want to interrupt the flow of conversation. "I understand you were popular with the male players when you and Reggie joined the bridge club."

"Maybe those guys viewed me as a fresh opportunity," Paige said. "But that was in their minds, not mine."

Peg took a swallow of tea and waited for Paige to continue.

"Besides, let me be clear. It wasn't just about *this*." Paige waved a hand to indicate her face and figure.

"What else?"

Paige reached across the table for the folder. She slapped it shut and tucked it back in her bag. "I own a successful business in town, and I'm also a local celebrity. People in my position get asked for stuff all the time."

"Like what?" Peg asked curiously.

"Jerry Watkins, for example. He has a son in college. He asked if I could pull some strings with the mayor to get the boy a summer internship in his office. Jerry thought it would look good on the kid's résumé when he applied to business school."

"And did you?"

"Frankly, I was a little annoyed by the request," Paige said shortly. "If I was going to call in a favor from the mayor, I'd rather do it on my own behalf. But Reg and I are members of the bridge club and I wanted to look like a team player. So I put out a few feelers to see if anything turned up. J.J. ended up interning with one of the city council members so that turned out all right."

Paige grimaced unhappily. "Better than Carrie's daughter, Madison, anyway. God knows how that gal ever managed to get herself a real estate license. Thanks to her mother, I got roped into giving her a job in one of my branch offices. Madison was barely even qualified to answer the phone. She didn't last long, and somehow I ended up getting blamed for it."

"That doesn't sound pleasant," Peg said.

"Believe me, it isn't."

"Did Stan ever ask you for any favors?"

Paige stared at her across the table. "You have a one-track mind, don't you?"

"When it comes to someone I know being murdered, perhaps I do."

"Then you should talk to the police," Paige said.

"I already did. I assume you did too?"

"Sure. They questioned everyone in the bridge club. For all the good it did them. They still don't have a clue who was responsible."

Peg had read every bit of information about the case that was reported in the local media. To date, they hadn't mentioned anything about suspects or a lack thereof, only that the investigation was still ongoing.

"How do you know that?" she asked.

"Like I told you, I'm a celebrity. In my line of work, I hear things. I hope they figure out who did it and arrest him. Stan was a decent man, you know?"

Peg nodded.

"He wasn't pushy like some of the other men in the club," Paige said. "Always talking about how important they *used* to be. As if I was supposed to be impressed by that. Stan was quieter than most. He didn't seem like the kind of guy who would have had enemies."

"It only took one," Peg said.

Chapter 22

Sunday morning, Rose got in touch with Carrie's bridge partner, Lacey Duvall. The two women agreed to meet in an hour at Bruce Park in Greenwich.

"Just so we understand each other, I'm only talking to you because Carrie asked me to." Lacey sounded annoyed. "So let's get it over with. Meet me at the park bench near the tennis courts and we can walk around the lake. One circumference and then I'm gone."

Bruce Park comprised more than twenty acres of open land just south of downtown Greenwich. It had sports facilities, hiking trails, and a playground. In the summer, the park was always filled with people. Rose arrived early and sat down on the designated bench. She didn't want to take a chance on missing Lacey.

The sun was shining in a bright blue, cloudless sky. Later, the day would be hot and steamy. But now, sitting in the shade of a leafy oak tree, Rose was almost cool in her shorts and T-shirt. The prospect of a stroll around the big pond was definitely inviting.

As she waited, Rose thought of the places she'd been and things she'd seen during the past several years. It was hard for her to understand how anyone could be unhappy surrounded by this much beauty, especially in a public park that was available to all. Lacey had chosen a wonderful meeting place. Rose could only hope that the fine weather and lovely setting would overcome her reluctance to talk.

Twenty minutes later, Rose was wondering if she'd been stood up when a metallic gray Tesla came speeding into the park. The car pulled into a nearby parking space and Lacey hopped out. She was dressed in lightweight shorts, running shoes, and a loose-fitting tank top. Her long hair was gathered into a single thick braid. The big black band around her wrist looked like a serious fitness tracker.

Like Rose, Lacey was in her sixties. Unlike Rose, she looked ready to run a mini marathon at a moment's notice.

Rose sighed and stood up. So much for her thoughts of a lovely stroll.

"Ready?" Lacey said as she approached. "Let's get going."

Before they'd even reached the path that wound around the lake, Lacey was already two strides ahead. At this rate, the only way Rose was going to be able to hold a conversation with her was if she shouted out her questions. And even then she probably wouldn't be able to hear the answers.

Abruptly Rose stopped walking. "I was thinking

we could talk about your relationship with Stan and the reasons you disliked him," she said to Lacey's departing back. "But if you'd rather I can take my speculations to Detective Sturgill instead."

Lacey spun around to face her. "I had no relationship with Stan Peters. I already told the detective that."

"Is he aware that Stan was married to your half-sister?"

Lacey shrugged. "I don't know. I didn't tell him. Someone else might have."

"That seems like important information. Why didn't you mention it?"

While Lacey paused, Rose covered the distance between them. She strode past her and kept going. After a moment Lacey caught up. The two women began to walk together.

"It would have complicated things for no reason. Stan's death had nothing to do with me. Why would I want to tell anyone about a prior connection that might make me look bad?"

"How would it do that?"

"You just said it yourself. Stan and I didn't get along." Lacey glanced over at her. "I assume Carrie told you that?"

"Carrie told me that Stan's wife, Bethany, was your sister. The other information came from somewhere else."

"Some*one* else, you mean." Lacey frowned as

if she was trying to guess who might have been the culprit.

Rose let her wonder. Lacey was setting a brisk pace, but now that she'd settled into stride, Rose was finding it easier to walk and talk at the same time.

"What was the problem between you and Stan?" she asked.

"I loved my sister," Lacey said.

Rose nodded.

"And Stan was responsible for her death."

Rose stumbled over a small crack in the sidewalk. Lacey reached over and grabbed her upper arm. She held Rose steady until she'd found her footing again.

"Thanks, I'm good. You just surprised me, that's all." Rose halted, so Lacey did too. "What do you mean Stan was responsible for your sister's death?"

"Exactly that. It was his fault. The mild-mannered man you met at bridge club? That wasn't the Stan Peters Bethany knew. She and Stan were married for fifteen years and toward the end they had some rip-roaring fights."

"All married couples disagree sometimes," Rose said.

Lacey gave her a nasty look and took off again.

"I'm well aware of that," she said as Rose scrambled to catch up. "I had three husbands before I figured out that I was much better off alone. But this was different. Stan wanted kids, and he blamed Beth because they couldn't have them."

"I assume they had the testing done," Rose said quietly.

"Oh sure, the whole nine yards. The problem wasn't Stan's fault, and he never let her forget it. At one point, they were all set to do in vitro fertilization, but then suddenly it didn't happen."

"Do you know why?"

"The cost is huge, more than ten thousand dollars every time you try. According to Bethany they had enough money saved up for two cycles. She'd already started doing the shots and everything. Then out of the blue Stan changed his mind. He said it was stupid to spend that much on something that might not even work. They had a huge fight about it. Bethany was really upset. She stormed out of their house and drove away."

Rose swallowed heavily. She was pretty sure she knew what was coming.

"Bethany was on her way to my place when the accident happened," Lacey said in a hollow voice. "She and I were on the phone, talking about her fight with Stan. Suddenly I heard Beth scream. Then I heard the crash. It was the most horrible thing I could ever imagine. It felt as though I was right there with her when the collision killed her."

Rose took Lacey's hand and gave it a gentle

squeeze. "I am so sorry. I can only imagine what a terrible thing that must have been to go through."

"It was the worst experience of my life," she said. "Even though it happened a long time ago, it still feels fresh in my mind. I had nightmares about it for years. Eventually I got some therapy and that helped. At least now I can remember Bethany without wanting to kill Stan for what he did to her."

Lacey frowned as she realized what she'd said. Her gaze slid Rose's way. "Don't get any ideas. That was wishful thinking, not an impulse I ever intended to act upon."

"It must have been hard for you, being in the bridge club with Stan," Rose said. "Considering what happened, I'd have thought you would never want to see him again."

"I didn't. But Carrie and I have been friends forever. She was excited about getting the club together, so of course I agreed to be her partner."

Lacey blew out a breath. Apparently it had nothing to do with being winded, because she was still moving right along. "Imagine my surprise when one of the other couples showed up with Stan in tow. There wasn't much I could say at that point, not with everybody else around. Afterward, I intended to tell Carrie she needed to make sure that I would never have to sit at the same table as Stan and his partner."

Rose started to comment, but Lacey was still talking.

"But you know what happened? The whole time we were there, Stan kept stealing looks over at me. I realized that he was just as uncomfortable with the situation as I was. So I never said a thing to Carrie. After that, whenever Stan saw me at the bridge club, I knew it made him think about Bethany. And I hope it made him feel guilty as hell."

Lacey stopped walking and turned to face Rose. Her lips curved in a cruel smile. "Knowing that Stan had to show up every week and look me in the eye? That was my own personal revenge."

Rose had turned off her phone while she and Lacey were walking. When she got back to her car, she discovered she had a missed call and a message from Violet Severson. Violet apologized for the short notice, and asked if Rose was free to join her and John at their club for lunch.

Rose quickly called back to accept the invitation, find out what time she should arrive, and inquire about a dress code.

"Don't worry about that," Violet told her. "John and I have our grandchildren for the weekend so we're spending the day at the pool. There's patio dining right next door and we have an outside table. We can eat and keep an eye on the kids at the same time. It's all perfectly casual. We'll see you in an hour."

Perfectly casual. At a country club. Right.

Rose ended the call and glanced down at her creased shorts and slip-on sneakers. She was sure this outfit wasn't what Violet had in mind.

There was just enough time for Rose to race home, change into a seersucker sundress and sandals, and make it back to the club's Greenwich address before the hour was up. Her gaze darted from side to side as she drove between a pair of stone gateposts, then up a wide driveway that bisected a perfectly manicured golf course. At the top of the hill, she could see a white two story clubhouse with double doors and tall Doric columns.

If Violet and John had wanted to make a statement by inviting Rose to meet them here, they'd definitely succeeded.

Rose passed a tennis complex. Its small lot was filled with cars whose price tags exceeded her entire net worth. She still hadn't seen any sign of a swimming pool when she arrived in front of the clubhouse. A young man dressed in crisp khakis and a club polo shirt hopped off a stool that was hidden behind one of the columns and came out to greet her.

Oh joy, valet parking.

"Can I help you?" he said. "You look like you might be lost."

"It's the six-year-old minivan, right?"

He grinned. "Actually, it was the expression on your face as you drove up. This place hits people like that sometimes if they haven't been here before."

"I can understand why. I'm supposed to be meeting some people at the swimming pool." Rose gestured toward the imposing building behind him. "I don't suppose it's in there?"

"No. We should have better signage." His voice lowered. "Members like to think that everyone who matters already knows where to go."

He leaned against the front of the van and motioned back the way Rose had come. "See that driveway just before you get to the tennis courts? Hang a right there and it will take you around the back of the clubhouse. Once you're there, you can't miss it."

"Thank you." Rose had never felt so out of her depth in her life. "Anything else I should know?"

The young man smiled. "The latch on the gate that leads to the pool area sticks. Don't let it pinch your fingers. And if you're going to be eating on the patio, don't order the egg salad. Other than that, you should be fine."

Rose found Violet and John seated at a shaded table on a terrace just beyond the club's Olympic sized swimming pool. She skirted carefully around a group of splashing children, then made her way past the lifeguard stand and a long row of chaise lounges. Most were occupied by younger women in designer swimsuits.

Violet stood up and waved as Rose approached. Her diamond wedding ring glittered in the bright sunlight. Her blond hair was held in place by a silk ribbon hairband. Even sitting poolside, Violet was wearing full makeup and jewelry.

"Well done," she said. "You found us."

If there had been any doubt of that, why hadn't Violet supplied her with better directions? "No problem," Rose said aloud.

As Violet retook her seat, John hopped to his feet to pull out Rose's chair. Since he'd allowed the women to seat themselves when they were playing bridge, Rose assumed these were his country club manners. She was pleased to see that her sundress fit right in with Violet's Lilly Pulitzer skirt and matching blouse and John's light blue golf pants.

Still on his feet, John lifted a hand and waved over a waiter. "Violet and I are drinking mimosas," he said to Rose. "Would you care to join us?"

"Umm . . . sure." Not much of a drinker, she didn't know what a mimosa was, though she was pretty sure alcohol was involved. The two tall glasses already sitting on the table looked innocent enough, however. "That would be fine," Rose said. "Thank you."

John placed the order and sat back down.

"Violet and I appreciate your joining us today. We wanted to have a conversation about what happened at the bridge club, and we thought that meeting in a less formal setting would help put everyone at ease."

Rose nodded, a reflex action. Offhand, she could hardly think of a time when she'd felt less at ease than she did right now. Unless it was when she'd been facing down that knife-wielding child.

The waiter returned with her mimosa and slipped it onto the table in front of her. Rose lifted the glass and took a sip. To her relief, she discovered that she hadn't requested anything too exotic. The drink merely tasted like fizzy orange juice. But despite its innocent guise, she was sure it would have a kick.

"Harriet! Lowell! Come over here." Violet beckoned toward a group of youngsters who were emerging from the pool. "I need to reapply your sunblock and there's someone I want you to meet."

Two children, a boy and a girl, separated themselves from the rest of the pack. Obviously brother and sister, the pair had sun-streaked hair and chubby cheeks. They were dressed in matching bathing suits and appeared to be six or seven years old. Their feet left a trail of wet footprints on the concrete deck around the pool as they came trotting over.

Violet reached into a canvas bag beside her

265

chair and came up with a hand towel and a tube of sunblock. When the two children reached her, she turned them around to face Rose and performed the introductions.

"Pleased to meet you," Lowell said solemnly. He was the older of the two. He stuck out his hand for Rose to shake. When his sister didn't follow suit, he remedied that deficiency with an elbow to her ribs.

Rose bit back a smile. "I'm delighted to meet you too," she replied as Violet began slathering lotion on their faces and bodies. "What a treat to have a pool to swim in on such a warm day. Do you enjoy swimming?"

"I do," Lowell said. "We both take lessons. But Harriet mostly just splashes around." Harriet nodded her head in agreement.

"Off you go," Violet told them. "It looks as though your friends have gone down to the playground. Why don't you join them?"

Pleased to have been excused, the children raced away. Violet recapped the tube of sunblock then carefully wiped off each of her fingers with the towel, before replacing both items in the canvas tote.

"They're adorable," Rose said. "You're lucky to have grandchildren."

"How about you?" asked John. "Any grandchildren of your own?"

"No, I'm afraid I never had children."

The time Rose had spent in the convent wasn't a secret, but talking about her past often led to numerous questions. It seemed easier not to elaborate. Rose took another sip of her mimosa instead.

"Harriet and Lowell are great kids," Violet said. "They go to Whitby School for the Montessori program. Of course they're both way ahead of their grade level. Lowell, especially." She glanced over at her husband. "I'm sure he'll follow John to Princeton one day."

"Let's not get ahead of ourselves," John said. "There's plenty of time before we need to worry about that."

He polished off his drink, then tapped the table beside the empty glass with his forefinger, indicating that he wanted another. The gesture barely registered with Rose, but their waiter caught it and quickly hopped to comply.

Violet leaned toward Rose across the table and said in a confiding tone, "John thinks I brag about our grandchildren too much. But I can't seem to help myself."

"You know I don't really mind that." John smiled indulgently. "A little bragging is to be expected. At least you're not soliciting our friends' help to advance the kids' careers."

Rose looked at him in surprise.

Violet saw her puzzled expression and said, "He's talking about Jerry Watkins."

"What did he do?"

"Tried to hit me up for a job for his son." John accepted his drink directly from the waiter's hand and took a long swallow. "The kid isn't even out of college yet. I don't know what he thought I could do for him now."

"Don't mind John. He's just feeling grumpy today," Violet said to Rose. "I think it's sweet the way Jerry dotes on that boy. He and Mae had three daughters first. I think they'd given up on having another child when J.J. came along. Jerry loves his girls, but when his son was born, it was as though he'd been waiting for him his whole life. I've heard him call J.J. his proudest achievement."

"That's because none of his other achievements are worth much," said John. He'd picked up a menu and begun to study it.

"Jerry told me he was an entrepreneur," Rose commented. "He said he'd put together some deals with other bridge club members, like Stan. Were you ever involved in that?"

"A few times, sure." John looked up. "It's not that Jerry didn't have some good ideas. Just that you had to pick and choose carefully because they didn't all pan out. Mostly I did all right. Once or twice, it went the other way. I think Stan might have been in one of those. But that was over and done with years ago. Let's talk about something of current interest."

What Rose really wanted to talk about was what kind of impropriety had led to John's retirement from his former job. She couldn't figure out how to raise the subject gracefully, however, especially not when she was sitting there as the Seversons' invited guest. Rose might be feeling out of place in this tony milieu, but she still had manners and knew how to use them.

"Violet and I asked you here today because we're aware that you and Peg have been asking questions of the other bridge club members," John said. "She and I find that behavior not only wholly unnecessary, but also offensive."

John clearly wanted Rose to understand that he was speaking for both himself and his wife. So why was Violet staring off into the distance while he delivered his lecture?

"Violet and I place a high value on our privacy," he continued. "It's bad enough that an acquaintance of ours lost his life in such a regrettable fashion. Worse still, that the police are involved."

Rose had to bite her tongue to keep from snapping back a retort. Under the circumstances, how could the police *not* be involved?

"We're taking steps to disassociate ourselves from the whole sordid situation. We'll be ending our membership in the bridge club and severing the friendships we formed there. In addition, I would like to make it perfectly clear that Violet and I have no intention of taking part in Peg's intrusive fact-finding mission."

A moment earlier, Rose had wanted to speak up. Now she was stunned into silence.

"I don't blame you in the slightest," John continued. "Obviously Peg is the problem. Perhaps you've also found yourself caught up in a situation beyond your control. In that case, you have my sympathies."

Rose caught a movement out of the corner of her eye. Violet had tuned back into the conversation. She was nodding too. That was just great. Apparently Rose had everyone's sympathy.

She didn't need that. What she did need was a good excuse to make a speedy exit from this increasingly awkward conversation.

John thwarted that idea by picking up another menu and handing it to her. Rose's fingers had already grasped the laminated sheet before she realized what she was doing.

"Now that we've gotten that bit of business out of the way," he said jovially, "let's eat, shall we?"

Chapter 23

When Paige finally left, Peg exhaled a huge sigh of relief.

She hadn't been able to get rid of the woman until after she'd given her a complete tour of her house and the surrounding property. That had taken nearly an hour to complete. During that time Peg had found herself answering more questions than she was able to ask.

It was no wonder Paige was so successful in her career. Her sales technique was eloquent and energetic. She knew how to take command of a conversation and steer it in the direction she wanted to go.

Grudgingly, Peg had to admire all of that. She just wished she hadn't wasted so much time to gain so little useful information.

As she was leaving, Paige handed Peg a thick file of real estate facts and figures. She must have spent hours compiling the data, which was too bad because Peg had no intention of reading it. She returned to the kitchen and shoved the file in a drawer where she wouldn't have to look at it.

Just a few feet away, Essie was standing up in her ex pen, whining under her breath. The small dog's eyes were trained on Peg. That wasn't entirely surprising since Peg had started talking to Essie the moment she'd entered the room.

Actually she'd been talking to the Toy Poodle virtually nonstop since she'd left the Grover sisters' home with Essie in her arms. This was the first time Peg had received a reply, however.

Though Essie hadn't been at Peg's house long, her demeanor had already begun to change. She wasn't as tense, and she'd become more engaged in the activity going on around her. Peg knew the presence of her other dogs was a huge asset. She was sure there must have been some interesting conversations taking place among the four Poodles.

Now Peg's dogs were standing beside the back door. The trio wanted to go outside and play. It looked as though Essie was asking to go with them.

"Is that what you're saying?" Peg bent down over the side of the ex pen. She reached out a hand and beckoned to Essie. "Do you want to go for a run too?"

The little brown Poodle pricked her ears. She walked toward Peg's outstretched fingers. As Peg leaned over to scoop Essie up with her hand, she heard the sound of a loud pop. The glass behind her gave a sharp crack as a jagged hole appeared in the big window at the front of the kitchen.

Peg knew the sound of gunshot when she heard it.

Reflex immediately kicked in. She grabbed Essie, then ducked down to the floor as a second shot shattered the window and sent shards of glass spraying across the room. The bullet whistled over Peg's head and smacked into the back wall.

Thankfully the big dogs were out of range of flying glass at the other end of the room. They whipped around and began to bark. Within seconds, they would come running to Peg's side. She had to stop them. There were splinters of glass all over the floor.

"Sit!" she commanded sharply. "Stay!"

The three black Poodles didn't look happy but they obeyed. Peg would apologize to them later.

She hunched down over Essie and she waited to see what would happen next. Peg's heart was racing. She was sure Essie could feel it beating in her chest. Rather than pulling away, however, the little Poodle nestled closer, as if proximity to Peg made her feel safe.

Thirty seconds passed in silence. It felt like an eternity. No third shot came ripping into the room. Maybe the gunman had fled. Or maybe he was still there, waiting for her to move.

That thought didn't bear considering. Peg had to move. She had no choice.

Bending low and cradling Essie to her chest, Peg inched across the floor. Glass crunched beneath her feet. Her phone was on the kitchen table. She lifted up a hand, fingers scrambling blindly over the wooden surface until she found the device and pulled it down.

Peg was shaking as she dialed 9-1-1.

"Nine-one-one. What's your emergency?"

"Somebody is shooting at me." She quickly supplied her address, then said, "Two bullets were just fired into my house."

"Is the shooter still there?" the operator asked.

"I don't know. And I'm not going to look outside to check."

"No, don't do that. Are you injured?"

"I don't think so. But there's glass everywhere." Peg realized her cheek was stinging. When she lifted her hand to touch it, Essie squealed in protest.

"Ma'am, what was that?" the operator asked urgently. "Are you all right?"

"Yes, sorry. That was a dog."

"A dog?"

The woman sounded so incredulous, Peg was almost tempted to laugh. But she was afraid that if she started, she might not be able to stop. Perhaps she was slightly hysterical.

That had certainly never happened before. Then again, Peg had never been shot at either.

"I have a patrol car on the way," the operator said. "It will be there in twelve minutes. Do you want me to stay on the line with you until the officer arrives?"

"No, I think I'm all right now." After the two shots were fired in quick succession, there hadn't been another one since. Hopefully the shooter had made his point and was long gone. "Thank you for your help."

Peg put the phone away and slowly levered herself up. Bits of glass coated her clothing and hair. They made a tinkling sound, raining down onto the floor around her as she rose.

Once on her feet, Peg didn't even glance in the direction of the window. Instead she quickly made her way to the back of the room. Her dogs were upset. They knew something was wrong and they wanted to help. They just didn't know how.

Peg crooned reassuringly under her breath. She patted each of the big Poodles in turn. Then she reached around Joker, opened the back door, and shooed all three dogs outside into the fenced field. Her backyard wasn't visible or accessible from the road. They should be safe there.

There was a crate on the back porch. Peg opened the door and slipped Essie inside. For the time being, it would be the best place for her.

That done, Peg turned back to survey the damage in the kitchen. Aside from the shattered window and the shards of glass glittering on the floor, everything looked much the same as usual. But it wasn't the same. Not even close. The pounding of Peg's heart could attest to that.

Peg strode through the kitchen, then down the hall to the front door. She flipped the dead bolt into the locked position. Peg had lived in this house for decades. She'd never felt unsafe here before.

Now she didn't know how to feel. The thought was unsettling.

Stan had been killed with a gun and now someone had taken a shot at her too. She and Rose had been poking around and asking questions. Somewhere, they must have touched a nerve.

Rose! Peg thought suddenly. What if the shooter had gone after her too?

Peg yanked out her phone and quickly put through the call.

"I just sat through the most awkward lunch of my life," Rose said when she picked up.

Peg sagged back against the wall. She expelled a breath in relief. Thank goodness Rose was okay.

"I can beat that," she said. "I've just been shot at. Twice."

"You win." Rose laughed. There was a pause as she waited for Peg to laugh too. When she didn't, Rose issued a shocked squeak. "Wait a minute. You were *serious?*"

"Yup."

"Oh my God!" For once, when Rose uttered those words, they didn't sound like a prayer. "What happened? Are you all right?"

"Mostly. Someone fired two shots into my kitchen. The dogs and I are fine, but I have a shattered window and at least one bullet in my wall. I already called nine-one-one. The police are on their way."

"Your friend, Detective Sturgill?"

"No, he works in Stamford. These will be Greenwich police."

Peg wasn't sure whether that was a good thing or a bad thing. On one hand, Sturgill would have immediately made the connection between Stan Peters' death and the shots that were fired today. On the other, he might have yelled at her for getting herself into this situation.

"Hang tight," said Rose. "I just had lunch at the Lakeview Country Club with John and Violet and I was on my way home. I'm just south of the parkway. I can be at your place in three minutes. Maybe less, if I ignore the speed limit."

Peg walked to the back of the house and checked on the Poodles. Everything was fine on that front. The three big dogs were lying in the shade, and Essie had settled down in her crate.

As she returned to the front door to wait for Rose, Peg realized that her hands were shaking. Now that she knew everyone was safe, a delayed reaction was setting in. Her fingers felt numb as she unlocked the dead bolt on the door when Rose's minivan came flying in the driveway.

Rose was the most principled person Peg knew. It was almost touching that she'd been moved to break the law on Peg's account. She opened the door as Rose came racing up the stairs.

"Really, I'm okay—" Peg began.

Rose didn't let her finish. Instead she threw her arms around Peg and smothered the words in a fierce hug. Caught by surprise, Peg initially stiffened. Then slowly her own arms lifted to circle tightly around Rose.

In all the time they'd known each other, had the two of them ever hugged before? Peg didn't think so.

Rose clung to Peg for a minute before stepping back to look her up and down. The scowl on Rose's face didn't bode well.

"I told you I'm fine." Peg went to brush a stray lock of hair back off her face, then stopped when her fingers were pricked by the slivers of glass that were still caught among the strands.

"You're not fine," Rose retorted. "You have a scratch on your cheek that needs to be treated and your blouse is torn."

"It is?" Peg looked down. A button had ripped free, leaving a small ragged hole. "Essie must have done that."

"Franny and Florence's dog?"

Peg nodded, then attempted a smile. It looked wobbly. "I was holding her. Don't worry, I didn't get shot."

"No, but you might be in shock," Rose said briskly. It was clear she wanted to take charge. "I saw the broken window on my way in. Someone made a great, gaping hole in your house. From outside, it looks gruesome. It probably looks even worse in here. What can I do to help?"

"Wait with me until the police get here?"

"Of course I'll do that." Rose turned Peg around and steered her toward the kitchen. "Why don't you sit down? Let me make you some tea."

The two women reached the doorway to the kitchen and stopped dead. A breeze was wafting through the broken window and glass covered most surfaces in the front half of the room.

"Okay, so we're not going in there." Rose quickly changed her mind. "At least not until I've had a chance to clean up."

"We shouldn't touch anything," said Peg. "Not until after the police have been here. We can go wait in the living room."

The living room was bright and spacious, and filled with furniture that looked as though it didn't see much use. In front of the fireplace, two chintz-covered love seats flanked a low coffee table. Peg and Rose both sat down.

Peg's silence indicated that she still didn't feel like talking about what happened. Rose didn't push her. Instead she used the time to relate what she'd learned about Bethany's death from Lacey. Briefly she considered mentioning her conversation with John and Violet, but under the circumstances that felt like a bit of a pile-on.

Five minutes later, the doorbell rang. Peg went to open the door. A patrol car was parked outside, and a uniformed policeman was standing on her porch.

Peg had expected that. What she hadn't expected was to see a second car turning off the road into her driveway.

Rose appeared behind her. "That must be Detective Sturgill," she said.

Peg frowned. "What's he doing here?"

"I called him from my car and told him what happened. He said he'd better come and take a look."

"Excuse me, ma'am," the policeman said. "I'm Officer James. I got a report of a drive-by shooting at this address?"

A drive-by shooting? Was that what they were calling it? If so, it had to be the first event of its kind ever to take place in back country Greenwich.

Peg and Rose shared a dubious look.

"I'm the one who called," Peg told him. "Please come in."

As the officer complied, Rose watched Detective Sturgill get out of his car. Peg gave Rose a none-too-subtle nudge in the direction of the steps.

"Officer James and I have things to discuss,"

she said. "Perhaps you could tell the detective that I'll be with him in a few minutes?"

"Of course," Rose replied. "Take all the time you need."

Chapter 24

Rose frowned as the door closed behind her. Judging by the look on Peg's face, she was in big trouble for contacting Detective Sturgill. But what else was she supposed to do? Peg had been shot at. Stan had been shot at, too, and now he was dead.

With everything that Rose knew, it only made sense to aim for the best possible police response. She wanted someone on the case who not only knew what he was doing, but who was also capable of seeing the big picture. Because despite what that patrolman had said, this was no ordinary drive-by shooting.

By the time she reached the foot of the stairs, Detective Sturgill had left the driveway. He was standing in the middle of Peg's front yard, shading his eyes as he stared up at the broken window. Rose walked over to join him.

"Thank you for coming," she said.

He glanced over at her and nodded. "Thank you for calling me. Does Peg have any idea what happened here?"

"I only arrived a few minutes before you did. She told me someone fired two shots into her house and that no one had been hurt."

"No one?" Sturgill looked surprised. "Someone else was here with her?"

"No." Rose smiled. "I think she was referring to her dogs."

"Oh, right. Those Poodles of hers. I've met them."

Rose knew the detective had met the dogs the week before when he'd come to talk to them about Stan's death. But now he seemed to be referring to an earlier acquaintance. Perhaps one that explained why Peg sometimes called the detective "Rodney."

Rose wasn't brave enough to inquire about that, not that she was given the chance. Sturgill was walking away from her again. This time he appeared to be striding a direct line between the shattered window and the road fifty yards away. Rose had little choice but to trail along behind.

When he reached the end of the yard, Sturgill squatted down to study the grass on the verge and the loose dirt at the edge of the lane. Rose had watched enough cop shows to guess that he was looking for tire tracks. Or maybe bullet casings.

"There's a bullet in Peg's kitchen wall," she told him. "Maybe it came from the same gun that killed Stan Peters."

The detective looked up at Rose with a bemused expression on his face. He seemed surprised to see that she was still beside him. "Ballistics will be able to tell us that."

He didn't sound happy about the prospect. Rose had no idea why. Peg was an old hand at dealing with the police, but this was all new to her.

"So that's a good thing," she said. "Right?"

"In theory, yes." Sturgill braced his hands on his knees and rose heavily to his feet. "But if the bullet in Peg's kitchen is from the same gun, then I'm going to start wondering why someone seems intent on bumping off the members of your bridge club."

His bushy brows lowered as he frowned at Rose across the small space between them. "Either that, or *someone*"—Sturgill glanced meaningfully toward the house—"is going to have to admit that despite our previous conversation, she's done some investigating of her own. If that's true, it would lead me to suspect that this shooting was meant as a warning rather than an attempt at a second homicide."

"Oh," Rose said. She carefully looked away.

Even that single word sounded like she was conceding too much. It occurred to Rose that this was a conversation Detective Sturgill ought to be having with Peg instead of her.

They'd started back toward the house when Peg's front door opened. Officer James came out. Peg was just behind him. In the interim, she'd cleaned up the cut on her cheek and changed her blouse. Peg glanced around the yard, locating

Rose and Detective Sturgill before turning back to the officer.

"I hope you're right and this was some teenagers blowing off steam," she said to him.

"Yes, ma'am." Officer James nodded. "I do too."

He got in his patrol car and backed slowly out of the driveway. Sturgill walked over to stand beside Peg. The two of them watched the officer drive away down the lane.

"You don't really believe that, do you?" he asked.

"No," Peg replied. "But at the moment, I don't know what to believe."

"I have a theory," Sturgill told her. "Let's go inside and talk."

Rose watched the two of them walk away. She wondered if they even remembered she was there. That was a disconcerting thought.

Then Peg paused and turned back. "You're coming, aren't you, Rose? I'm sure you'll want to hear what Detective Sturgill has to say."

Having already heard what he was thinking—and had implied—just minutes earlier, Rose wasn't sure either of them wanted to hear more from the detective. Particularly not Peg. Nevertheless, she once again followed along.

Inside the house, Peg waved Rose and Detective Sturgill toward the living room while she went to check on her dogs. Rose sat down on one of the love seats. She expected Sturgill to take the other. Instead he remained on his feet. He walked around the room, examining the antique captain's desk in the corner and checking out the framed photographs that were displayed on various tabletops.

Peg returned shortly with a smile on her face—the first smile Rose had seen from her today. She could guess what that meant. Peg's kitchen was a disaster, but her Poodles were fine.

As Peg took a seat beside her, Detective Sturgill ambled over to the other love seat and sat down opposite them. His feet were set wide apart. He braced his elbows on his upper legs and lowered his shoulders by leaning forward. Rose wondered if that was an interrogation technique meant to make him look less threatening.

If so, it wasn't working.

"Start from the beginning and tell me everything that happened," he said to Peg.

Rose had asked the same question and barely gotten a reply. Peg was eager to supply the detective with much more detail, however. Rose listened to the recital in silence—and at some points, with her heart in her throat. She couldn't imagine being on the receiving end of an attack like that.

Peg had obviously rallied during the time she'd spent talking to Officer James. Earlier, Rose had thought she might be in shock. Now Peg looked pleased to be the center of attention, relating her story as if the shooting had been an adventure rather than potential catastrophe.

"If you don't mind, I'm going to discount the rowdy teenager story and cut straight to the chase," Sturgill said when she was finished. "And I want an honest answer. What have you two ladies been up to that would make someone send you a threatening message so you'd cut it out?"

Rose and Peg shared a look.

"I guess we've asked a few questions about Stan," Peg said.

"You talked to the other bridge club members?"

Rose and Peg both nodded.

Sturgill closed his eyes briefly. He looked as though he might be praying for patience. "I think I asked you not to do that, didn't I?"

"We thought we could help," Peg said. "Rose and I were sure the other players would talk to us more readily than they would to the authorities. We hoped we'd be able to gather some pertinent information for you."

"And did you?" he asked. "I'm here now. Let's hear what you've got."

Rose went first. "Carrie Maynard had an affair with Stan. She said they parted amicably but I'm not sure that's true. Stan, John Severson, and Jerry Watkins all did business together over the years. Sometimes the deals were successful, sometimes not. Maybe there's bad blood there. Stan's now-deceased wife, Bethany, was Lacey Duvall's half-sister, and Lacey blames Stan for her death."

Rose paused to wait for a reaction. She'd thought that last tidbit was particularly compelling, but Detective Sturgill didn't look impressed.

"Is that it?" he asked.

"No," Peg chimed in. "John Severson was engaged in some kind of wrongdoing that resulted in his expulsion from his high profile job. Obviously that doesn't speak well of his character. Mick Doran credits Stan with pro- viding the assistance that enabled him to open his own car repair business. But how well is his garage actually doing? Maybe he owed Stan money that he wasn't able to repay. Paige and Reggie Greene were cheating at our card games, and Bennett Jones was gambling on them."

"You two have gotten yourselves mixed up with a real bunch of winners," Sturgill said. "But none of that sounds to me like enough of a motive to commit murder."

Peg glared at him. "Well then, what have you got?"

Detective Sturgill almost smiled. "You know I'm not going to tell you that, Peg. First, because it's official information. And second, because based on past experience, you'd probably find a way to use it to get yourselves into even more trouble."

"Then just tell us this." Peg refused to be put off. "We know the police have been looking into other areas of Stan's life. Based on the knowledge you've compiled, do you have a strong suspicion about who might have killed Stan? Are you close to making an arrest?"

"Once again, I have nothing to say on the subject." Sturgill stood up, signaling that the conversation was over. "But I will say this. Those bits and pieces of information that the two of you have cobbled together? To me, they don't seem to be worth the risk of what happened here today."

He turned and marched out of the living room. Peg and Rose hopped up and went after him. The detective let himself out of the house, but when he reached the porch, he decided that he wasn't yet finished making his point.

He turned and nailed Peg with a hard glare. "You've made yourself a target, Peg. I'm sure that's not what you meant to do, but sometimes actions have unintended consequences. Especially when you're dealing with people who might be desperate and who aren't above using lethal means to fight back."

Peg didn't reply. There didn't seem to be much she could say.

"Officer James is young. Maybe he hasn't seen

as much as I have, so he jumped to what seemed like an easy answer. But the three of us know better, don't we?"

Rose and Peg mumbled their assent.

"What happened to that bullet? He take that with him?"

"Yes," Peg confirmed.

"Good. I'll touch base with the GPD, let them know we need to coordinate, and get something moving there. I'll also arrange for them to send a patrol car down your lane every so often to keep an eye on things."

Sturgill paused again. This time, he looked back and forth between Rose and Peg. "But you have to do your part too. Leave the investigating to the professionals. Am I making myself clear?"

Maybe he suspected he wouldn't like Peg's answer, because he didn't wait to hear it. Instead, Sturgill stomped down the stairs, got in his car, and drove away without looking back.

Rose released her breath as the detective's car disappeared from sight. "That was interesting," she said. "I've never been yelled at by a member of the police force before."

Peg's gaze swung her way. "Really?"

"Of course not. I'm a model citizen."

"I am, too. But sometimes things happen."

Rose definitely wasn't going to ask what kinds of things those might be.

"Besides, you shouldn't take it personally," Peg

added. "I think Rodney was mostly yelling at me."

As if anyone was surprised about that.

The two of them went back inside. Peg closed and locked the door behind them. Then she started down the hallway. "Let's go clean the kitchen and get something tacked up over that open window. The Poodles have been stuck outside for nearly an hour. I want to get the glass picked up, so I can let them back in."

Peg used a broom to sweep up all the debris she could see. Rose followed with a vacuum, making sure that none of the smaller shards of glass were missed. When the floor was clean, they wiped down the counters and the tabletop. Peg replaced the bedding in Essie's pen. Rose washed out and refilled the Poodles' water bowls.

They ignored the hole in the wall where Officer James had dug out a bullet. That was a problem for another day. The broken window was of more immediate concern.

"I'll have to call and see how quickly I can get the glass replaced," Peg said. "In the meantime, I have a tarp in my garage that we can use to cover the hole."

Once they'd fetched the tarp and a toolbox, it only took a few minutes to complete the task. Rose stood on a step stool and held the plastic sheeting in place while Peg hammered the tacks into the window frame. Then they both stood back and studied their handiwork.

"That'll do," Peg decided.

Rose thought their quick fix looked appalling. Until the window was repaired, it would serve as a grim reminder of what had taken place. But no one had asked her opinion, so she didn't offer it.

Peg strode to the other end of the room and opened the back door. She didn't even have to call the Poodles. As soon as they saw Peg, all three jumped up. They raced across the yard and into the kitchen.

Rose's eyes widened at the sight. It was like being charged by a herd of buffalo. She quickly ducked behind the table to avoid being run over. Peg calmly sidestepped the oncoming horde and walked out onto the porch. She returned a moment later with a small brown ball of fluff in her arms.

"What's that?" Rose asked.

"This is Essie." Peg glanced at her in surprise. "Franny and Florence's Poodle. I told you she was here."

"Yes, but . . ." Rose gestured toward Joker and Coral who were slurping up water from the two bowls. "When you said she was a Poodle, I thought she'd look like them."

"Poodles come in three sizes. Essie's a Toy Poodle. They're little."

Rose drew closer for a better look. She lifted a tentative hand to stroke Essie's soft hair.

"Do you want to hold her?"

"No!" Rose jumped back.

"Just as well," Peg said. "Since she hasn't met you before, Essie might not have liked that. If you want to get acquainted with her, you should sit on the floor."

"No, thank you." Rose wasn't sure if Peg was kidding. And she had no intention of finding out. She pulled out a chair and sat down at the table.

"Now you've been warned off twice," she said. "Once by an unknown person with a gun, and the second time by Detective Sturgill. What do we do next?"

Peg deposited Essie on the floor and joined Rose at the table. "The same thing we were doing before."

Rose glanced at the tarp-covered window. "Are you sure that's safe?"

"If someone already thinks I'm a threat, I don't know how our stopping what we're doing is going to change that. I think we should redouble our efforts to figure this out, so the police can arrest the guilty party. That's what would really make me feel safe."

Rose nodded. She could see that. But where did they go from here? What had they overlooked?

"When you spoke with Paige, did you tell her

you knew that she and Reggie had been cheating at bridge?"

"No," Peg admitted unhappily. "I probably should have. But since I'd gotten her to my house under false pretenses, I wasn't exactly occupying the moral high ground. What about you? At your lunch with John and Violet, did you ask him why he'd been fired from his job?"

"I couldn't." Rose sighed. "He'd already made it clear that he was angry about us invading his privacy. After that, I didn't have the nerve."

"A fine pair of detectives we make," Peg muttered.

"Detective Sturgill would agree with you."

Rose jumped in her seat. Something cold and wet was pressed against her calf. She peeked down under the table. Essie was sniffing her leg. The brown Poodle looked up and their eyes met. Rose had no idea what she was meant to do in this situation.

"Good dog?" she tried.

"Who are you talking to?" asked Peg.

"Essie. She's licking my leg. And it tickles."

"Drop your hand down slowly. See if she'll let you pet her."

Rose stared at Peg. "Why would I want to do that?"

"Because it would be good for her. Essie made the first move. Now you should reciprocate."

"Maybe I should just move my leg."

"That won't help at all. Go ahead. Just give her a little pat so she knows it's a good thing to make friends."

"Essie and I aren't friends." Rose glanced down again. "At best, we are approximal acquaintances."

"Oh pish," Peg replied. "Essie likes you. That means you and she are friends."

Peg wasn't going to give up. Rose knew that. Peg never gave up until she'd had her way.

Rose slid her hand down off her lap. She wondered if the front end of the dog might want to bite her. Just in case, she aimed her hand toward the tail. Her fingers grazed the length of Essie's back.

The Toy Poodle didn't seem to mind her touch. She was soft all over. And Rose didn't even get nipped. She took that as a win.

"Why you?" Rose asked when Essie had moved away.

"Why me, what?"

She flicked a hand toward the tarp. "Why did someone come after you and not me? We've both been asking questions."

Peg considered that. "I don't know. Maybe I made someone mad."

"It wouldn't be the first time," Rose allowed.

"Or maybe it's down to location. You live on a busy street. My house is more remote. Someone firing a gun here would be less likely to be seen."

Rose nodded. That made sense.

"Or maybe it's because I'm the brains of the operation."

Rose choked on a laugh. "You mean the troublemaker."

"That too," Peg agreed. She didn't sound displeased either way.

Chapter 25

Peg awoke the next morning with a renewed sense of resolve. After she'd let the Poodles outside for their morning run, she brewed a cup of strong tea and sat down at the kitchen table to plan her day.

At the top of her to-do list was arranging to get her window fixed. Just below that was getting in touch with Bennett Jones or Sue Richey. Of all the members of the bridge club, that engaged couple were the only people neither she nor Rose had spoken with yet. It was time to remedy that.

Peg tried four different glass repair shops. The first appointment she could get was three days away. The glass man had sounded almost eager when she described the problem. Apparently she was his first gunshot victim. Peg didn't think that was anything to brag about, but at least now she had something scheduled.

After that, she looked through the contact information Rose had given her. Phone numbers were listed for both Bennett and Sue. She decided to try Bennett first.

Her call went to voice mail. She left a message and Bennett called her right back. He recommended they meet at a Starbucks in downtown Greenwich.

Peg liked that idea. Neutral territory, and even

better, a very public place. Just in case Bennett had been her trigger-happy visitor the day before. She approved on both counts.

"Will Sue be joining us?" she asked.

"No," he replied quickly. "In fact, I won't even tell her where I'm going. This whole situation has been very upsetting for Sue. The less she thinks about it, the better."

Peg knew she was meant to admire Bennett's protective instincts. Instead, she thought Sue might be better off having the opportunity to make her own decisions. She wondered if Bennett feared they'd be discussing things, like his gambling habit, that he didn't want his fiancée to know about.

Hope came over and rested her head in Peg's lap. Peg ran her hand down the curls on the Poodle's neck, then scratched behind her ears. Looking into Stan's death was making her suspicious of everyone's motives. Maybe she was being unfair to Bennett. The times she'd seen the couple together, they'd appeared to be very much in sync. It was possible Bennett really was looking out for Sue's best interests.

"What do you think?" Peg asked.

Hope lifted her head. Her tail waved back and forth. She liked being asked for an opinion. Happily she wriggled her body closer to Peg.

"You're no judge of character," Peg said. "You like everybody."

Hope jumped up and draped her front legs across Peg's lap. She pressed her graying muzzle against Peg's chin. Now the two of them were nearly eye to eye. Just the way they liked it.

The other three Poodles were asleep around them. Essie was in a dog bed, curled up next to Coral. Everyone was getting along so well that now she was able to be loose with the bigger dogs when Peg was there to supervise.

Essie had even begun coming to Peg for affection, just like the other Poodles did. She still had a long way to go. But it was another step in the right direction, and Peg was happy to see it.

The Starbucks Bennett had chosen for their meeting was just off Greenwich Avenue near the Board of Ed building. Midmorning, the coffee bar wasn't crowded. Peg arrived first. She bought herself a chai tea latte and a large blueberry scone, then sat down at a table toward the rear of the room to wait.

Bennett came hurrying in ten minutes later. He was a good looking man in his late fifties, the youngest member of the bridge club. He was also taller than Peg, which in her experience didn't happen often. The lenses of his glasses lightened from opaque to clear as he gazed around the small room. Seeing Peg, he gave her a wave of acknowledgment, then went to buy himself an iced coffee.

"Sorry about that," Bennett said. He set the tall cup down on the table, then slid into the seat opposite her. "I always forget how hard it is to find a parking space on Greenwich Avenue. I circled the block twice and ended up on Mason Street."

"Have you lived here long?" Peg asked curiously.

"Actually I live in Stamford now, but I grew up in Greenwich. I remember what it used to be like in the old days."

"Me, too," she said.

The two of them shared a smile. Bennett made himself comfortable. That was good, though Peg didn't intend for it to last.

"How well do you know John Severson?" she asked.

A look of surprise, quickly suppressed, crossed Bennett's face. Peg had been hoping to catch him off guard, and obviously it had worked. Bennett was expecting another line of questioning entirely. She would get to that in a minute.

"Well enough, I guess," he said carefully.

"Why did he leave his corporate job?"

"He retired."

"Voluntarily?"

Bennett gave Peg a shrewd look. "That's an interesting question."

"I'm hoping you have an interesting answer."

"I don't," he replied. "John had a golden parachute. He took it. End of story."

"Not necessarily," Peg said.

Bennett shrugged. "You'd have to ask him about that. Look, I thought you asked me here to talk about Stan."

"Him, too." Peg nibbled around the edges of her scone. "Tell me about Stan."

"He was one of the good guys. I can't imagine why anyone would have wanted to hurt him."

Peg repeated her earlier question. Hopefully she'd get a better result this time. "Did you know him well?"

"I'd say so." Bennett took a sip of his coffee as he considered his answer. "He and I originally met on the golf course. That was years ago, right after his wife died. You know about her?"

Peg nodded.

"Her death must have been a real tragedy. Stan was just wrecked for a long time afterward. I was single then, and we hung out quite a bit in those days. I took him to the horse races at Belmont. He and I played some poker. Once we went on a trip to Vegas. Stan had been bugging me to join the bridge club for a while. When Sue and I got together, it just seemed like the right time."

"So you haven't been a member long," Peg said.

"Not compared to the rest of those guys." Bennett laughed. "Maybe five years or so. And before you ask, yes it took me a while to pop the question. Sue and I had both been married before and she wanted to take things slow. That was fine by me. I didn't care how long we took to make our relationship official, as long as it got done in the end."

"Congratulations on your perseverance."

"There was never any doubt about that. I knew right from the start that Sue was worth waiting for."

Peg appreciated the sentiment, but she needed to get back on track. She hadn't come to talk to Bennett about his love life. She broke off a piece of her scone and popped it in her mouth. "It sounds as though Stan must have enjoyed gambling just as much as you do."

Bennett wasn't fooled by her deliberately casual tone. "What do you mean by that?"

"You just mentioned a trip to Las Vegas. And I saw you collecting your winnings at the bridge club last week. Was Stan ever involved in betting on the games?"

Bennett sat in silence for a minute. Peg sipped her tea and waited him out. Someone had raised the threat level in her life rather dramatically the day before. She would spend as much time as it took to get answers.

"Let's get something straight," he said finally. "What you saw was perfectly innocent. All I do is offer a little action on the games to anyone who might be interested. I handicap the players and fix the odds accordingly. But you need to understand that I don't do anything to influence the outcome of the games."

"You're sure about that?"

"Hell, yes, I'm sure. And I ought to know."

Of course he would *know.* Whether or not he was telling Peg the truth was another matter.

"Was Stan ever part of your betting pool?" she asked.

"No. Never," Bennett said firmly. "He knew about it, though. Stan didn't approve. He was afraid I'd get caught and the bridge club would be disbanded." His gaze narrowed to a hard stare. "I hope that's not what you're trying to accomplish?"

"Not at all." Peg held up her hands in a gesture of innocence. "I'm just trying to learn more about Stan."

Bennett grabbed his cup and slurped down half his iced coffee. All this talking must be thirsty work. "Look, you want to know something about Stan? Here's what I can tell you. For him, it wasn't about the betting. He just liked to win. You know what I mean?"

A nod seemed called for. Peg obliged him.

"Stan was a better golfer than I was. That was why he liked playing with me, because most days he could beat me handily. Mick is far and away the best player in the bridge club. That's why Stan had him as his partner. Those guys win way more rubbers than anyone else because of Mick's prowess. Poker nights, Stan didn't even seem to care how big the pot was, he just wanted to be able to rake the chips over to his spot at the end of a hand."

Peg had been about to reach for another piece of her scone. Now her hand went still. "Poker nights?" she said.

"Yeah, sure. Me and most of the guys from the bridge club get together to play poker a couple Friday nights a month. I mentioned that earlier."

No, he hadn't. Not exactly. But at least he was mentioning it now.

"Usually the games are at my house. Sometimes at Stan's or Mick's. Since we're the ones who are single, that just makes sense. Having a guy's wife hanging around the place when you're trying to play serious cards can be a real buzzkill."

"Unless she wants to play too," Peg mentioned.

Bennett just shook his head. Apparently that wasn't happening.

"Which of the men from the bridge club play with you?"

"John, Jerry, Stan, Mick, and I are the regulars. Reggie shows up about half the time." Bennett stopped and smirked. "He'd probably come more often if Paige didn't keep him on such a tight leash."

That sounded like just about everyone to Peg. "When was the last time you got together for a poker night?"

Bennett thought back. "Probably ten days ago."

That would have been just a few days before Stan was killed.

"Did anything unusual happen that night?"

The question seemed to require some serious consideration. Peg went back to demolishing her scone.

"Now that you mention it, there was something," Bennett said eventually. "Stan and Jerry got into a quarrel at the end of the night."

"Over what?"

Bennett shrugged. "Nobody knew what set them off. Later on, sometimes things get rowdy. You know."

"No," said Peg. "I don't."

"Then let me set the scene for you. By the time we've been drinking and playing cards for three or four hours, we're all pretty well lubricated. So it's not like we're on our best behavior. Usually when an argument breaks out—which, let's face it, could be over anything from baseball stats to which actresses look best naked—everyone else jumps in and chooses sides. But this time, it was just Jerry and Stan."

Bennett had told her to imagine the scene. So Peg did just that. Immediately something occurred to her. "So Stan and Jerry couldn't have been sitting at the poker table when the fight started."

"Yeah, you're right. Jerry had gotten up to go

to the bathroom. On his way back, he stopped on the other side of the room to look at something. Then he called Stan over to have a conversation about it."

"What was Jerry looking at?" Peg asked.

"I have no idea. There were some shelves on the wall. Maybe something there."

Bennett shrugged again, as if he couldn't care less. His indifference made Peg want to reach across the table and smack him.

"And you couldn't hear anything they were saying?"

"To tell the truth, I wasn't even trying. I was on a hot streak at the time. I just wanted both of them to shut up and sit back down so we could deal the next hand."

"Did Stan and Jerry eventually come back to the table and rejoin the game?"

"Now that you mention it, no. Stan did. He was pumped. We dealt him right back in. But Jerry, he looked sick." Bennett frowned. "Maybe that was the problem. Anyway, after that he cashed in his chips and left."

"Is that how your poker games usually work?" Peg asked. "Can anyone leave whenever they want?"

"If someone's winning big, no one wants them to skip out until the rest of us have had a chance to get some money back. But as I recall, Jerry had already lost a bundle that night. So no one was going to insist that he hang around and prolong the agony."

Bennett glanced over at the door. He looked like he was getting ready to move on. Rather than pressing him further, Peg changed the subject. "I assume you were questioned by the police like everyone else."

"Sure." He lifted his cup, tipped back his head, and polished off his drink. "Some detective asked me a lot of questions."

"Did you tell him what you just told me?"

"No. Why would I? I wasn't even thinking about it at the time. Everything the detective wanted to know was about the bridge club. And anyway, the other thing wasn't a big deal. Just two guys having a bad night. What goes on at the poker game is like that commercial about Las Vegas, you know?"

"What happens there, stays there?"

"Precisely. Nice talking to you, Peg." Bennett shoved back his chair and stood up. "Along those same lines, I'm going to assume that what we covered here is just between us."

Like hell, thought Peg. The idea was so ludicrous she almost laughed. Then she realized what Bennett was worried about.

"You'd prefer I don't repeat any of this to Sue," she said.

Bennett lifted his hand in a small salute. "Thanks for understanding."

Before the Starbucks door had even closed behind him, Peg already had her phone out. Her first thought was to call Detective Sturgill. Surely he would be interested in this new information.

Then just as quickly, she realized there was no way she could give it to him. It hadn't even been twenty-four hours since the detective had warned her, very firmly, to stay out of his investigation. This meeting with Bennett was exactly the kind of thing he hadn't wanted her to do.

Peg's second thought was to wonder what Rose was up to this morning. Maybe she was watching her tomato plants again and would like to have some company.

A month earlier, Peg couldn't have imagined caring about Rose's opinion on anything. Now she not only cared, she couldn't think of a better person to share her thoughts with.

Peg picked up her phone again and put through the call.

Chapter 26

The kitchen at the Gallagher House was small. Appliances took up most of the available space. Even with both windows open in the hope of catching a stray breeze, the room still felt warm. A ceiling fan did little more than push the same tepid air around.

Rose and Maura were sitting at a tiny table pushed up against one wall. They'd been making a supermarket shopping list when Rose's phone rang.

Rose saw Peg's name on the screen and snatched up the device. She hoped nothing else had gone wrong. With Peg, you never knew.

"Are you at the Gallagher House?" Peg asked.

"Yes—"

"Good. I'm coming over. We need to talk."

"We're talking now," Rose pointed out. For all Peg's peremptory ways, at least this didn't sound like an emergency.

"I'm already on the turnpike. I'll be there in ten minutes."

Peg disconnected the call without waiting for a reply. Typical.

When Rose put down the phone, Maura was staring at her across the table. She'd been raking her fingers through her short brown hair. Now it was standing up in tufts.

311

"That didn't sound like it went well," she said.

It took Rose a moment to realize that Maura had been listening to her conversation. "That's just Peg's way. There was some trouble at her house yesterday. So if she wants to be bossy today, I'm willing to cut her some slack."

"What kind of trouble?"

"Someone shot out one of her windows."

"With a gun?" Maura's eyes widened. She'd experienced violence in her life, but she'd never been threatened like that.

"Yes, with a gun." It took effort for Rose to sound less disturbed about the event than she felt.

"Your friend Peg sounds like a dangerous woman to be around."

"What happened wasn't her fault," Rose said firmly.

She refused to accept Detective Sturgill's opinion. Because if she had to concede that Peg was to blame for the shooting, that meant Rose was equally to blame. They'd both been guilty of snooping around.

Rose definitely liked the no-fault theory better.

Maura didn't look convinced. "Is she bringing that big scary dog with her?"

"Hope isn't scary. She's a Poodle. I'm pretty sure they're mostly harmless."

"So you say. All I saw was a bunch of big white teeth. You'd better be careful when she's around."

Rose smiled. "Peg or the Poodle?"

"Both," Maura said stubbornly.

It only took a few minutes to finish the shopping list. Rose folded it up and tucked it in her purse. She'd been about to go to the supermarket. Now she'd wait to see what Peg wanted first. Maybe she'd been up to something interesting that morning. In fact, where Peg was concerned, that was pretty much a given.

Rose found herself humming with anticipation. When Maura left to straighten the living room, Rose got up and went outside. She was on the front porch when Peg's maroon minivan slid into a spot beside the curb in front of the house next door.

Rose walked down the steps to meet Peg on the sidewalk. "Let's go around back and sit outside."

"More plant watching?" Peg looked amused.

"The tomato plants are doing just fine. But it's hot in the house. At least the air is moving out here."

Peg gazed up at the tall house as they walked around it. "With that many floors, you need air-conditioning."

"Maybe it'll happen someday," Rose said with a shrug. "If the budget ever allows. There always seems to be something more important that we need to get to first."

The chairs were already set up in the shade provided by a neighbor's leafy tree. Rose headed that way. "Besides, we'll have more privacy out here. I assume there have been developments?" She tried not to sound too eager as they both took their seats.

"Indeed," Peg replied. "Well, one anyway. I talked to Bennett this morning. He was the last person on my list."

"Was Sue there too?"

"No, he made some excuse about her being too upset to talk about what happened. I thought it sounded like he didn't want her there. Like maybe he was afraid of what she might hear."

Rose turned to face her. "I assume you're referring to Bennett's gambling?"

"Yes. He had to have known I'd be grilling him for information. Everybody in that bridge club knows what we're up to before we even get a chance to do it."

"They're a tight group," Rose agreed. "Carrie once said something about the club being almost as close as family. It probably isn't just us they're keeping tabs on. I bet they all mind each other's business too."

"That's hardly a comforting thought," Peg said. "It means that if someone in the club pulled the trigger, some other member probably has a pretty good idea why he or she did it."

"Which is why we need to get this figured out. Tell me what you learned from Bennett."

"I may be inching closer to uncovering

something interesting. Bennett told me that in addition to playing bridge, the men in the club also hold a semi-regular poker game. It takes place a couple of times a month and moves around between the houses of the single players."

Rose thought for a moment. "That would be Stan, Mick, and Bennett." She glanced at Peg. "Unless Bennett doesn't count as single because he and Sue are engaged?"

"Not only does Bennett count, but he's probably the one who came up with the idea. It sounds as though he'd be happy to place a bet on just about anything, including whether or not the sun will come up tomorrow morning."

"And you think that Stan's death could have been connected to the poker game?"

"Maybe." Peg stopped and frowned. "No, strike that. More than maybe, I think there's a strong possibility. At least in a tangential way."

Rose laughed. "If you put any more qualifiers in that reply, you might as well just say no."

"I need you to understand that I'm only guessing."

"Fine by me," Rose replied. "We've been guessing about everything else all along. So what's the tangential connection?"

"The most recent poker game took place ten days ago. It was held at Stan's house. And at one point during the evening, he and Jerry got into an argument."

"Over what?"

"That's just it," Peg said. "Bennett didn't know. He made sure to tell me that plenty of alcohol is served at these poker games, and that things tend to get rowdy as time goes on. Apparently it's not unusual for the guys to be arguing about all sorts of things by the end of the night."

"So what made that particular disagreement stand out in his mind?"

"Two things. First, that it was only between Stan and Jerry. And second, that it didn't happen over the poker table where everyone else could jump in and take sides. Jerry left the room, and when he came back, he seemed to notice something on a shelf. He called Stan over and that's when they began to quarrel."

"You know what my next question has to be," said Rose. "What did Jerry see that set him off?"

"Bennett had no idea. Nor did he care. He was much more interested in getting back to his poker game."

"What kinds of things would a man be likely to have on his shelves?" Rose mused. "Books, maybe? Some kind of plaque or commendation from work? Possibly photographs or souvenirs from places he'd been?"

"It could have been any of those things," Peg said unhappily. "The person who could answer that question is Detective Sturgill. I'm sure he's been inside Stan's home."

"And he's the one person we can't ask."

Peg nodded. They were in complete agreement about that.

"What happened after Stan and Jerry had words?" Rose asked. "Did they both go back and sit down at the poker table again?"

"Stan did. Jerry didn't. He left."

"The implication being that he was too angry or upset to hang around?"

"Maybe. Bennett was also open to the possibility that Jerry didn't feel well."

"He could have been right," Rose pointed out. She hated setting aside the only clue they might have. "That poker game took place before last week's bridge club meeting. Stan and Jerry both attended, and there didn't appear to be any acrimony between them then."

Peg thought back. "As I recall, Mae and Jerry were among the stragglers that day. So they missed most of the pregame chitchat. Maybe that was on purpose. Then the Watkins played their first rubber with Sue and Bennett."

"For the second rubber, Stan and Mick were with us," Rose mused. "I didn't notice anything amiss."

"I didn't either," Peg replied. "But that doesn't mean much. I hardly had a chance. Mick was throwing down cards at lightning speed. I was more worried about playing the wrong suit than I was about watching Stan."

"So whether by accident or design, Jerry and Stan didn't really have an opportunity to interact during the meeting," Rose summed up.

Peg got up and walked a small circle around the yard. There wasn't much to see, but she was hoping that the movement would get her brain in gear.

"Don't step on my tomatoes," Rose told her.

Peg sniffed. "Only an optimist would call those scraggly shoots tomatoes. They look as though they're a very long way from bearing fruit."

"You'll see." Rose was complacent. Having Ivy as a secret weapon had given her a boost of confidence. Especially since Ivy had reassured her that the plants were progressing nicely.

"Your mention of photographs a moment ago reminded me of something." Peg stepped carefully around the two cultivated rows and returned to her seat. "Weren't Jerry and Stan two of the men who had known each other since high school?"

"Yes, and Reggie was the third. Jerry mentioned that when I was having lunch with him and Mae. He said that he and Reg were the same year and Stan was a year behind them."

"That shoots my theory then. I was thinking maybe what Jerry saw was something like a class photo."

Rose felt a quiver of excitement. "You may be on to something. Because it could have been a team photo. Jerry told me they all played high school sports together—" Abruptly she stopped speaking.

"What?"

"I just remembered something else Jerry said. When I asked him about Stan, he said that they'd lost touch after high school until the bridge club brought them back together."

"So?" Peg asked.

"He also told me that outside the bridge club, he never spent any time with Stan because the two of them didn't have anything in common."

"That's not right." Peg realized what Rose was getting at. "Bennett said both those men were regulars at the poker games. I'm sure he wouldn't be mistaken about that. He strikes me as the kind of man who counts his winnings before he even sits down at the table."

"So Jerry was lying to me," said Rose.

"It certainly appears that way."

"Why would he lie about that?"

"Maybe he's hiding something." Peg liked that idea. "Some connection to Stan he doesn't want anyone to know about."

"But that's just it," Rose frowned. "The other club members already know about the guys' poker night. We're the only ones who didn't."

"Us—and possibly the police. Maybe what the other members know doesn't matter to Jerry, because they're not the ones who are trying to put clues together and come up with an answer."

"My head hurts," said Rose.

"Literally or figuratively?"

"Both. I've probably been thinking too hard. But at least it looks like we're finally getting somewhere. What's our next step?"

Peg stood up again. Now that things were falling into place, she was filled with a sense of urgency. And she wanted to be moving.

"We can't afford to lose any more time," she said. "We need to get someone else who was at that poker game to tell us what they saw."

"Good luck with that," Rose grumbled. "We've already bothered everyone else. I'm sure they're not eager to talk to us again."

"I never spoke with Reggie Greene," Peg commented. "When Paige came to my house, she was alone. She was so excited about the prospect of getting the listing, she wasn't about to let poor Reg get in the way. I think she would have dumped him by the side of the road if he'd tried to come along."

"You're sure he was there that night?"

"No, but I can check." Peg took out her phone and sent Bennett a text. A reply came right back. "Reggie was there," she said with satisfaction. "Now all we have to do is convince him to talk to us. That's your job."

"Why me?" asked Rose.

"Because I'm the intimidating one. You said

so yourself. Reggie probably gets enough of that kind of treatment from his wife. Having the opportunity to talk to a sweet, unassuming woman like you will come as a relief."

Rose laughed. "You think I'm sweet?"

"Not really. But I'm pretty sure you can fake it better than I can."

Rose stood up and walked away to make the call. Peg glared after her. She'd wanted to listen to Rose be persuasive. Maybe she could pick up a few pointers. Now that wasn't going to happen.

Two minutes later, Rose was back. "Paige is at work, but Reggie is home. He said he'd be happy to talk to us."

"Great," Peg replied. "When?"

"Now." Rose was already heading toward the side of the house.

Peg jogged to catch up. *"Now?"*

"Well, as soon as we can get there. The Greenes live in Belle Haven. I told him fifteen minutes."

"Fifteen minutes?" Peg was beginning to sound like an echo.

Rose spun around and propped her hands on her hips. "Weren't you the one who just said that we didn't have time to lose?"

"That does sound like me," Peg conceded.

"Well, this is me not wasting time," Rose snapped. "Now hurry up. We need to get moving."

Chapter 27

Peg had no idea Rose could run that fast. But there she was outsprinting Peg to the front of the Gallagher House where both their vehicles were parked. Those skinny legs of hers could really move when they needed to.

"Hop in," said Peg, stopping beside her minivan. "I'll drive."

Belle Haven was a residential neighborhood on the south side of Greenwich. It was only a short trip—back the way she'd just come—on the Connecticut Turnpike. Rose drove like somebody's ancient granny, or perhaps like an ex-nun. If Peg was behind the wheel, she figured she could cut their drive time in half.

In moments, they were on their way.

"Goodness!" Rose's hands clutched the door handle as the minivan shot up the on ramp to the turnpike. "I know I told you to hurry, but haste won't help if we don't arrive in one piece."

"No worries on that score." Peg cast a quick glance back, then merged into traffic. "I'm a great driver."

The horns that were blaring behind them seemed to offer a different opinion. Rose deliberately kept her gaze trained forward. Whatever was going on back there, she didn't want to know. At least the road in front of them was clear.

The Greenes' home was a cream-colored mansion with a mansard roof, a porte cochere, and a three car garage. It wasn't right beside the water, but Peg was willing to bet that the upper floor offered an unobstructed view of Long Island Sound. She parked the minivan on one side of the circular driveway.

"Wow." Rose's gaze went up, and then around, as she got out of the vehicle. "This place is amazing. I had no idea Paige was doing this well selling real estate. Maybe you should let her sell your house. You could probably make a small fortune."

"I don't want a small fortune," Peg replied. "I just want to continue living in the home I shared with Max. Is that too much to ask?"

Rose felt a pang, as she was sure she was meant to. Chastened, she shook her head.

Peg was already moving past her toward the front steps. "Quit gawking and come on. Reggie should be waiting for us."

When Peg rang the bell, Reggie answered the door himself. Though not particularly handsome, Reg had even features and warm brown eyes. His body, dressed in crisp khakis and a polo shirt with an upturned collar, was trim and fit for his age. He greeted them with a welcoming smile.

"Rose said you needed to ask me something important with regard to Stan's death," he said.

"I'm not sure I'll be able to help, but I'm happy to try. We can talk in my study."

Reggie led Peg and Rose down a wide center hallway with a marble floor. As they passed a pair of double doors that opened into a sumptuous living room, Rose stopped and stared. Peg had to poke her in the side to get her moving again. Reggie must have been accustomed to that kind of reaction. He paid no attention to their momentary lapse in manners.

His study was a cozy room with wood paneling and burgundy leather furniture. There was a scrollwork patterned rug on the floor. Prints of schooners sailing on open water covered the walls. Reggie sat down in a well-padded armchair and waved Peg and Rose to the matching couch.

"I've heard you two have become the modern day Hardy Boys of our little bridge club," he said. "Everyone is buzzing about it. To tell the truth, I'm quite put out that it took you so long to get around to me."

"There was certainly no slight intended," Peg told him with a coy tilt of her head. "We were saving the best until last."

Rose snorted under her breath. She was tempted to return the poke she'd just received. Except to her surprise, Peg's flirty manner seemed to be having the desired effect. Reggie treated them both to a wide smile.

"I'm happy to be of assistance," he said. "Stan

was a lifelong friend. His death has been a devastating blow."

"I understand that you, Jerry, and Stan had all known each other since high school," Rose said.

"That's correct."

"So you must have also known Stan's wife, Bethany?"

"We'd met on occasion, but I wouldn't say I knew her well," Reggie replied. "As you probably know, Bethany died a long time ago."

Peg and Rose both nodded.

"It was a real shame what happened. Her loss really hit Stan hard. He and I were golfing buddies and I think that helped. Getting out on the course gave him a way to fill the empty hours outside of work."

"Bennett told me that he and Stan also played golf together," Peg said. "Were you all part of the same group?"

"No. Stan and I usually played at Lakeview. Bennett isn't a club member." Reggie sat back in the cushy chair and crossed his legs. He wasn't wearing socks. "I imagine he and Stan got together at a public course. Not that there's anything wrong with that, of course. Variety is the spice of life, as they say."

"Indeed," Peg murmured.

"Are Jerry and Mae members of your country club?" Rose inquired.

"They used to be, once upon a time. But then

Jerry let their membership lapse. He said he'd decided that country clubs were elitist, but frankly I think it had more to do with the fact that he was looking at the cost of four college tuitions for those kids of his. That has to be enough to give anyone sticker shock."

"Jerry does join you at the Friday-night poker games, however," Peg commented.

"Oh yeah, sure." Reggie nodded. "Jerry'd never give that up. Nor would I. After you've been married awhile, it's nice to have an excuse to get out of the house and hang with the guys."

Rose looked as though she wanted to say something uncomplimentary. Instead she flattened her lips and kept quiet about that remark. Peg did too. They didn't have to agree with Reggie's views on married life. They just needed to keep him talking.

"We heard there was an incident at the last poker game," Peg said. "Could you give us your impression of what happened?"

"An incident?" Reggie's look of confusion wasn't entirely convincing. "I'm afraid I don't know what you're talking about."

"We were told that Stan and Jerry got into an argument," Rose said.

"Oh, that." Reg dismissed the comment. "It was nothing."

"We also heard that Jerry left Stan's house right after it happened," Peg added.

"Yeah, I guess he did."

"Do you know what they were fighting about?"

"It wasn't a fight," Reggie corrected. "More like a heated conversation. And trust me, that's not the first time something like that has happened. In fact, it's pretty normal. The rest of us were at the poker table halfway across the room. We hardly took any notice. I don't think anyone heard what was being said."

"I was told it had to do with something Jerry saw. Possibly something on a shelf," Peg prodded. "And that Jerry called Stan over to ask him about it. Did you happen to see what it was?"

Ten minutes earlier, Reggie had been offering to help. Now he was squirming in his seat. He closed his eyes briefly. Peg wondered if he was hoping she and Rose would disappear while he wasn't looking.

"Here's the thing," Reggie said, sounding pained. "I can't go against the bro code."

Peg glared at him. "Surely you're not serious. The bro code, indeed. That's an excuse for teenagers to use, not grown men. You just told us that Stan was a lifelong friend. You offered to be of assistance. And now you find yourself unable to answer a simple question?"

"Umm . . ." Reggie's shoulders slumped. His gaze went to the door as if he was looking for a means of escape.

Peg wasn't having that. She'd get up and bar

the door if she had to. "Yes?" she prompted.

"It's not about me. It's Paige. She told me to stay out of this. She's concerned that even the perception that she and I are involved in a murder investigation could be bad for her business."

Peg sat up and squared her shoulders. The more Reggie shrank down into his seat, the larger she became. Peg had meant it when she'd told Rose that some people deserved to be intimidated. And apparently Reggie was one such person.

"Would you rather answer our questions?" she inquired crisply. "Or would you prefer to be interviewed by the police? Detective Sturgill and I are old friends. I'd be happy to call him and ask him to drop by."

"Don't do that," Reggie sputtered. "That's a terrible idea."

"Then you need to help us. Something Jerry saw in Stan's home led to their argument. I'm guessing you know what it was. A book? A photograph? Perhaps a school picture?"

Reggie grimaced. He was clearly irritated and he took his time before answering. "You're right," he said finally. "It was a picture. A small one in a silver frame. The two of them were acting so squirrelly that I got curious. So later when I was leaving, I took a look. Information is always a useful thing to have. I'd imagine that's something you understand yourself."

Peg ignored the dig. And besides, he was right.

"Tell me what you saw. What was in the picture?"

"That's the weird part. It wasn't anything special. Just a photo of some kid. A teenage boy on a beach. He looked a little familiar to me, but I had no idea why. I thought maybe it was Stan when he was a kid."

Reggie had known Stan when he was a teenage boy. Presumably he would know what Stan looked like then. Peg didn't bother to point that out.

"What else?" she said.

"What do you mean?"

"So far, you haven't given me anything that explains why two men would have gotten into a heated discussion over it. Besides the teenage boy, what else was there to see?"

"That's what I'm trying to tell you. Nothing. It was just some dumb vacation shot. Blue sky above, blue water behind. With a kid standing front and center."

"That doesn't help," Peg snapped.

"What do you expect me to do about that?" Reggie whined. "I told you in the beginning that I didn't know anything. It's not my fault that I was right."

Peg wanted to argue with him. She would have, too, except that Rose reached over and laid a quelling hand on her arm. Peg was tempted to push it away, but she suspected Rose had a point. They'd probably already learned everything from Reggie that they were going to.

"Thank you for your time," Rose said. She stood up to leave. "You've been a big help."

Peg growled under her breath. In what world had Reggie been a big help? Certainly not Peg's.

Nevertheless, she got to her feet too. It was either that or take the chance that Rose might attempt to drag her from the room. As if she could have made *that* happen.

"It's been lovely talking to you," Peg said. "You and Paige have a beautiful home."

Rose tore a piece of paper off a small pad on the desk. She wrote down her phone number and handed it to Reggie. "Peg and I are working closely with the police. We know you want to do everything you can to help bring Stan's murderer to justice. If you think of anything else to tell us, please don't hesitate to call me."

Rose and Peg made it out the door, across the driveway, and into the minivan before Peg began to laugh. *" 'Peg and I are working closely with the police'?"* she mimicked. "Where did that come from?"

"You should talk," Rose retorted. *" 'It's been lovely talking to you. You and Paige have a beautiful home.' "*

Peg turned the key in the ignition. "I may have been laying it on a little thick, but at least I was telling the truth."

"So was I. After a fashion, anyway. You did some good work in there. I'd just about given up on getting anything useful out of Reggie. Then you turned into Scary Peg and suddenly he was blurting out everything he knew."

The first time Rose had called her that, Peg had been offended. Now she just smiled. "I have to admit it felt kind of good."

"I should hope so. You were most impressive. I should start taking notes so I can figure out how to do that myself."

Peg slanted Rose a look. "Please don't. I'd hate to think that I was becoming a bad influence on you."

"You're the worst," Rose agreed. She didn't seem perturbed by that in the slightest. "I can't remember the last time I had this much fun."

Chapter 28

Peg stopped the minivan at the end of the Greenes' driveway and looked both ways. "Now where are we going?"

Rose didn't even hesitate. "Port Chester."

"Mick?" Peg guessed.

"Right. He wasn't just Stan's bridge partner, he was also one of his best friends. And he's likely to have been at Stan's house that night. Let's go see what he has to say about that photograph."

This time, when Peg parked in front of the garage at Doran's Auto Works, two of the bays were in use. A shiny yellow sports car was up on a lift in one. A silver Audi was parked with its hood in the air in the other. Mick was standing beside the car, leaning down into it. It looked like he was making an adjustment to the engine.

"Just the man we wanted to see," Rose said. "That's handy."

As they approached, Mick glanced up, then abruptly straightened. He was holding a wrench in one hand and had a grimy rag in the other. His sneakers lacked shoelaces and there was a grease stain on the front of his T-shirt. Mick didn't look pleased to see them.

"You know I'm trying to run a business here, right?" he said.

"We only need five minutes of your time." Peg glanced at the mechanic working in the adjacent bay. "Privately?"

Mick scowled. He set down the wrench and dropped the rag on top of it. "I guess we can talk in the office. You've got five minutes. That's all I can spare."

Peg and Rose followed him around the corner into the cluttered room. As they entered, Mick reached up and turned on a table fan that was sitting atop a file cabinet. The small breeze made the papers on his desk flutter.

"Air conditioner broke," he said. "Fan'll have to do."

There was a chair behind the desk, and another one in front of it. Mick ignored both seats, so Peg and Rose remained standing too. Apparently they weren't going to be staying long.

Mick crossed his arms over his chest. "What's this about?"

"We have a couple more questions for you," Peg said.

"*For* me?" He grunted. "Like you're doing me a favor? Seems to me that I answered enough questions the first time you came by."

"We're grateful for your previous help," Rose said. "But now Peg and I think you may have additional information that will point to why Stan was killed. I'm sure you'd like to see the person who's responsible brought to justice."

"Justice won't bring Stan back," Mick said. "And I already told Peg everything I know. Which, with regard to his death, is basically nothing."

"This is about the poker game you attended the Friday before last," she told him. "It took place at Stan's house."

"Yeah. So what?"

"We heard that Stan and Jerry Watkins got into an altercation at the end of the evening."

"Altercation." Mick snorted. "That's too big a word for what actually happened. Just a couple of guys raising their voices and shoving each other around for a minute. When guys get together to play cards and bet money, sometimes tempers fray. It's nothing we haven't seen before."

"Yes, but this time one of those guys was shot dead four days later." Peg's voice sharpened. "I'd imagine that's something you haven't seen before."

"Again," Mick growled, "I don't know anything about that."

Rose stepped forward. "We just want to ask you about a photograph Stan had at his house."

"A photograph?" Mick repeated incredulously. "You're kidding, right?"

"No, Mick, we are not kidding." Peg was losing her patience. "This is serious business. Someone took two shots at me yesterday afternoon. I hope it wasn't you."

"Hell, no." His face blanched. "It wasn't me. Is that the truth?"

Rose and Peg both nodded.

"Damn," Mick swore.

"My thoughts exactly," Peg said. "That's why we're hoping you'll be willing to help us."

"I would if I could. But I have no idea what you're talking about. I don't know anything about a picture."

"There was something on one of Stan's shelves that served as a catalyst for the argument between him and Jerry. We were told it was a photograph."

Mick just shrugged.

Peg tried again. "You said a few minutes ago that their voices were raised. Could you hear anything that was being said?"

"No, not then. We weren't close enough for that. And besides," he added, "it wasn't as if we were listening. The rest of us were just waiting for things to calm down so we could get back to playing cards."

"Stan returned to the table," Rose said. "But Jerry cashed in his chips and left."

"That sounds right—" Mick began.

Peg interrupted him. "Wait a minute. What did you mean when you just said, 'No, not then.' Did you hear something about the dispute at another time?"

"Maybe. I guess so. But it didn't have anything to do with that picture you're asking about."

Peg and Rose shared a look. They waited for him to continue.

"A couple minutes later, play still wasn't happening because Bennett was the bank and now he was busy dealing with Jerry. So the rest of us are still sitting around. Stan's chair was next to mine. He came back to the table and he had this smirk on his face. Like whatever had gone on between the two of them, Stan figured he'd come out on top. And Stan was a guy who liked to win."

Peg nodded. She'd heard that before.

"Anyway, as Stan sits down, he looks over at me and says under his breath, 'It serves him right.' "

"Serves who right?" Rose asked. "Jerry?"

"I assumed that was who he was talking about."

"Did you know what Stan meant when he said that?"

"I figured I could take a pretty good guess."

Peg waved a hand impatiently, prodding him to keep talking.

"Years ago, Stan got involved in a business deal Jerry was putting together. Jerry had pitched it to him as a 'sure thing.' This was back when Stan was married to Bethany. They wanted kids, but they'd run into problems. The next step they needed to take was major league expensive. So Stan figured he could raise some quick cash by going in on Jerry's deal. He was hoping to surprise Bethany with it."

"But that didn't happen," Rose said.

"No, it didn't." Mick shook his head. "Not even close. Jerry's sure thing went belly-up and Stan lost all the money he'd invested. He had to confess what he'd done to Bethany and they got into a big fight about it. She got mad and ran out of the house."

Mick paused and swallowed heavily as if he didn't want to finish telling the story. Rose couldn't blame him. She knew what had to be coming next.

"Bethany never came back," he said after a pause. "That was the night she died."

Rose sighed on an exhale and remained silent. Each time she heard the story it felt like a gut punch.

Peg, however, still had questions. "Did Stan blame Jerry for what happened?"

"On some level, sure," Mick replied. "I think he had to."

"And yet they remained friends," Peg said. "Or at least friendly enough to play cards together."

Mick shrugged. "I didn't understand it either. But Stan was the kind of guy who kept his own counsel. He only told people as much as he wanted them to know. There were some things you just couldn't ask about."

"Did you tell the police that story?" Peg wanted to know.

"No. It never even occurred to me to mention it.

The whole thing was over and done with nearly twenty years ago. So it's not just old news, it's like ancient."

"Maybe not," Peg muttered.

"Besides," Mick continued, "Stan was the one who lost out on that deal. So if someone was going to get killed over it, I'd have figured it would be Jerry. You know?"

"I agree with you," Rose said when they were back in the minivan. "Mick's story may be old news, but I'm willing to bet those events had some bearing on what happened last week."

"Where to next?" Peg asked. She was driving, but Rose had come up with a couple of good ideas. Peg was hoping she might have another.

Rose considered for a minute, then said, "Riverside."

Peg glanced at her across the seat. "Who's in Riverside?"

"Carrie. She's another member of our little group who knew him better than most."

"The torrid affair?" Peg cocked a brow.

"Precisely." Rose settled back in her seat.

It occurred to Peg that Rose might be shocked right down to her toes to learn how many women in the bridge club had known Stan *better than most,* to use her parlance. She'd mentioned those group shenanigans earlier, but apparently Rose had put them out of her mind. If that was the case, Peg wasn't about to remind her.

While Peg drove, Rose texted back and forth with Carrie. "She's home," Rose said after she received the first reply. "She's expecting us," she said after the second.

"Stop right there," said Peg. "Don't tell Carrie why we're coming over. I'd rather be able to watch her reactions when we ask our questions."

"Good luck with that. It's not as if Carrie doesn't know what we're up to. Our amateur investigation isn't a secret from anyone anymore. She's probably already rehearsing her answers."

"I doubt that." Peg flashed a cheeky grin. "After all, she has no idea what we're going to ask."

Carrie's gray and white cat was lying in her front yard when Peg and Rose drove up. "That's Stella," Rose said as they got out of the minivan.

Peg walked over to where the cat was stretched out on a patch of sunny lawn. "Hello, Stella."

The cat opened her eyes and looked at Peg dismissively. Her tail flicked up and down. Then she turned her head away and went back to sleep.

"I don't understand cats," Peg said.

Rose was a few feet away, already knocking on Carrie's front door. "That's all right. I don't understand dogs."

"If I greeted a dog, it would at least have the courtesy to sit up and acknowledge me."

The door opened. Carrie looked at the two women. "Who are you talking to?" she asked Peg.

"Stella. But it appears to be a one-sided conversation."

Carrie shrugged. "That's because she doesn't know you."

"That's because Stella doesn't *want* to know me."

"That's hardly her fault," Carrie said. "You interrupted her nap."

"Peg talks to dogs," Rose explained. "And when she does, they answer back."

"You're a dog whisperer." Carrie sounded pleased. "I've never met one before. You should try whispering to Stella."

"I tried," Peg said. "But apparently I'm dog specific. May we come in?"

"Of course." Carrie stepped back out of the doorway. Rose and Peg followed her inside. They all found seats in Carrie's cozy living room. "Rose said there was something you wanted to talk to me about. I'm assuming that means Stan."

"Yes," Rose said. "During the course of your relationship with him, did you ever visit his house?"

"Of course. He lived in a cute little ranch near Bulls Head. Not much space, but then he didn't need much. Bachelor quarters. You know what that's like."

"Peg and I were wondering if you might have

noticed a photograph of a teenage boy that was on a shelf in his living room."

Carrie snorted out a laugh. "That's a stretch. A massive one. I haven't been in Stan's house in close to ten years. There may have been pictures in his living room, but I never paid any attention to them. When Stan and I were together, I had much better things to do than admire his decor."

"Oh." Rose could feel her cheeks heating with a blush. "Of course."

"Besides," Carrie added, "if the photograph you're talking about is current now, ten years ago that teenage boy would have been in grade school."

"Right again," Peg conceded unhappily.

Carrie leaned forward in her seat. "Why are you so interested in that photograph?"

"We think it caused an argument between Stan and Jerry Watkins a few days before Stan died."

"That's odd," Carrie said.

"We think so, too."

"Stan had always wanted kids," Carrie mused. "I suppose he might have had a picture of someone else's child." She paused and thought some more. "Although . . ."

Carrie's voice trailed away. Rose and Peg sat and waited. They didn't want to interrupt her train of thought.

"Although?" Peg prompted after a minute had passed.

"There was this one time . . ."

Peg frowned when Carrie stopped speaking again. Rose kicked Peg in the ankle, a warning to control her impatience. Rose knew enough about counseling from Peter to realize that they would learn more by letting Carrie proceed at her own pace.

"It probably doesn't mean anything," Carrie said slowly.

"Go on," Peg prompted. Rose ground her teeth.

"It was just a comment Stan made once. There was a soccer match on TV, and he mentioned that he'd recently watched a local school game. He thought it was funny that the parents were so intense, like they all thought their little kids were going to grow up to be the next Pelé."

Carrie shrugged. "I thought we were just making conversation, so I said something like, 'What were you doing at a school game? Did a friend of yours have a child playing?' And suddenly Stan just froze. It was really weird. Then he changed the subject so fast it made my head spin."

Rose leaned forward in her seat. "What did you make of that?"

Carrie looked bemused. "I haven't thought about that day in years. But now, thinking back, I remember at the time the way he acted made me wonder."

"Wonder what?" asked Peg.

"Whether when Stan couldn't have a baby with Bethany, he'd had one with someone else."

"That was interesting," Peg said when she and Rose were on their way back to the Gallagher House. "Do you think Carrie could be right?"

"I don't know," Rose replied. "Obviously Carrie was there with Stan and we weren't. But her conclusion sounded far-fetched to me. And suppose Stan did have a child outside his marriage. How would that be connected to his death?"

Peg apparently didn't have an answer for that either. "We'll think about that overnight," she said. "Then tomorrow we'll touch base and see what brilliant ideas each of us has come up with."

Rose didn't expect to be having any ideas overnight, much less brilliant ones. But since she had nothing useful to add now, she was more than willing to table the discussion.

Peg dropped Rose off in front of the Gallagher House. Peter was inside.

While she'd been away, he'd decided to do something about the fact that the shelter's dining room needed a fresh coat of paint. Rose walked in to find him up on a ladder, scraping away a section of blistered paint above a window.

"Mauve," Peter said, glancing down at her. "Why would anyone think that was a good shade for a dining room? It's a depressing color. More like to put you off your food than make you want to eat."

"Beatrice Gallagher was full of curious notions," Rose replied with a smile. Seeing Peter always lightened her mood. "And since one of them involved turning this house into a women's shelter, I'm not inclined to complain."

"I'm not complaining either. Just stating a personal preference." He nodded toward two cans of cream colored paint on a nearby drop cloth. "In two days this room will look entirely different. Did you have a good time with Peg?"

"I had an interesting time with Peg."

"Nothing new about that." Peter climbed down off the ladder. Rose had been keeping him apprised of everything that had happened over the past week. So for the sake of his wife's safety, he knew which questions needed to be asked. "I hope there were no more shots fired?"

"Thankfully, no," Rose reassured him. "From that perspective, everything was quiet."

"And from other perspectives?"

"It feels as though Peg and I turned up more new questions than we did answers."

"That's good," Peter said.

She looked at him in surprise. "It is?"

"Of course. It means you're broadening the scope of your thinking. Ideas you hadn't previously considered are now part of the conversation. New questions present the possibility of new answers."

"I thought the whole point was to narrow things down," Rose grumbled.

"That part will come."

"Will it?" Rose wasn't so sure.

"Of course. You and Peg are both intelligent, motivated women. Plus, you have the tenacious Detective Sturgill on your side. After you've explored all possible options, one of you is bound to come up with the winning theory."

He made it sound so easy. Rose hoped Peter was right.

That night after dinner, her phone rang. The screen identified Reggie Greene as the caller. *Reggie Greene?* What could he possibly want?

"Hello?" Rose knew she sounded uncertain.

"Rose, this is Reg." He, on the other hand, sounded very sure of himself.

"Yes, Reg. How are you?"

"I'm fine, thanks for asking. Something occurred to me after you and Peg left earlier. I had to do a little digging around to make sure I was right. But you told me to call if I thought of anything?"

"Yes, of course," Rose agreed, her voice stronger now. "Thank you for getting back to me."

"You know how I said that the kid in that picture looked familiar, but I didn't know why? I figured it out."

"That's great," Rose said. "Who was it?"

"Jerry and Mae have a son, J.J. Jerry thinks the sun rises and sets on that boy. The kid's in college now, but Jerry got the idea that Paige could pull some strings and get him a cushy summer job in town."

Rose nodded. She'd heard a similar story from John and Violet.

"Jerry gave Paige a copy of J.J.'s résumé. As if a kid has done enough stuff to even need such a thing," Reg added mockingly. "Anyway, the résumé had his picture attached. It was the same boy."

It took a moment for Rose to absorb that information. And its possible ramifications. Maybe it meant nothing. Stan and Jerry were friends, after all, and plenty of people had told her how much Stan liked children. Or maybe it meant everything—and provided Rose and Peg with the key to Stan's death.

"Just to be clear," Rose said slowly. "The boy in the photo you saw at Stan's house and the picture of Jerry's son on the résumé were the same person?"

"Correct," Reg said. "Does that help?"

"It does indeed," she assured him. "You've been a big help. Thank you for letting me know."

Rose disconnected the call with Reggie and immediately dialed again.

"Grab a chair and sit down," she said breathlessly to Peg. "You'll never guess what just happened."

Chapter 29

Peg awoke the next morning to a ringing phone. The device was on her bedside table. With one eye open, she maneuvered around Hope and Coral to reach it. As her fingers closed around the phone, she recalled her conversation with Rose the night before. Suddenly Peg was wide awake.

Perhaps this was another fresh and illuminating insight from Rose. Against all odds, the woman was proving to be an unexpectedly useful partner. That was high praise coming from Peg. Useful people were her favorite kind.

She picked up the phone and slid her thumb up the screen.

"This is Franny Grover and you have my dog," her caller announced. "It's been three whole days. How is Essie doing?"

"Good morning, Franny." Peg braced a pillow against the headboard, then pulled herself up so she was leaning against it. That meant Hope had to rearrange herself so the length of her body was still pressed against Peg. "Essie is doing very well. She's relaxed and happy, and she's interacting with me and my other Poodles. Last night she had a bath and a little grooming session."

"I hope you didn't cut off all her hair!"

"No, I just did some gentle trimming. Now you can see her pretty face."

"That's just what I want to do, see her pretty face," Franny said firmly. "You said I could come and visit."

"Of course you can." Peg reached down and ran her fingers through Hope's topknot. The big Poodle stretched out her legs and leaned into the caress. "Whenever you like."

"This morning suits me. That's why I'm calling. I know you said you'd take good care of her. But I want to see for myself that Essie is all right."

"Then you should come," said Peg. "Essie and I will be waiting for you. Will Florence be with you?"

"No, it's just me. Contrary to what everybody thinks, my sister and I don't go everywhere together. We're not joined at the hip, you know."

"Of course not," Peg agreed. "Shall we say ten o'clock?"

"Make it nine," Franny replied. "At my age, I don't sleep much. I've already been up for hours. You're lucky I'm not standing on your doorstep already."

Peg ended the call, then glanced at her bedside clock. It was just after seven. Rose had a husband and a job. She was probably awake.

"Are you busy this morning?" she asked when Rose picked up.

"When this morning?"

"Nine o'clock."

Rose laughed. "You work fast. Where are we going now?"

"I'm not going anywhere," Peg said. "Franny Grover is coming here. She wants to visit Essie and see how's she's doing."

"Who's Essie?"

"The little brown Poodle you met on Sunday."

"If you say so."

Peg could picture Rose shrugging, as if the small dog was the farthest thing from her mind. Which she probably was.

"This will be a great opportunity to pick Franny's brain," Peg said. "Maybe she has something to add to what we've already learned. You and I made a pretty good team yesterday. I figured you wouldn't want to miss this."

"We do make a good team." Rose sounded pleased. "I'll be at your house by nine."

As soon as Peg put down the phone, all four Poodles jumped to their feet. First thing in the morning, they knew it was time for a trip outside. Joker, Hope, and Coral had been sprawled across the covers on Peg's bed. Essie was safe inside a crate on the floor.

Peg reached down and undid the latch. The little Poodle's tail was whipping back and forth. When the gate opened, she sprang out into Peg's arms.

"Yes, I know. Your bladder is smaller than theirs." Barefoot, dressed in her pajamas, Peg was already heading toward the bedroom door. "Don't worry, we're on our way. I'll have you outside in no time."

As she hurried down the hallway, Peg was struck by a sudden memory. On cold winter mornings, she and Max would play rock, scissors, paper to see which one of them had to get out of their warm bed to put the Poodles outside. Max had been adept at reading Peg's mind. He nearly always won.

She heaved a sigh as the big Poodles danced around her bare feet. Even after all these years, she could still be ambushed by unexpected images of her life with Max. Rather than being a source of comfort, the memories only renewed her sense of loss.

It was a good thing Franny and Rose were on their way over. That would give her something else to think about today.

Franny arrived at eight-thirty.

She was standing on Peg's porch, staring in the direction of the broken window when Peg opened the door. Wearing a bright yellow sundress and large sunflower earrings to match, Franny took a moment to turn her gaze back to Peg. Her eyes widened when she saw the three big black dogs crowding the doorway.

"Those aren't Poodles," she said. "They don't look anything like Esmeralda."

Having just been groomed, Essie looked a good deal more like Peg's Poodles than she had upon her arrival. Peg decided to let Franny discover that for herself.

"You're early," she said instead.

"I got impatient. So sue me." Franny strode past Peg into the house. "Florence figured you for some kind of miracle worker. I'm more of a skeptic. Essie's coming home with me today."

"That's up to you," Peg said mildly.

"You're darn right it is." Franny had stopped in the hallway. She didn't know which direction to go.

Peg pointed toward the kitchen. The three Poodles trotted down the hall ahead of them.

"Essie's in an exercise pen in my kitchen. I'm sure she'll be happy to see you."

"She never has been before," Franny muttered.

"Give her a chance," said Peg. "You may be pleasantly surprised."

"Give her a chance? What's that supposed to mean? I've given her plenty of chances."

"It means don't rush her. Essie's probably spent most of her life having things happen to her that she had no control over. So she learned to be defensive. Now we're letting her make some of her own decisions."

Franny glared at Peg. "By 'we,' you mean you."

"Yes, me." Peg paused in the doorway. "And you're in my house now, so you can follow my rules."

Essie had been lying in her bed. When the Standard Poodles preceded Peg and Franny into the room, she jumped up and raced to the side of the pen to touch noses with them. Her expression was bright and eager.

"That's different," Franny said.

"I should hope so," Peg replied. "That's the whole point. Take a seat on the floor."

Franny looked dubious. "In my dress?"

"Yes, in your dress. The floor's clean. But I can get you a towel to sit on if you like."

"No, I guess I'm all right." Gingerly Franny lowered herself down. "Don't let those big dogs trample me."

"I'll try not to." Peg smiled.

"That's not funny," Franny groused. "I'm old. For all you know, I might have brittle bones. At my age I have to be careful."

"That's why the big Poodles are going to lie down and we're going to let Essie come to you." Peg opened the door to the ex pen, then she sat down on the floor too.

"She looks funny," said Franny. "Although not as funny as that one." She flicked a hand in Joker's direction. "What's he got on his head, dreadlocks?"

"They're ponytails," Peg told her. "He's a

show dog. He needs his hair long for the ring. At home, I band it and wrap it to keep it out of his way. And Essie looks different because she was groomed."

"I can see her eyes now." Franny smiled as the little Poodle hopped out of the pen and started toward them. Essie's head and tail were both up. It was clear she recognized Franny. Even so, she held back for a few seconds.

Franny started to move toward the little dog. Peg put out a hand to hold her back. "Give Essie a minute. This is all new to her."

"I'm not new. She knows me."

"She knows you at your house. She doesn't know you here."

"That's the dumbest thing I ever heard."

Peg just shrugged. "Ignore her for a minute. Let's talk about something else."

"Okay." Franny's head swiveled around. Clearly she had an idea. She pointed at Peg's tarp-covered window. "What happened there?"

"Bullet holes," Peg said.

"Holy crap. Where'd they come from?"

"A gun presumably."

"Yeah, I got that part." Franny's gaze came back to Peg. "Were you here when someone shot up your house?"

"I was."

"You're lucky to be alive, then. Who did it?"

"I don't know. Neither do the police. If I had to

guess, I would say it was the same person who shot Stan."

"Because you've been too nosy," Franny said.

"That's a matter of opinion."

Essie had made her way over to Franny. Now she was sniffing the older woman's hand. If Franny continued to sit quietly, Peg was pretty sure the little Poodle would climb up in her lap. Luckily Franny was still distracted by her conversation with Peg.

"When did that happen?"

"Sunday afternoon," Peg said.

"Essie was here then."

"Yes, she was. Luckily both bullets were fired high in the air. None of the Poodles were hurt."

"But they could have been," Franny insisted. She seemed to be pondering something.

Peg was about to ask what when the doorbell rang. That was bad timing. Predictably, the three big Poodles jumped up and went racing out of the room.

"That must be Rose," Peg said.

"What's she doing here?"

"Visiting." Having just been called nosy, there seemed to be little point in telling the truth. "Rose is my sister-in-law."

"And your bridge partner."

Peg pushed herself up off the floor. No doubt about it, that used to be easier. "Yes, she's that, too."

"The two of you don't look like you have much in common."

Peg had been on her way out of the room. Now she stopped and looked back. "What makes you say that?"

"It's just an impression I got. Florence and I are like two peas in a pod. You and Rose are more like a tomato and a baseball bat."

Peg laughed in spite of herself. Franny was pretty perceptive. "I wouldn't be surprised if you feel the same way about Florence occasionally."

"Yeah, that's true." Franny grinned. "But luckily, the feeling passes."

"It took you long enough," Rose said when Peg opened the door.

The big Poodles were milling around their legs. Rose stepped carefully around them to come inside. Absently, she reached a hand down and gave Coral a pat. Peg noted the move but didn't comment. She'd make a dog lover out of Rose yet.

"I know Franny's already here. Her car's in the driveway," Rose said. "You said nine o'clock, didn't you? I hope I haven't missed anything."

"Franny was anxious to see Essie. She showed up early. And the only thing you've missed is her calling me nosy."

Rose laughed. "That's all right, then. Maybe she'll like me better. Most people do."

In the short amount of time since Peg had left the

kitchen, Franny had succeeded in coaxing Essie up into her lap. The Poodle was lying down across the woman's legs and Franny was stroking her back.

"That was well done," Peg said, pausing to take in the scene.

"She likes me," Franny said happily. "It's about time. Hello, Rose. I hope it's okay if I don't get up?"

"Perfectly," Rose replied. "You and Essie look very comfortable just as you are. It's nice to see you again."

"Is it?" Franny shifted slightly to face the kitchen table where Rose was taking a seat. "How come?"

"Because I suspect it will be some time until the bridge club gets going again, if indeed it ever does. Peg and I would be sorry to lose the connections we've made there."

"Maybe some of them." Franny looked skeptical. "But it seems like you and Peg have been pretty suspicious of the rest of us."

"Not you and Florence." Peg rejoined Franny on the floor.

"Oh yeah? Since when?"

"You'd hardly be likely to risk Essie's life by firing bullets into my house while she was here," Peg pointed out.

"You're right about that." Franny gazed down at the little Poodle. Essie's eyes were closed. She seemed to be taking a nap.

"Peg and I were hoping that you might be able to help us with some information," Rose said.

"Maybe," Franny allowed. Her attitude appeared to be softening. "About what?"

"A few days before Stan was killed, he hosted a poker game for the men in the bridge club."

"Stupid poker nights," Franny muttered. "No women allowed."

"Would you have played if they were?" Rose asked curiously.

"Of course. Me and Florence, both." Franny cackled. "We'd have fleeced those guys good."

"At one point during the evening, Jerry saw a photograph that belonged to Stan," Peg continued. "He called Stan over and they had angry words about it. The picture Jerry saw was of his son, J.J."

Peg had thought Franny might be surprised by the information. Instead she looked cagey. That told Peg pretty much everything she needed to know.

"So?" Franny demanded.

"We're wondering if you know why that picture was there."

"Why me?"

"It's like I said the last time we spoke. Older women are often overlooked. Even when they know more about what's going on than anyone else. I'm sure you talked to the police. Everyone in the bridge club did. But I'm also betting that you and Florence know more than you told them." Peg leveled a stern look her way. "Am I right?"

Franny hesitated before replying. "Could be you are."

"Will you tell us what we're missing?" Rose asked.

"Maybe you think I owe you, because of what you've done with Essie."

"No," said Peg. "I did that for her sake."

"Doesn't matter. That wouldn't have made a difference to me." Franny stared at the shattered kitchen window. "But that does."

Peg nodded. She felt the same way.

"Before someone took a shot at you, I'd have said that the secrets I've kept were none of your business. But now it looks as though this whole mess has become personal for you too."

"It has," Peg agreed. "Why don't you and I join Rose at the table? Essie can go back to her bed. Rose will make coffee, and I'll get out some cake. And when you're ready, you can tell us whose secrets you've been keeping."

"What kind of cake?"

"Double fudge," Peg told her.

"How big a slice am I getting?"

"As big as you want."

"It's a deal," Franny said.

Ten minutes later, the three women were seated around the butcher block table. Rose and Franny had coffee. Peg was drinking tea. A chocolate fudge cake was on the tabletop between them. Peg cut off three generous slabs, put them on plates and passed them around.

Rose accepted hers without an objection. Peg didn't say a word about that. She waited until Franny had taken four big bites before pressing her to speak.

"I'm getting around to it," Franny said. "Just give me a minute to prime the pump first."

Peg ate more of her cake. That wasn't a hardship. Even Rose was slipping tiny morsels into her mouth.

"Okay," Franny finally said when her cake was almost gone. "This is what we're going to do. I have a story to tell. But you ladies have been doing an awful lot of poking around. So rather than me repeating things you already know, I'm going to let you talk first. Afterward, maybe I can fill in a few gaps."

Peg and Rose both nodded. That sounded fair.

Rose began. "Stan and Jerry have known each other since they were in high school. Jerry calls himself an entrepreneur. He puts deals together and sometimes his friends get in on them. Mostly they make money, at least according to Jerry. But not always."

Peg took up the story from there. "Stan and his wife desperately wanted children, but she couldn't get pregnant. Stan took part in one of Jerry's business deals hoping to raise money for fertility treatments. Instead, he ended up losing the money they'd already set aside."

"You've heard how Bethany died?" Franny asked.

"Yes," Peg and Rose said together.

"Stan was a mess after that," Franny said. "It was like he'd lost everything in the world that mattered to him. Florence and I were worried about him. A lot of his friends were. Eventually some time passed, and things began to seem a little better."

"We know that part, too," Peg said impatiently.

"I figured as much, but I'm just setting the stage. If you don't like the way I'm telling things, I can stop right now."

Rose spoke up quickly before Peg had a chance. "The way you're telling it is perfect. Please ignore Peg and go on."

Unexpectedly Franny grinned. "I can't ignore Peg. She's the one with the cake."

Peg took that as her cue. She cut another slice and put it on Franny's plate. Franny nodded her approval before she resumed speaking.

"One day out of the blue, Mae Watkins came to see me. She said she had something private to discuss. She didn't even want Florence to know. I couldn't imagine what it was going to be about. Then she told me, and it was a doozy."

Peg started to say something. Rose quickly shushed her.

"Mae said she needed my help," Franny continued. "She was forty-five years old and pregnant. She was going to get an abortion, and she needed someone to accompany her to the clinic, then see that she got home safely. Mae had no one else to turn to. She said she hoped that a liberal old hippie like me would understand and support her decision."

"And did you?" Rose asked.

"It wasn't up to me to judge." Franny was firm about that. "But I did ask her if Jerry was aware of what she intended to do. Mae started to cry. Next thing I know, the whole story came pouring out."

"The child was Stan's, wasn't it?" Peg said.

"He was." Franny looked back and forth between them. "You two must be smarter than the rest of us thought. Mae and I have been keeping that secret for twenty years. If you'd have asked me two weeks ago, I'd have said that nobody but she and I were ever going to know about it."

"Did Stan seduce Mae to get back at Jerry?" Rose asked.

"Mae never said that in so many words." Franny dug into her new piece of cake happily. "But if I had to guess, I'd say that's the gist of it."

"Stan seemed like an unlikely Lothario," Peg mused.

Franny swallowed, then said, "Jerry and Mae's

marriage was already in trouble, so it didn't take much. Jerry cared more about his business than he did about his wife and daughters. When Stan started to pay attention to Mae, she was ripe for the picking. Mae said it had been a long time since a man had made her feel important. Stan gave her that."

"And then she got pregnant," Rose said.

Franny frowned. "I gather that was a complication that neither one of them had foreseen."

"So Stan knew about the baby?" Peg asked.

"Yes, Mae told him. And apparently he couldn't have been happier about that development. Mae didn't tell him about her abortion idea. He probably would have been horrified by that."

"But Mae obviously changed her mind," Rose pointed out.

"She did. Once Mae stopped and really thought about it, she decided she couldn't go through with her plan. In the end it turned out that all I had to do for her was lend moral support."

Franny paused for more cake, then added, "That, and congratulate Mae when she announced the pregnancy like it was the first time I was hearing about it. Then the baby came, and it was a boy. Right away, Jerry was crazy about him. The irony of the whole situation was, that baby boy saved Mae's marriage."

"I'm guessing Stan must have followed his son's upbringing from afar," Peg said.

Rose nodded. "And that would explain why he and Jerry continued to remain friends."

"Right on both counts," Franny said. "And Jerry was never the wiser."

"Until ten days ago," Peg pointed out.

"J.J. is in college now. Legally, he's an adult," Rose mused. "I wonder if Stan put that picture out on purpose. Maybe he decided it was time for him to have a more meaningful relationship with his son."

"That's not going to happen now," said Franny. "Someone made damn sure Stan would never have the chance."

Chapter 30

"Someone?" Rose said incredulously. Franny had finished her cake and left a few minutes earlier. "She must share the same suspicions we do."

"And yet she didn't mention them to the police," Peg replied. "Why do you suppose that is?"

She lifted Essie's plush bed out of the ex pen and put it down in a corner of the kitchen. Then she emptied out the small water bowl and gathered up the dog toys. After that, she folded up the ex pen and set it aside. Franny had been so impressed by Essie's improvement that she'd agreed to leave her dog with Peg until the end of the week. It was time for Essie to graduate to having the run of the house.

"Because until Franny heard what we know, she didn't have all the information," Rose pointed out. "She and Florence were never invited to the poker games. She wouldn't have known about the argument between Stan and Jerry. As far as she was concerned, the secret she'd been keeping for twenty years was still safe. She had no reason to break Mae's trust by revealing it to the police."

"She must know better now," said Peg. "I wonder what she'll do next."

Rose stood up. She gathered the empty cake

plates and carried them over to the sink. "I know what we're doing next. You need to call Detective Sturgill and tell him everything we've learned."

"Detective Sturgill doesn't want to hear from me. He couldn't have been more clear about that the last time we spoke."

Clearly Peg was still stinging from the rebuke she'd received on Sunday. Rose didn't care.

"That was two days ago. Everything's changed since then."

"We know that. But he doesn't."

"Which is precisely why you need to talk to him." Rose had been running warm water over the plates. Now she turned away from the sink and beckoned. "Give me your phone."

Peg plucked the device off the counter and handed it over. Rose scrolled through the contacts, then looked up. "You don't have his cell phone number?"

"Certainly not," said Peg.

"He's your friend. You call him Rodney."

Peg shrugged. "Apparently he and I aren't as close as you think. *You're* the one who got him over here the other day. It's more likely he'll listen to you than me."

Rose sincerely doubted that. But now she was annoyed.

"Well, he's going to have to listen to one of us," she said. "And if you're not going to call him, I will."

That turned out to be easier said than done. Rose input the number for the Stamford PD and was connected to the officer at the front desk. She asked to speak with Detective Sturgill, only to be told that he was unavailable.

"This is important," Rose said. "I have information regarding the murder of Stan Peters."

"Ma'am, you can leave that information on our Hot Tips hotline. If we have any questions, someone will get back to you."

"I would like a return call from Detective Sturgill," Rose said firmly. "My name is Rose Donovan. He'll know who I am. Yes, Rose. Like the flower."

Peg watched with some amusement while Rose spelled her name, then recited her phone number twice. She then asked the officer when the detective might become available. The man didn't have an answer for that either.

Rose disconnected the call, then smacked her phone down on the tabletop. It wasn't nearly as satisfying as slamming down a telephone receiver, but it was the closest she could get.

"Bureaucracy is a pain in the posterior," she said.

"I'd have said the same thing about Rodney the other day." Apparently, Peg wasn't going to let that go.

Rose smiled reluctantly. "I'd imagine he's sorry he lost his temper. But he thinks you gave him a reason to. He worries about you, Peg. And that isn't the worst thing."

"It isn't the best thing," Peg muttered.

"Either way, it doesn't matter now. We need Detective Sturgill. And although he doesn't realize it yet, he needs us too. I hate that there's nothing we can do now but sit around and wait."

"I share your frustration," Peg said. "You and I have done our part. We put together all the pieces and figured out who killed Stan. It has to have been Jerry, lashing out in anger after discovering that the son he adored wasn't really his."

Rose nodded in agreement.

"So now it's time for the big reveal. Rodney should be listening in amazement as we lay out all the clues, then telling us how brilliant we are. And instead . . ." Peg slashed a hand through the air. "*Pffft!* Nothing. I don't know where we went wrong. This never happens to Melanie."

"Maybe it does, and she just doesn't tell you."

"No, that's not possible," Peg said. "Melanie tells me everything."

Rose didn't believe that for a minute. If Melanie was apt to tell anyone everything it was probably her Standard Poodle, Faith.

"So now what do we do?" she asked.

"Let's take a walk."

Of all the ideas Rose might have come up with, that wasn't one of them. "Why would we want to do that?"

"For one thing, exercise is good for us. For another, until Rodney deigns to get back to us, we have nothing better to do." Peg was already heading for the back door. "Plus, the Poodles will love it."

"They're coming too?"

"Of course they're coming." Peg reached down and scooped up Essie. When she opened the door, the three big dogs went racing out into the yard. "They'll be leading the way."

"Fine." Rose sighed.

It didn't look as though she had a choice. It was a good thing she'd put on sneakers that morning. Peg's idea of a walk was probably more of a hike. At least she had her phone with her, so she'd be ready to answer when Detective Sturgill called back.

They were barely out the door and Peg was already setting a brisk pace. Coral, Hope, and Joker ran ahead toward a gate in the back of the fenced-in field. Peg had put Essie down in the grass. The two of them were striding after the Poodles.

Rose was bringing up the rear. Again.

"Where are we going?" she asked.

"The Greenwich riding trails run through all the properties in this area. The GRTA keeps them very well maintained, which makes them a marvelous place to walk."

"Riding trails." Rose stopped. "Like horses?"

"Yes, horses." Peg looked back at her. "There's nothing to worry about. They're usually very well behaved."

"Usually? What happens when they're not?"

"In that case, it's best if you stay out of the way."

Rose would be happy to stay out of the way. Right now, Peg's living room was sounding like the perfect place to do exactly that. Except that Peg was already unlatching the gate and drawing it open. The Poodles darted through the opening and took off running. Of course, Peg followed. Which meant Rose had to, too.

A hundred yards beyond the fence they picked up the riding trail. Rose was relieved to see that there wasn't a horse in sight. As she and Peg strolled along the manicured path, the Poodles raced circles around them. Joker led the way, chasing every rabbit or squirrel he could find.

Essie's shorter legs meant she had a hard time keeping up. After the first few minutes, Peg leaned down and picked her up. The little dog appeared to enjoy the view from Peg's arms as much as she'd relished running with the big dogs.

The trail wound around the fringes of a grassy meadow, and then through a patch of woods. The air was cooler there, and slightly damp. The loamy dirt felt like a cushion beneath Rose's feet. After walking in the summer sun, it was a relief to be shaded by the trees.

And still, Rose's phone didn't ring.

"Cut that out," Peg said when Rose pulled out the device and looked at its empty screen for the third time. "Staring at it won't make it ring."

"I can't help it. What's taking Detective Sturgill so long to call back?"

"Maybe he's busy."

"Maybe he didn't get my message."

"Maybe he got the message and he doesn't want to talk to you," Peg retorted.

"You're the one he doesn't want to talk to," Rose said. "Maybe he's hoping someone shot at you again."

Peg laughed. "In that case, he'd definitely call back—if only to make sure it was true."

Rose stuck the phone back in her pocket and kept going. Peg's idea of a walk was apparently a two mile trek. For all Rose knew, there might not even be cell service out on the horse trails. Not that it mattered, because Detective Sturgill wasn't returning her call.

Forty-five minutes later, they were back in Peg's kitchen. The Poodles went running to the water bowls. Rose sat down at table. Her fingers drummed impatiently on the wooden surface.

"Do you think I should leave another message?" she asked.

"No, I think you should take a deep breath and relax."

Rose stared at her. "You're usually the impatient one. I'm supposed to be calm and serene. I feel like we've reversed personalities."

"Heaven forbid," Peg muttered.

Rose smiled. For some reason, the fact that she could still get under Peg's skin made her feel better.

Abruptly the big Poodle's heads lifted in response to something only they could hear. Water dripped from their muzzles as they spun around to face the front of the house. A moment later, they took off running. Essie scrambled to keep up.

"Someone's here," said Peg.

Rose stood up. "Maybe it's Detective Sturgill."

Peg walked over to the window, pulled the edge of the tarp aside, and looked out. "No. It's Mae Watkins."

"Mae?" Rose said, surprised. "What does she want?"

"I have no idea." Peg was already striding out of the room. "But I expect we're about to find out."

"Maybe Franny called her," Rose said, hurrying along behind. "Maybe she's come to ask us to keep her secret. Or to plead with us not to turn Jerry in."

Peg nodded. "Pretend you don't know anything. Play dumb and let her do all the talking. Who knows? Maybe we'll learn even more secrets."

She stepped around the Poodles and opened the

front door. Mae was coming up the steps. She was dressed in stretchy jeans and a long T-shirt. A bulky purse was slung over her shoulder. Mae's hair needed to be combed and the expression on her face was grim. Rose thought she looked like she'd left her house in a hurry.

"What a lovely surprise—" Peg began.

Mae shrieked and jumped back as the big Poodles swarmed around her legs. Rose could sympathize with Mae's reaction. She extended a hand to draw Mae into the house.

"Don't worry. The Poodles look fierce but they don't bite," she said. "Peg and I were just about to have chocolate cake. Would you care to join us?"

Peg threw Rose a startled glance, then realized she was meant to play along. "Yes, please do."

"No, I don't want any cake." Mae glared at both of them. "We need to talk."

"Of course," said Peg. "Let's go into the living room."

"Not with those animals."

"Standard Poodles," Peg corrected gently. Rose could tell she was biting her tongue. "They're very friendly."

"They're too big and there are too many of them. Can't you put them outside?"

Peg snapped her fingers and the three black Poodles followed her down the hallway. Essie remained behind as Rose led Mae into the living room. The small dog lay down under the coffee table. Mae hadn't noticed Essie, and Rose wasn't about to point her out. Mae didn't need any more distractions. Rose wanted her to be thinking about what she'd come to say.

Peg was back in no time. Obviously she was just as anxious as Rose was to find out why Mae was there. Rose and Mae were sitting on the love seats, facing each other across the low table. Peg sat down beside Rose. They looked at Mae expectantly.

"I guess you two must be feeling pretty proud of yourselves," she said. "Franny called and told me that you'd wormed some information out of her. *Private* information." Her gaze hardened. "Things that have nothing to do with you. Things that no one else was ever meant to know."

Peg stiffened. Rose attempted to look penitent. Now that Mae was talking, she hoped Peg didn't blow it by jumping in to defend herself.

Mae folded her hands in her lap. Her fingers twisted into a tight knot. "So I need you to tell me what you intend to do with that information. Considering it's my life you're about to ruin, I think I have a right to know that much."

"Nobody wants to ruin your life," Peg said quietly.

"You know as well as I do that it won't matter," Mae said with a sneer. "Unless we can come to an agreement, it's going to happen regardless. For the second time, I'll be used by someone to further their own selfish ends. As if how I feel, or what I care about, means nothing. Once again, I'm just going to be collateral damage."

Rose hadn't expected to feel sorry for Mae. To tell the truth, she hadn't given Mae much thought at all. She'd gotten so caught up in following the trail of Stan's killer that she'd never stopped to consider who else might end up getting hurt when the truth came out. Not that Mae was entirely blameless. She'd begun a chain of events that had gone on to spin wildly out of her control. Now it was too late for Rose and Peg to back away. Even if they wanted to help her, it was impossible.

"The first time someone used you," Peg said. "You're talking about Stan?"

"Of course," Mae snapped. "I thought Stan cared about me. He made me feel like I was the most important woman in the world. Until I found out that everything he'd told me was a lie."

"By that time you were pregnant," said Rose.

Mae's lips flattened into a thin line. "I thought about ending it. Franny admitted that she'd told you about that. But I changed my mind—just like you two need to change yours. You had no right to go poking around in people's personal lives. And now your little game has to stop before it goes too far."

Rose listened incredulously. Stan had been shot dead. How could Mae not realize that things had already gone much too far?

377

"That's not going to happen," Peg told her. "We know what Jerry did."

For a moment, Mae looked surprised. Then she quickly rallied. "What Jerry did? How about what Stan did? He seduced me! Everything that happened was his fault."

When neither Rose nor Peg replied, Mae reached for her purse. "I have money," she said. "Tell me what it will take to keep you two quiet."

"A man has been murdered," Peg said. "No matter what you do, you won't be able to cover that up."

"I can and I will," Mae insisted. "One way or another, the information Franny gave you is never leaving this room."

Rose and Peg shared a look. Mae's words sounded so melodramatic, Rose was almost tempted to smile. There was no way Mae could keep them from telling the police everything they knew. What Stan had done was wrong, but Jerry had taken a life. Rose and Peg would do whatever they could to see that he was brought to justice.

Then Mae looked at Rose and her eyes narrowed. Abruptly Rose's amusement faded. She was reminded of the steely gaze of a cobra about to strike. It occurred to her that she might have misjudged the situation.

Mae reached into her purse. When her hand withdrew, her fingers were wrapped around the grip of a sleek black pistol. Rose heard Peg gasp. Her own breath caught in her throat.

Mae cradled the weapon with surprising familiarity. She lifted it and leveled it at them across the table. Her forefinger curled around the trigger.

"Like I said, one way or another. Your choice."

Chapter 31

"There's no need to threaten us," said Peg. She was amazed by how calm her voice sounded. And also by how wrong she and Rose had been. Peg had been guilty of the same mistake she'd accused others of making: she'd overlooked the older woman. Having jumped to the conclusion that Jerry was the one who'd pulled the trigger, she'd never stopped to consider that Mae herself should also be a suspect.

"It was you." Rose sounded just as shocked as Peg felt. "You're the one who shot Stan."

"It had to be done," Mae said practically. "Stan made me a promise and he broke it. Twenty years ago he swore that if I had his baby, he would never bother me or the child again. The man was a liar. I never should have listened to anything he said."

Mae scowled as if she couldn't believe how gullible her younger self had been. "Now that J.J.'s grown, Stan decided he wanted to have a relationship with him. He wanted *my son* to know who his real father was. I couldn't allow that to happen."

"Of course not," Peg agreed. It was easy to go along with whatever Mae said when the woman had a gun pointed at her chest. "It must have

381

been bad enough that he'd already let the news slip to Jerry."

"You better believe it. Jerry was livid when he found out. But we'd been able to get past that. Jerry knew he was J.J.'s father in every way that mattered. He'd raised J.J. and been his role model. He was there for the camping trips, the braces, and J.J.'s broken arm. Jerry loved his son too much to ever turn his back on him."

"Good for Jerry," Rose said. "You married a fine man."

Mae rolled her eyes. "Don't think you can get out of this by humoring me. Sugarcoating the situation isn't going to help any of us."

"If you were still in control of the situation at that point," Peg said, "why go after Stan?"

"I couldn't take the chance that when J.J. learned the truth, he'd choose to let Stan be part of his life." Mae's anger at the thought was palpable. She'd begun to quiver in her seat. "Jerry never would have been able to handle that. I couldn't allow it to happen."

Peg snuck a glance at the handgun. It had been bad enough when the weapon was merely pointed at her and Rose, but now it was shaking. She could only hope that Mae's trigger finger wasn't shaking too.

"Put the gun away, Mae. I know you don't want to use it again."

"You're right, I don't. I didn't want to have

to use it the first two times either." Mae looked in the direction of Peg's kitchen. "Frankly, I'd rather never have to fire it again."

"Are you planning to shoot both of us?" Rose inquired.

Mae paused to think, as if the question hadn't occurred to her previously. "No," she decided. "Just one of you should be enough. That'll scare the other one into keeping quiet."

"Not if it's Peg," Rose said. "She doesn't scare that easily."

Peg frowned. What was Rose up to?

"Maybe you should stop and think this through." Rose kept talking. "There were extenuating circumstances for the first murder. But two people killed by the same person with the same gun? That begins to look like a bad habit."

When the cushion shifted beneath her, Peg realized Rose was engaged in some kind of subtle movement. Then she caught on. All that talking was a distraction. Beneath the table, Rose had wedged the toe of one sneaker onto the heel of the other. She was maneuvering the shoe off her foot.

A shoe? Rose's shoe against Mae's pistol? *That was her plan?* As ideas went, it was pretty terrible. But perhaps it was better than nothing.

"Shut up, Rose," Peg said, deliberately drawing Mae's attention her way. "You're not helping."

"I don't need help," Mae snapped. "What I

need is a promise that neither of you will ever repeat what Franny told you."

"I promise," Peg said. She held up one hand. "Girl Scout's honor."

Rose grunted under her breath as the sneaker finally popped off her foot. That small sound was followed by an audible snarl from Essie. The shoe must have kicked her when it slid free. Rose froze in place.

"Girl Scout's honor," Peg repeated loudly, but it was too late.

Mae wasn't looking at Peg anymore. She'd leaned over slightly to peer beneath the table. Then she reared back in horror. "There's something under there!" she squealed. "What is it?"

"Another Poodle." Suddenly Peg stopped worrying about her own safety. If Mae shot Essie, there was going to be hell to pay.

"I told you to get rid of the dogs," Mae snapped.

"No, you told me to get rid of the big dogs."

"Well whatever it is, keep it away from me!"

Essie growled again. This time the menace in the sound was more pronounced. Clearly the small dog didn't like Mae's tone.

"Stop yelling," Peg said. "You're scaring her. Essie came from an abusive situation. You're probably triggering harmful memories."

Mae glared at Peg across the table. "Of all the idiotic ideas—"

Rose saw her chance and went for it. She

snatched up her shoe and hurled it at Mae's gun.

Mae had been looking at Peg, but she caught the movement out of the corner of her eye. Reflexively, she dodged to one side. The flying sneaker missed the pistol and hit her in the chest.

Mae's legs swung beneath the table as she tried to right herself. One of her feet connected with Essie. Teeth already bared, the small dog jumped out from her hiding place. She issued another snarl, then grabbed Mae's ankle and bit down hard.

The woman screeched and flailed her hands. The gun dropped from her open fingers. Dodging away from Essie, Mae didn't even seem to notice that she'd lost her weapon.

Peg was already up and on her way around the table. She swooped down and picked up the gun. Now Mae was slapping at the Toy Poodle with both hands. When Essie let go and retreated back under the table, Peg was pleased to see that Mae's leg was bleeding.

"Touch that dog again and you'll be sorry," Peg said ominously. Then she looked down at Essie and her tone lightened. "Good girl! That was well done. Now come to me where you'll be safe."

As Essie complied, Rose's phone began to ring. Her hands were shaking as she took it out and looked at the screen. "It's Detective Sturgill. He's returning my call."

"It's about damn time," Peg said.

385

• • •

"You'd think he would have been happier that we wrapped up his case for him," Rose said two hours later. She and Peg were in Peg's kitchen sharing another piece of cake.

In the interim, two squad cars—one from Greenwich, one from Stamford—and Detective Sturgill had all come and gone. Mae was in custody, her gun had been taken into evidence, and Essie had been hailed a hero.

Somehow the little Poodle had received more credit for having nabbed a killer than Peg and Rose had. Peg was amused that Rose sounded disgruntled about that.

"He will be once he has a chance to sit down and think things through," she replied complacently. "The connection between Stan and J.J. was the key piece of information. Rodney would never have been able to discover it without our help."

Rose delivered a second sliver to both their plates. Two weeks earlier, Peg might have gloated. Now she pretended it was nothing out of the ordinary.

"Are you going to tell Peter about what happened here this afternoon?" Peg asked as she dug in again.

Rose licked a smidge of frosting off her fork as she paused to consider. "Most of it, but not everything."

Peg suspected Rose would be leaving out the part about Mae pointing a gun at them.

"I wouldn't want him to worry," Rose added.

"Of course not."

"Are you going to tell Melanie?"

"Every single second," Peg replied. "She'll be sorry she missed it."

"It's because she wasn't here that you and I got together," Rose pointed out.

"Maybe," Peg considered.

"But we did a good job."

"We did, but we could have done better. Mae must have seen my broken window from the outside when she pulled in the driveway. I should have realized something was up when she didn't even ask about it."

Rose nodded. "And I should have given more thought to Jerry's excessive devotion to his son. More than one person remarked on it, but I wasn't paying enough attention."

"We'll do better next time," Peg said.

"Next time?" Rose sounded pleased.

"Of course." Peg smiled. "Problems like this one crop up more often than you might think. At our ages, exercising our brains is a good thing. I intend to do so at every opportunity. And if you know what's good for you, you will too."

After all the excitement died down, Peg had a busy week.

She got her window fixed and judged another dog show. A few days after that she returned Essie to Franny and Florence. The sisters were as delighted to have their Poodle returned to them as Essie was to be back home. Peg's remedial mission had come to a satisfying end.

Peg heard on the local news that Jerry had retained the services of a top lawyer who'd quickly gotten Mae out on bail. She received an email from Carrie announcing that the bridge club had been permanently disbanded. And she spent endless hours enjoying her Poodles' company.

Even with all that going on, Peg realized that her days suddenly felt less full—and less fulfilling. It wasn't hard to figure out why. Her bridge partnership with Rose hadn't been a complete success, but once the two of them had pushed past that rocky beginning, their alliance had worked out even better than Peg had dared to hope. She'd enjoyed chasing clues and brainstorming with Rose. Now that they no longer needed to spend time together, Peg was forced to admit that she missed her sister-in-law's company.

Peg mulled that over for a day. Then she did something about it.

The following afternoon, she showed up at the Gallagher House. Rose's minivan wasn't parked out front, but when Maura answered the door, she told Peg that Rose was in the office. Maura stared pointedly at the small dog crate Peg was carrying.

"Thank you," Peg said, ignoring the woman's unspoken question. "I know the way."

Peg walked straight down the hallway, rapped once on the office door, then pushed it open. Rose was sitting at the desk, staring at a row of figures on her computer screen. She glanced around, then jumped up from her chair.

"Peg, what are you doing here?"

"I brought you a present."

Rose's gaze dropped to the enclosed crate. Her eyes widened. Then she frowned. "Tell me you didn't bring me a puppy."

Peg was just high-handed enough to do something like that. Since she adored dogs, she thought everyone else should feel the same way.

"Of course not," Peg replied. "Why would I do that?"

She set the crate down on the floor, unlatched the door, and drew it open. For several seconds nothing happened. Peg remained standing. There was a smug smile on her face. In Rose's experience, that didn't necessarily bode well.

Rose approached the crate and leaned down, curious to see what was inside. After a moment, a tiny orange and white kitten popped her head out of the opening. She looked around briefly, then hopped over the lip of the crate onto the rug.

The kitten gazed up at Rose. Her green eyes blinked as the two of them assessed each other. Her white-tipped tail flicked back and forth.

"Oh my," Rose said, delighted. "She's adorable. Where did she come from?" Her hand reached out to stroke the kitten's silky head.

"A neighbor's cat had kittens in the spring. I knew they were looking for homes for them. So after I'd delivered a stern lecture about the benefits of spaying and neutering, I brought one home with me. I thought perhaps you might like a new friend."

Rose sat down cross-legged on the rug. When she patted her lap, the kitten climbed up her leg and butted its small head against Rose's hand. "What's her name?"

"She doesn't have one yet," Peg replied. "That's up to you. Assuming you want to keep her."

"Of course I want to keep her." Rose tore her eyes away from the tiny cat to look up at Peg. "I've wanted a cat forever. How did you know?"

"Call it an educated guess."

The kitten had navigated her way over Rose's hip and was climbing up her shirt. Rose's head was tipped downward. There was a big smile on her face. "Thank you."

"You're welcome."

"I know you lead a busy life, but I hope you'll make time to come and visit us." Rose plucked the kitten off her shirt and cradled her in her arms. It didn't look as though Rose would be standing up again anytime soon.

Peg pushed the crate out of the way and sat down on the floor too. "Whenever you like," she said. "I'm sure I can find the time."

"Good." Rose nodded. "Marmalade and I would enjoy that."

"I would too," Peg agreed. Then, "Marmalade? That's a big name for a very small cat."

"She'll grow into it," Rose said happily. She glanced over at Peg. "By the way, I got a postcard from Melanie and family this morning. They're passing through Ohio and expect to be home in a day or two."

"Is that so?" Peg leaned back against Rose's desk and made herself comfortable. "That trip flew by, didn't it? It seems like I barely even had time to notice they were gone."

Center Point Large Print
600 Brooks Road / PO Box 1
Thorndike, ME 04986-0001 USA

(207) 568-3717

US & Canada:
1 800 929-9108
www.centerpointlargeprint.com